With Love,
MISS
AMERICANAH

With Love,
MISS
AMERICANAH

Jane Igharo

FEIWEL AND FRIENDS

NEW YORK

A Feiwel and Friends Book
An imprint of Macmillan Publishing Group, LLC
120 Broadway, New York, NY 10271 • fiercereads.com

Our books may be purchased in bulk for promotional, educational, or business use. Please contact your local bookseller or the Macmillan Corporate and Premium Sales Department at (800) 221-7945 ext. 5442 or by email at MacmillanSpecialMarkets@macmillan.com.

Library of Congress Cataloging-in-Publication Data is available.

First edition, 2024
Book design by Maria W. Jenson
Feiwel and Friends logo designed by Filomena Tuosto
Printed in the United States of America

ISBN 978-1-250-87337-8
10 9 8 7 6 5 4 3 2 1

*For everyone who, despite fear and uncertainty,
left their home in search of another*

Chapter One

I. FEEL. LIKE. AN. IDIOT.

I'm walking down the busy street with an urgency that makes my movement uncoordinated. My legs fumble over each other in a hasty attempt to pass the elderly couple in front of me and get to my destination.

I'll admit, this is a low point for me. I've hardly left the house since my family and I moved to America a month ago. But today, I threw on a stain-free sundress, quickly slicked down my edges with my favorite fruit-scented gel, and rushed out the front door looking like a civilized person.

All this to save an old DVD player.

At first glance, a passing stranger might look at the blanket in my arms and assume I'm cradling an adorable baby or a helpless puppy. Their last guess would be a DVD player on the verge of death. The chunky, outdated technology has a disc stuck inside it, and while the situation might seem trivial, to me it is a full-blown emergency. Hence my clumsy march to the tech repair shop.

A mild breeze, laced with the smoky scent of barbecue, tousles my long braids, and I shake the displaced locks from my line of vision, squint against the sun's glare, and hurry past a restaurant with a grinning cartoon pig on its front window. When I arrive at my destination, I release a deep breath. Before leaving my house, I googled "DVD player repair." That search brought me here—to Tech and Techies. I open the door, and a bell chimes. There are only a few customers in the small space; some examine the displayed computers, while others go through the products that seem to be in an unorganized cluster on shelves.

"Hey," the girl behind the counter says, jutting her chin to me.

"I . . . um . . . er . . . hi."

Upon arriving in America, I developed a new personality trait: extreme awkwardness. It started in the airport. In the swarm of travelers, I became very aware of myself—of the color of my skin and my intonation—for the first time in my life. In the melody of American accents, my Nigerian accent stood out like an off-key note. When a uniformed man with an air of authority requested to see my passport, I froze and babbled. Thankfully, my mother and sister intervened.

Since we arrived, I've noticed Esosa, my younger sister, speaking with a convincing American intonation. I can't do that. I only know how to sound like myself.

"Need something?" The girl at the counter speaks again. She looks about fifteen. She's wearing heavy, dark makeup that's harsh against her lily-white complexion. When she blows her bubble gum, it pops, then flattens on her pierced nose.

"Um . . . yes. I need help," I answer in an unsteady voice.

"Yeah. We don't do animals. The vet's a few blocks down."

I look at my arms and instantly understand her assumption. "It isn't an animal."

"Okay. Well, we don't do babies either. Dr. Mason's across the street."

"It isn't a baby."

The girl blows another bubble. She watches me blankly as the pink gum expands and pops. Clearly, she isn't willing to waste any more words on our exchange.

I approach her and place the bundled DVD player on the counter. "I need this fixed. Please."

"O-kaa-aa-aay." She drags the word, extending the two syllables into six. "A few questions. One, what is it?"

"A DVD player."

"Okay. Why is it in a blanket?"

"I walked here. I wanted to give it some cushion just in case I dropped it."

"Right."

Even with her deadpan expression and flat tone, her judgment comes off clearly. I really regret leaving the house, but there's little I can do about that now. I sigh and shift my weight from one leg to another. "So? Can you . . . fix it?"

"We repair phones, computers, game consoles. Not that."

"Um . . . I don't understand. Why not this? According to Google, you fix electronics. This is an electronic."

"But is it? Or is it just a piece of junk?" She pulls a lock of brown hair behind her multi-pierced ear and shrugs.

"Come on, Jade, just look at it." The disembodied voice that comes from behind makes me flinch. The guy standing two feet from me is tall. He's wearing sunglasses, a baseball hat, and a large hood over the baseball hat. Only the lower half of his face is visible. He's left a lot to my imagination when I would rather see the face of the person coming to my aid. "Just plug it in and have a look," he goes on.

"Ugh," the girl—Jade—grumbles, then grabs the cord and plugs it into a socket. "What exactly is the problem?"

"There's a disc inside," I explain hurriedly. "It's stuck and won't come out."

She pushes multiple buttons with no true coordination, like I did at home. When nothing happens, she scoffs. "Like I said, it's a piece of junk. Toss it."

"What about your dad?" the hooded guy says to Jade. "Maybe he can figure it out?"

"He's at an appointment. Won't be back for another hour."

"An hour." I frown, but nod. "Okay. I'll come back."

"Mind if I try something?" the hooded guy asks, moving to my side.

"Um . . . I . . . I . . . ." Surprised by both his question and his sudden proximity, I stutter.

"Promise I won't destroy it. Well, I'll really try not to." He smiles. It's a nice smile, infectious too, because the corners of my lips immediately turn up. He accepts my smile as permission, and then he fists his hand and bangs it on the DVD player.

"Oh, my God!" My eyes go wide. "What are you doing? Do you want to destroy it completely?"

"Nah. That was definitely not the plan." His lips shrink into an apologetic smile. "I was just trying something, and I really hope it works." He presses the Open/Close button, and to my surprise and total relief, the disc slides out.

"Oh, my God." I expel a loud breath. "It worked."

"Yay," Jade says in a monotone. "Hooray." She grabs her phone and stares at the screen.

I ignore her and celebrate by bouncing on my toes. "I can't believe you fixed it. Thank you so much."

"Don't mention it. I think I just got lucky." He looks from me to the ejected disc and smiles. "*Sixteen Candles.* My mom's always going on about this movie. Never seen it, though. Is it good?"

"It is. I had a few minutes left when it stopped working."

It really was a shame when the DVD player malfunctioned at a pivotal moment in the movie—just when Jake Ryan surprises Samantha at the church. The urge to know what happened next pushed me to declare a state of emergency.

"Well, let's hope it's good now." He presses the Open/Close button several times to confirm the device does exactly what it's supposed to do. Thankfully, it does. He reaches behind the counter and unplugs the cord. After wrapping the blanket around the DVD player, he extends it to me. "Protect it at all costs."

I laugh. "Of course. Thank you."

"Still think it's a piece of junk," Jade adds, without looking away from her phone. "Ever heard of streaming a movie? Life made easy."

I roll my eyes, and even though the hooded guy is wearing tinted glasses, I have a feeling he does too.

Outside the store, the sun hangs a little lower than it did minutes ago. The barber across the street flips the sign on the shop door from OPEN to CLOSED, and the dry cleaner two stores down does the same. The once busy street is growing empty, many customers and shop owners ending their day at five o'clock. While some cities never sleep, Bellwood, where my family immigrated to, has an unofficial yet respected curfew. The scenic town is located in New York State's Hudson Valley and has a mixture of groomed greenery and picket-fence houses. Lampposts with ornate designs almost seem like accessories on the impeccably clean streets lined with small commercial buildings that are white or brick. It's the kind of close-knit, my-nose-in-your-business town where everyone knows everyone, where news travels too fast, and neighbors gift each other pies and casseroles and other American dishes I have only heard of but have never tried. It's also the kind of town where a very small percentage of the residents look like me.

My father would not have liked it here. His picture of America involved neon lights and glass skyscrapers, a multicultural hub with a liveliness that wasn't set to start and end by a clock.

When I asked my mother why we couldn't live in New York City like Dad would have wanted, she told me to be grateful we didn't have to struggle like many new immigrants. She told me to be thankful my uncle—my father's older brother, who has lived in America for twenty-four years—is a generous and kind man with the means to take care of us. I *am* grateful. But sometimes I think if we lived in the part of America my father imagined, he would feel more present. Alive.

I sigh and look over at the children's performing arts studio beside the dry cleaner—Little Big Star. Through its large window, a group of girls dance in sync; they leap in the air and then twirl on their toes. I stop walking and watch, immersed in their performance. I've walked past the studio a few times, during the rare occasions my mom forces me to leave the house and run errands with her. Each time, I've stared through the window and watched either a dance routine or a musical performance. The music and voices always fill the streets, faint but still audible. Usually, I'm captivated until my mom calls for my attention. Today, the thing that diverts my focus from the studio is the sound of quick footsteps moving toward me.

"Hey." The hooded guy from Tech and Techies jogs forward and stops once he reaches me. His breath is quick and short. He looks at the studio briefly, a small furrow between his eyebrows, then turns to me. "Don't judge me," he says with a hand on his chest. "I'm a little winded. Coach's gonna have to whip me back into shape during practice." He laughs, but I frown, completely confused and slightly uneasy.

Why is he following me? To be more precise, why is he running after me in a disguise?

As if sensing my apprehension, he takes a step back. "I must be freaking you out right now. I didn't mean to. I was just . . . um . . . sorry." He smiles timidly, and I relax. Despite his getup, he doesn't seem like a threat.

I study him through narrowed eyes. "Why are you dressed like a burglar on a budget?"

He chuckles. "What?"

"You know—the glasses, the hat, the hoodie. It looks like you're about to rob a house but can't afford a proper disguise? Hence being a burglar on a budget."

"Well, I would like to point out that most burglars are on a budget. Hence them being burglars."

"And I would like to point out that smart burglars invest in good disguises and really commit."

"Well, I guess I'm not a very smart burglar."

"Yeah," I agree. "It seems like you aren't."

It occurs to me, as we're both smiling, that I haven't stammered or paused awkwardly since we started speaking. I've forgotten about my accent and the feeling of inadequacy I developed since moving here. I don't know where that feeling has gone, but I hope it stays at bay until this conversation ends.

"I'll admit," he says, "this is a terrible disguise. But I'm not a burglar. Promise. I'm actually trying to avoid some people." He turns around and surveys the street. When he's satisfied with his inspection, he faces me again. "My friends."

"You're trying to avoid your friends? Why?"

"I've spent the whole summer with them. I just needed a break, you know? Some time to myself. So I planned to grab a video game from Tech and Techies and go home to chill before any of them see me."

"Oh." I glance at his empty hand. "Where is the game?"

"Well, I didn't get a chance to grab one. I was looking through the stack when . . ."

"You came to the rescue of my DVD player."

He laughs. "Yeah. And then after you left, I—"

"You ran after me." I frown, then lift an eyebrow. "Why?"

"Well, I noticed your accent. I wanted to tell you I like it."

"Accent? What accent? I don't have an accent."

"Um . . . I . . ." He bites his lip. "Right. Sorry. My mistake."

"Relax. I'm just joking." I smile, and my cheeks grow warm. He likes my accent, one of two things that make me stand out in Bellwood. "I'm from Nigeria. I just moved here."

"Really? That's cool. Did your whole family move too?"

I consider the question, then shake my head. My father's absence is still new to me. Sometimes I forget he's gone. I laugh; I get wrapped up in a movie about American teenagers; I meet a peculiar guy in a terrible disguise, and my grief is temporarily suspended—hanging over my head like a hammer, waiting for the precise moment to fall and hit me with a staggering force.

This is the moment.

A tightness gathers in my chest, and my heart thumps. I have taught myself how to survive these moments, how to contain my grief until I am alone, behind a closed door.

First, I shut my eyes.

Second, I breathe with intention.

In and out.

Slow and steady.

Third, I imagine my breaths as a tide of cool blue water flowing through me—dousing the flare of emotion and then soothing the disquiet.

"Hey." His voice is gentle, laced with a touch of concern. "Are you all right?"

I open my eyes and nod. "Yes. But I need to go. Thank you again for your help."

"Yeah. Sure. And sorry for . . . you know. Keeping you."

I start to leave, then stop. "You know what's unfair?"

He shakes his head.

"The fact that you've been staring at my face this entire time, and I don't know what you look like."

"Yeah." He smiles, nodding. "I guess that's unfair." In one swift motion, he pulls the sunglasses from his face.

I don't mean for it to happen, but it does—automatically, as if my body is programmed to react to his striking hazel-green eyes.

Soft flutters explode in my stomach, then intensify and travel like a ripple through my whole body. I'm dazed until he takes a small step toward me.

"Are you okay?"

"Um . . . yeah . . . yes." I force my eyes away from his and look toward the path that leads home. "I should go. Bye."

With the DVD player pressed to my chest, I rush down the street. There's an irrepressible urge at the pit of my stomach, compelling me to turn around. To look at him. One more time.

So I do.

Chapter Two

MY UNCLE IS AN ATTORNEY. HIS WIFE, SARA, IS THE chief of surgery at Bellwood General Hospital.

They are rich.

It's why they can afford to live in the part of Bellwood where the houses are bigger.

Still holding the DVD player, I walk along the path that divides the main house and the guesthouse. That's where my mom, my sister, and I live—in the three-bedroom guesthouse that's the size of many picket-fence houses a few streets away.

My mother is right. We're lucky to have Uncle. He's generous and kind. When he would visit my family in Nigeria, he would bring a suitcase of gifts—clothes, novels, electronics, and expensive perfumes my mother never let me use. We didn't ask for those things and the other things he did for us. My mother worked as a doctor at a government hospital, and my father was a biology professor and dean of the life sciences faculty at the University of Benin. He also had side businesses that generated additional income. We lived comfortably. But that didn't stop my uncle's generosity. He wanted us to have more. A year ago, during his annual visit to Nigeria, he spoke to my father about us moving to America.

"You have a PhD in biology," he said to my father in our living room. "Ivie has been a doctor for over ten years. You're both educated, professional people. This will make your application strong."

"Mm-hmm," my father replied, stroking his bearded chin.

"You have been putting this off for years—for far too long. Let's start the application process now. Maybe within a year, we will all be together. Adrian and Naomi can get the chance to grow up with their cousins. And Enore and Esosa can have a wide range of opportunities. Eh?"

My father agreed. We started the applications. Everything was going well. And then we went to Lagos for a health check—a standard part of the process. That's when they found a lump in my father's lung. The doctors said it was inoperable. It was too late. My father had gone months ignoring his shortness of breath, his fatigue, and his weight loss. Though with the diagnosis and a precise prediction of his life span, the symptoms intensified, as if acknowledging the disease instantly made it more aggressive. Within weeks of his diagnosis, he became frail.

We watched him die slowly, our goodbye gradual, extensive, and agonizing.

Two months after his funeral, we moved to America. My mother was eager to leave Nigeria—to put distance between us and the scene of our loss. We packed what we could and left so much of him behind—his collection of fountain pens, his Fela records, his academic books with colorful notes sticking out of them. All I brought to America were fragments of him—pieces of his identity that don't paint a complete picture of the man he was. His T-shirts hang in the closet in my new room. His gold necklace with a small cross pendant is on my nightstand. His brown leather watch is strapped to my wrist—slightly loose, but secure. I've worn it every day since we arrived. It's the least I can do. There are no memories of him here, so I carry a part of him with me and conjure up moments that could have been.

The front door opens unexpectedly, and my sister and cousin step out of the main house. They're laughing, but stop the moment they see me. Their eyes shift to my arms.

"Did they fix it?" Esosa asks.

"Yes," I say. "It's fixed."

"Good, so you can come out with us."

"We're gonna meet up with some of my friends and grab something to eat," my cousin Adrian says. "It's gonna be chill. You should come."

"No. I'm okay. Go ahead."

"You can't stay inside that house forever, watching those movies," Esosa says. "It's not . . . healthy."

"Yeah. I second that," Adrian adds.

They make me sound like a loner. I'm not. I've just been preparing myself before fully interacting with my new environment and the people in it. I'm a preparer. A meticulous one. It's the reason I asked Adrian to give me a complete rundown of what to expect from high school when it begins next week. As I go into my senior year, it's important I know the social norms—the dos and don'ts of an American high school. But Adrian, who was born and raised in America, couldn't spare the time for a lesson.

"Look, cuz," he said to me just two weeks ago. "Summer is almost through. I can't afford to waste . . ." He cleared his throat. "I mean spend the last days drawing a map of high school for you." He ruffled his long curly hair, then blew out a breath. "Look. There's gonna be a party at the beach tonight. You should come—get to know some people before school starts up. It'll be fun."

I turned down his invitation because going to a party meant diving into socializing. And I don't dive. I watch the water first, studying the nature of it before gradually, and I mean *gradually*, dipping my toes into it.

After a moment of thinking, Adrian snapped his fingers and grinned. "I've got an idea. Hold up." He left my bedroom and returned minutes later with a box. "These should help. If you want to know about high school, watch these."

"What are they?" I asked.

"Naomi's collection of movies." He placed the box on my bed and opened it. "I'm surprised she didn't take them to college with her, seeing how obsessed she was with them."

DVD cases filled the box. I picked one and read the title. "*Mean Girls.*" My stare shifted to Adrian. "How is your sister's collection of movies supposed to help me?"

"They're movies about high school—every single one of them. If you want to know what to expect from an American high school, watch these."

"Okay. But are they accurate?"

"Um . . . they're informative," he answered with a shrug.

"Come *na*," Esosa says to me now. "Come out with us. You might have some fun, make some friends. I've made a few already."

Of course she has. My sister is not like me. She doesn't watch the water to study the nature of it. She doesn't dip her toes in gradually.

Esosa just dives in. She looks at me now, her brows bent, asking me to dive in with her.

But I don't know how to do that.

"Have fun," I tell them.

"But you've been—"

"It's fine, guys," Auntie Sara says, cutting off her son. She stands under the doorframe and smiles warmly. "You two go ahead. Enore can hang out with me." She waves goodbye to Esosa and Adrian and motions for me to enter the house. "Come on, honey. You can help me with dinner."

The interior of the house is as extravagant as the exterior. A grand staircase curves against the wall, and behind it, there's an entryway that leads to the kitchen.

I place the DVD player on the white countertop, where there's a vase of sunflowers, and Auntie Sara frowns.

"What's that about?" she asks.

"It stopped working, so I took it to get repaired."

"Well, we can always get another. That one is pretty old."

"That's okay. It's working now. He fixed it." The corners of my lips twitch as a smile forms.

"Who fixed it?" Auntie Sara's eyes narrow, suspicious and curious.

"I don't know his name."

"Well, what does he look like? Do you remember?"

I remember the color of his eyes clearly, but what's most memorable is how they made me feel. Though I'd rather keep that information to myself. "I wasn't paying attention to how he looked."

"Hmm." Auntie Sara lifts her chin and examines me from a high angle. "All right." A moment passes, and she turns away. Her black bone-straight hair, tied in a low ponytail, swings as she moves around the kitchen. After rinsing a bunch of green onions in the sink, she places them on a wooden chopping board. "Help me cut these?"

"Okay." I lather my hands with soap, rinse, then start chopping. "What are you making?"

"Just something quick and simple—shoyu ramen. It's going to be very spicy—just how your uncle likes it."

"That's how I like it too."

"I know," she laughs. "Nigerians love spicy food. Because of your uncle, my taste buds have adapted."

Auntie Sara is Japanese American. She and my uncle have been married for nineteen years. I first met her when I was twelve. During one of my uncle's trips to Nigeria, he brought his whole family along. Adrian, who was also twelve at the time, was set on finding reliable internet access. Naomi, their oldest child, who currently goes to MIT, was set on sightseeing. Auntie Sara, however, was quiet and reserved. Not because she was shy. She was just comfortable. She didn't act like a foreigner—demanding the conveniences she had in her country or constantly looking to be wowed by something new. She was just chill. Back then, liking her was as easy as it is now.

"Enore, honey," she says, scooping a mixture of garlic and ginger from the food processor. "I think it would do you some good to leave the house at some point."

"I left today. And I went to choir practice last week."

"I mean leave the house to socialize with people your age—not a bunch of middle-aged and elderly women in a church choir."

"But I like singing in the choir." For years, I was part of my church choir in Nigeria. When my family moved to Bellwood, I joined the Holy Trinity choir because it's what my father would have wanted. He would have encouraged me to audition, saying something along the lines of *Enore, don't be stingy with your gift. Share it.* I joined because of him, because it would have made him proud.

"I know you love singing," Auntie Sara continues, "but I didn't think your one effort at socializing would be joining the church choir. I want you to make friends. Friends your own age. Hopefully when school starts next week, you'll make some."

I shrug. "Maybe."

"Honey, I just want you to get settled here. I want you to feel like you belong here. Like this is your home."

I've lived in America for a month, but I still don't know how to exchange one home for another, one country for another. I feel suspended, caught between two places, between the *before* when everything was normal and the *after* when everything changed.

I miss my dad. In a way that is almost intolerable. I've missed people before—my mother when she went to Abuja for a month to stay with her sister who had a baby, my uncle when he returned to America after every visit with us, Esosa one weekend when she stayed at a friend's. But whatever I felt then seems so shallow compared to what I feel now. I never knew missing someone could be excruciating.

"Enore," Auntie Sara says. "Do you understand what I'm saying, honey? I'm a little concerned."

"Don't be," I tell her while forcing a smile. "I'll make friends. I'll be fine."

That's what everyone wants to hear. And I wish it were true, but I can't ignore my grief. It's constantly present, lurking and slithering with a slickness that makes it obscure until it takes me by surprise.

Chapter Three

MORNINGS IN AMERICA ARE QUIET. THAT'S ONE OF the first things I noticed when we moved. Before daybreak, nothing indicates the beginning of a new day except an alarm going off. In Nigeria, there were various early-morning sounds.

First, the crow of a rooster from a distant compound. To this day, I don't know who, in our middle-class neighborhood of professionals, owned a rooster. But after the loud cock-a-doodle-doo, Mama Ebenezer would step out of her apartment. She lived below us in a two-story fourplex and hated the fruit trees that lined our gated compound. Whenever the leaves fell, they drifted to her verandah, and it drove her mad. She would wake up at the crack of dawn and sweep with a palm broom, separating mango and guava leaves from the sand-coated pavement while humming a Catholic hymn.

Minutes after she went inside, Dr. Abraham would try to start his 1966 Peugeot that should have been in a junkyard rather than in our compound. Some days, he got lucky and could drive the beat-up car to work. But on the days he was unlucky, he would grunt while looking under the hood, and his wife would stand at the door of their apartment, bouncing their baby on her hip and ranting about how cheap her husband was.

For a moment, I stay in bed and imagine these sounds are around me, that distance hasn't stifled the pulse of Nigeria. I imagine nothing has changed. And then the alarm on my nightstand goes off.

After a deep sigh, I sit up. It's seven o'clock on the first day of school. The outfit I plan to wear is on a velvet armchair at the end of the room. It's a plain black T-shirt, blue skinny jeans, and white Converses—the perfect outfit for someone who wants to go unnoticed. Through my research, a.k.a. the sixty teen movies I've now watched, I have learned that below the radar is the safest place to be in high school. It ensures survival. And that's my goal—to survive high school.

When I'm dressed, Esosa walks into my room with her hands behind her back. The gloss on her lips matches the buds of pink roses on her dress. Some of her short box braids are up in a double topknot; the style enhances her oval face—her cheekbones that have a layer of shimmer on them.

My sister and I don't look much alike. While she has our father's honey-brown complexion, I have our mother's warm chestnut. Even though I'm two years older, she's taller, with long legs she has trained to be graceful. The parts of us that are similar—our upturned eyes and round, full lips—look different on her once she's exaggerated them with makeup. Our slight similarities are only apparent early in the mornings before she's sat in front of a mirror to highlight and contour her features, using techniques I know absolutely nothing about.

Back in Nigeria, while still refining her skills as a makeup artist, she worked on middle-aged women whose idea of makeup involved drawing a sharp black line over their excessively plucked eyebrows. Her clientele later expanded to brides and birthday celebrants. Usually, her weekends were fully booked. I know she's already started building a client base here. She's been going to parties with our cousin, mingling and advertising her work on her always stunning and flawless face. She's spent the last weeks announcing her presence in Bellwood and will likely walk into school today with an entourage already assembled.

"Your outfit is . . ." She squints while studying me. "Underwhelming."

"That's intentional."

"Oh. I see." She nods slowly. "Well, would you like me to do your edges?"

"I already did them."

"But you never really do them right." She pulls her hands from her back, revealing an edge brush and a container of gel. "I could help."

After glancing at the mirror on my vanity, I sigh. She's right. I'm not skilled in the art of swooping my edges into a perfect half circle. "Okay." I sit on the bed. "But be fast."

The cool, sticky gel glides on my forehead as Esosa uses the brush and her finger to style my baby hair.

"So," she says. "How are you feeling about school?"

I look at her standing over me and shrug.

"Are you excited?"

Again, I shrug.

Esosa asks no more questions. She does my hair, then takes a step back to inspect her work. "Perfect."

I don't have to look in the mirror for extra validation. I trust Esosa blindly. "Thank you."

"You're welcome." She slumps into the spot beside me and huffs. "I'm a little excited about school. I'm also . . . nervous. And angry.

21

And really sad." She rests her head on my shoulder. "Is it crazy that I feel all these things at the same time?"

"No. It isn't." Since my dad died, there hasn't been a moment where I've felt only one emotion. Since his death, happiness is no longer just happiness; it's something sweet mingled with the bitter taste of guilt and anger. It's exhausting and confusing. I squeeze my sister's hand and assure her again. "It's not crazy."

"I just wish . . ." Esosa takes in a sharp breath but doesn't finish her sentence. She doesn't have to.

"I know, Sosa. I know."

After a moment where we both say nothing, she lifts her head and looks at me.

"Are we going to be fine?" she asks. "Are we going to be fine here? In this country? Without him?"

I imagine a future where the pain of our loss is less and things are better, but my pessimism blurs that image. For my little sister, I want that picture-perfect future to be bright and vivid—enough that the hope of it helps her through today and tomorrow and all the days ahead.

"Yes. We're going to be fine." I force those words out of my mouth and beg for the skills to make them sound believable. "We're going to be just fine. I promise."

Esosa nods, then sighs.

"*Oya.*" I stand and take her hand, pulling her up and then toward the door. "Let's go have breakfast."

When we walk into the kitchen, our mother gasps. "You both look beautiful."

"Thank you." Esosa grins and spins around, her dress flaring above her knees.

"Sit and eat." My mother sets down two plates of fried eggs and toast, and Esosa and I sit at the wooden counter. As we eat, she stands above us, watching with a small smile.

When I was younger, I used to stare at my mother while she got dressed or cooked, thinking she was the most beautiful woman. I'm seventeen and still watch her with the same admiration. The sunlight streaming through the gaps in the blinds beam on her chestnut-brown skin. Her hair, dense and springy with tight curls, hovers above her shoulders. In Nigeria, people would say she looks like the Nollywood actress Genevieve Nnaji. My father would disagree firmly. "*Abeg,*" he would say. "My wife is finer." That always made my mother laugh.

"So?" she says, looking from me to Esosa. "The first day of a new school. Are you both nervous?"

"A little, but I'm excited too," Esosa answers.

"Good." My mother looks at me. "Enore?"

If I tell her the truth, that I'm not only nervous but terrified, she'll worry for the rest of the day. "Me too," I lie. "I'm excited."

She presses her lips in a firm line, clearly not convinced. I'm sure she's going to ask me more questions, but a knock at the front door comes just in time.

"It's not locked," she shouts.

Seconds after the door creaks open, Uncle Davis appears in the kitchen. He's wearing one of his gray suits, appearing both professional and authoritative. He looks like my father the same way Esosa and I look like each other—similar in fewer ways than in more. The only things they have in common are their round eyes and pointed nose that dips slightly at the tip.

"Good morning," he says, cheerful. "It's a big day. Are you guys ready?"

"Absolutely." Esosa attempts to take her empty plate to the sink, but Mom gestures for her to leave it.

"Go ahead. I don't want you to be late."

"Yeah. We should get going," Uncle Davis says. "Adrian is already waiting in the car."

"Okay." Esosa grabs her bag off the floor and slings it over her shoulder. "Bye, Mommy. Have a nice day."

"You too. And be good. Don't look for trouble o."

"I won't. But if it comes my way, I will handle it."

"Esosa," Mom says sternly. "Behave."

"Don't worry." Uncle Davis stands in front of Esosa, theatrically shielding her from our mother's glare. "She'll behave." They rush out of the kitchen and then out of the house, laughing.

The room is quiet for a moment, and I breathe deeply before standing and grabbing my bag.

"Enore." Mom edges toward me. "Are you okay?"

"Yes. I'm fine."

"Why don't I believe you?"

I shrug.

"I am your mother. I know when—"

A loud honk cuts her off. These interruptions keep coming at the perfect time.

"That's Uncle. I should go."

Slowly, she nods. "Okay. But wait." She turns to the refrigerator and pulls out two brown paper bags. "Here. Lunch for you and your sister."

"But Adrian says they serve lunch at the cafeteria."

"Well, just in case you don't like the food."

"Thank you." I take the brown bags and examine them. "What is it?"

"Sandwiches. Turkey. Sara said it's a standard lunch here."

I'm relieved she didn't say tuna or egg. My research has proven that people with tuna or egg sandwiches don't do well in high school.

"So, what are you going to do while we're gone?"

"Study for my medical licensing exam. Maybe I will go to the library. But I'll see you after school. I'll be right here," she assures me. "You can tell me all about your day. Okay?"

"Okay. Bye." I turn to the door but pause and look at her when she calls me.

"Don't get carried away," she says. "No distractions. Remember the reason you're going to school. Remember the reason your father and I wanted you and your sister to come to this country. Make us proud, eh?" She blinks quickly, pushing back the tears in her eyes.

With a firm grip on my bag strap, I do the same and nod. "I will."

Chapter Four

BELLWOOD HIGH IS A MASSIVE REDBRICK BUILDING with a clock tower. I peer through the car window at the crowd entering the school, and my stomach tightens.

"You guys ready?" Uncle Davis asks, tapping his fingers on the steering wheel.

"Just a sec." Adrian looks in the mirror, gathers his silk curls in a bun, and grins at his reflection. "Okay. All good. See ya, Dad." He steps out of the car and gestures for me and Esosa to do the same.

"Everything okay?" Uncle Davis turns to the backseat. "You guys a little nervous? There's nothing to worry about. Adrian will be there if you need anything. And if you need to reach me, you can do so on these." He opens the glove compartment and pulls out two phones. "One for you and one for you."

I stare at the iPhone in my hand while Esosa squeals.

"Really?" she asks. "Our phones from Nigeria only work here with Wi-Fi. It's been such an inconvenience."

"Well, I couldn't possibly send you to high school without functional phones, could I?"

"Thank you, Uncle," we say together.

"You're welcome. I've saved my number in both. If it's too much, just call me. And I'll pick you up."

"That won't be necessary," Esosa says. "We'll be fine. Right, Enore?"

"Yes," I say, nodding. "We'll be fine." I've spent weeks preparing for this. The DVDs Adrian gave me were my only source of preparation, but they were informative. The first movie I watched was *Mean Girls*. It terrified me. But *High School Musical* eased my nerves slightly. *Heathers* and *Jawbreaker* revived my angst, and *Bring It On* was a surprise antidote. In the past weeks, I have watched sixty teen movies, a genre I didn't know existed until recently. They've been entertaining, engrossing, and educational. I've studied the social landscape of an American high school and have put together ten rules that will lead me down a straight and narrow path to graduation. If I follow all my rules, this day and the days following should be perfectly ordinary.

"Okay." Uncle Davis smiles. "Well, have a nice day."

I exhale, step out of the car, and walk up to the building.

This might as well be a scene in a teen movie—the first day of school for the new girl in town. In *Mean Girls*, Cady moves from Africa to America. On her first day of school, she walks to the doors alone—dazed and terrified. Rightfully so, because people bump into her without apologizing, a football flies right across her face, two students scuffle like amateur wrestlers, and someone tosses a burning book on the grass. It's total chaos. Thankfully, my walk to the school doors isn't that eventful.

With my sister and cousin, I cross the threshold and enter the building.

"I could help you guys look for your locker and your first class," Adrian offers, stopping in the middle of the busy hallway.

"No," Esosa says. "It's okay."

"Yeah," I agree. "Go ahead so you're not late for your class.

Besides, I have my schedule." I pull out the folded paper from my pocket. "Don't worry."

"Are you sure? 'Cause I don't mind."

My sister and I nod.

"Okay," he says. "See you guys later."

He means after school. With our different schedules, we likely won't see each other until then.

"Hey," Esosa says when it's just the two of us. "Put my number in your phone." She calls out the digits, and I save them. "Text me, so I have yours."

"Okay."

Her phone pings with a message, and she smiles. "Ah. There's nothing like the sound of an iPhone notification." Her smile flattens as she watches me. "Text me throughout the day. Just so I know you're okay."

"You too," I say.

"I'll let you know I'm alive with a series of hilarious GIFs."

A moment of silence passes between us. I want to say something about the situation, about the huge change we're currently experiencing, about how scared I am. But I don't.

"We're going to be okay, right?" my sister asks, her fake but believable American accent still intact. "Right, Enore?" She's looking for the same assurance I gave her earlier this morning.

"Yes," I answer. "We're going to be fine. No shaking."

She smiles. "I'll see you later." When she turns around and walks down the hallway, people respond to her confident strut by receding slightly and making way for her. Typical.

The time on my phone reminds me I have five minutes to find

my first class. Quickly, I shuffle through the crowd and glance at the small plaques on the doors with engraved numbers and letters. My search makes me completely oblivious to the traffic in front of me. I bump into someone, then stumble backward and hit someone else.

"Um . . . sorry," I say to the tall red-haired girl glaring at me.

My apology means nothing to her. She rolls her eyes and walks away.

Has this one mishap earned me a high school nemesis, someone who will remember this incident and enact her revenge over the course of the year? I curse under my breath, then turn around to offer another apology. Hopefully, this person is more forgiving.

"Sorry." I'm too embarrassed to make eye contact. "That was an accident." Based on the size and style of the white-and-green sneakers I'm staring at, it's possible I bumped into a guy.

"Don't worry about it." The deep masculine voice confirms my hunch. "I wasn't really paying . . ." He trails off, and his shoes shift toward me. "Wait a minute. Don't I know you?"

"Um . . . no. I don't think so. Sorry again. Bye." I turn around but only take a step forward. Again, I'm looking at white-and-green sneakers. The guy I just apologized to stands in front of me.

"I do know you," he says. "*Sixteen Candles*."

I squint and sort through my mind, trying to make sense of those words. *Sixteen Candles*. When things become clear, I look up and smile. "Burglar on a budget."

He laughs. "I actually have a name, you know."

"You also have hair." Wavy black hair; some locks fall backward while some dangle on his forehead, right over his hazel-green eyes that are set on me.

Seeing him like this—without tinted glasses, a baseball hat, and an oversized hoodie—helps me realize something I didn't when we first met. He looks like the male lead in a teen movie—the one that girls pine and scheme for. Seriously, he could go up against the best of them—Jake Ryan, John Tucker, Troy Bolton, Aaron Samuels, Noah Flynn. The only difference is his skin, his golden-brown complexion. He isn't white. The male leads in the movies I've watched are usually white. I think of two rare instances when they weren't—*#Realityhigh* and *Love Don't Cost a Thing*.

"Did you think I was bald?" he asks.

"I didn't know what to think. You left a lot to the imagination."

He bobs his head. "Yeah. Well, I'm totally disguise-free now, so how about an official introduction?" He extends his hand to me. "Davi Santiago."

"Enore Adesuwa."

We shake hands the exact moment the school bell rings. There's a sudden eruption of chaos, and I don't have the time to appreciate the fact that we're touching and it feels kind of nice. People leaning against lockers immediately stand upright. Conversations end as small groups break apart. People walk quickly while I'm frozen, dazed, and clueless.

"What class do you have?" Davi asks.

"Um . . ." I look at my schedule. "AP Calculus. But I'm not sure where that is."

"Wait a minute." He glances at the paper in my hand, then smiles. "Looks like we're in the same class."

"Really?"

"Yeah. Come on. It's this way."

On our walk to class, that involves multiple turns on the first floor, people say hi to Davi—too many people. Some smile, some pat his shoulder, while others bump his fist. I watch the interactions thoughtfully and come to an obvious conclusion.

He's popular.

Damn it.

I am dangerously close to breaking a rule.

Rule #1: Avoid interacting with or befriending anyone who is popular.

It's one of my most important rules. If I associate with someone who is popular, I can't achieve my goal of going unnoticed. Maybe eventually, I'll walk down the hallway and people will know my name. Maybe they will invite me to parties. And maybe for a while, it will be nice, like it was for Cady in *Mean Girls*. But as that movie and others like it prove, the climb up the social hierarchy is always fun, but the fall is long and hard.

We enter a classroom, similar to the ones I've seen in movies. Here, the rows of single desks differ from the wooden, two-person desks in my old school. Back then, I would sit with my best friend, Tolu, whispering and laughing whenever the teacher turned away. Tolu and I were never apart because, unlike the schools in America, we didn't have to gather our belongings at the sound of the bell and switch classes. We had every subject in one classroom. The teachers did the moving, while we sat under the perpetually swirling ceiling fan, jotting down the lesson on the blackboard, whispering jokes whenever we got the chance, and looking through the window for a distraction in the courtyard.

I take a seat in the back of the class, and Davi settles into the seat beside me.

Rule number one rings in my head, and I break eye contact with him and focus on the teacher—a tall white man with a sparse ponytail.

"I hope you all had a good summer," he says. "I see a lot of familiar faces and one new one." His stare zooms in on me, and I shrink in my seat. "Hello there. You must be . . ." He glances at the clipboard in his hand and then back at me. "Enore. Welcome to Bellwood High. I'm Mr. Mitchell." His smile is so expansive, his eyebrows shoot up. "I like to start the first day back with a little warm-up exercise—have everyone talk about what they did during summer. Why don't you start?"

Every single person in the room turns to me, and I dig my teeth into my lip. This is really the worst-case scenario for someone who wants to go under the radar.

"Go ahead," Mr. Mitchell encourages me. "No need to be shy."

"Um . . ." I look at Davi, and when he smiles and bobs his head, something tense inside me loosens. I don't expect that to happen— for the tension to just dissolve, but it does. I exhale and shuffle in the chair, no longer slouching. "I moved to America. From Nigeria. That's what I did during the summer."

"Damn!" a guy with wild curly blond hair says. "I only moved from my bed to the couch." He and the rest of the class laugh, and I worry they might be laughing at me, but then Wild Curls nods and says, "Nigeria. Cool."

"What part of Nigeria are you from?" Mr. Mitchell asks.

"Edo State—the southern region."

"Well, welcome to America and Bellwood."

"Thank you."

He turns to another student, and I stun myself by raising my hand.

"Um . . . excuse me."

"Yes, Enore." Mr. Mitchell looks at me expectantly.

"My name. You aren't saying it correctly."

"Oh. I'm sorry." He glances at the clipboard. "I pronounced it the way it's spelled. But please tell me the right way."

"It's pronounced Eh-no-ray."

He nods and repeats the syllables. "How was that?"

It was better but not perfect. He doesn't have the rhythm any Nigerian could easily convey. But maybe I should get used to people saying my name like this—with a layer of it stripped away. "Yes." I nod at Mr. Mitchell. "You got it."

Class ends ninety minutes after it begins, and it's a relief to learn I have no more morning classes with Davi.

"I can still walk you to your next class—show you where it is," he says while shoving books into his bag.

Even with my rule, I can't turn down his offer. I don't know my way around yet, and it's nice to have a guide. "Thank you. That would be helpful."

As we walk, he gets more attention. I wonder what clique he falls under. He's popular, yes. But is he a jock? A rich kid? Or just one of the school's extremely attractive people? I need specifics. Just then, I remember what he said when we met.

"You mentioned something the other day. Something about a coach?"

He nods. "Yeah. Coach Bathurst. The football coach."

"You're on the football team?"

"Yeah. We have our first away game next week. And debate club also starts next week." He blows out a breath. "The madness begins again."

"You're in the debate club?"

"Yeah."

A football player who's in the debate club and also in AP Calculus. Usually teen movies paint the popular jock as an idiot with high expectations of his future but no ambition beyond sports. That clearly isn't Davi.

"Your next class," he says when we stop at an open door.

"Thank you."

"I noticed we have the same lunch period. We could have lunch together. Um . . ." He clears his throat. "With other people too."

Other people. That would likely include the rest of his clique—the popular kids. The thought of eating lunch with them unnerves me.

The second bell rings, and Davi looks down the hallway. "I gotta go, but I'll see you in the cafeteria later?" He smiles sweetly, and my resolve slips away.

"Okay," I say.

"All right. Cool. See you later." His smile expands, and he turns and walks away.

It hasn't even been a day yet, and here I go about to risk my whole plan for a boy.

Chapter Five

EVERY TEEN MOVIE HAS CONVINCED ME A HIGH school cafeteria is a terrifying place to be, especially when you're new and know no one.

That's why I don't go to the cafeteria during lunch.

Davi's smile and the look in his eyes when he asked me to join him couldn't change my mind. In fact, those were more reasons to stay away.

I considered eating lunch in the bathroom. It's the go-to place for people with no friends in high school, but how can anyone possibly eat with the stench of pee in the air? I decided to go outside and sit on the bleachers instead. Here, the air is fresh and warm, and the cloudless sky is radiant. There's a gym class in progress. Girls wearing the same blue T-shirt with the school's logo run around the track field while a teacher with a firm grip on a whistle urges them to move faster. This really is the perfect entertainment.

I'm not sure how many lunch periods I'll spend like this. If I put in the effort—socialize and eat in the cafeteria—I'll likely make some friends, maybe two or three just as determined to go unnoticed. I'm not a shy person. In Nigeria, I had a good number of friends. We certainly weren't popular. Popularity was left to the bad boys, the star athlete, and the kids who were dropped off at school in luxury vehicles, courtesy of their wealthy parents. In Nigeria, those were the qualifications to being popular. There weren't cheerleaders or prom king and queen. If you didn't fall under the three categories, you existed below the radar. That's where I was in Nigeria, and that's where I want to be here.

I open the brown paper bag my mother handed me this morning. Without the turkey sandwich, I would starve right now. After taking a bite, I pull out the flyer I shoved in my pocket earlier. Seconds after the lunch bell rang, I attempted to rush through the school doors and step outside, but a blond girl with bright eyes and a wide smile forced the flyer in my hand and spoke with the sort of enthusiasm that was frightening. Even though I didn't hear a thing she said, I smiled and nodded while moving to the door. Now I smooth out the wrinkles on the rumpled flyer until the words on it are visible.

AUDITIONS FOR BELLWOOD'S ANNUAL MUSICAL!
MONDAY. 3:30 P.M.
THE AUDITORIUM.
DARE TO BE SEEN.

An invitation to audition for anything has never been so intimidating—*dare to be seen*. Well, I certainly don't want to be seen. The sort of attention you get from standing on a stage is particularly the kind I want to avoid. My fingers curl against the paper, ready to crumple it and toss it aside. But I pause and stare at the word *musical*. In my school in Nigeria, there were no musicals. We had our annual cultural dance, where students from similar tribes organized and performed a choreographed folk dance. I, being part of the Edo tribe, would dress with the traditional red velvet cloth around my chest and coral beads in my hair. With a white handkerchief in my hand, I would move with the calm and elegance associated with Edo dancers. The Igbos, with their energetic dancing, always stole the show. And I suppose I was okay with that, with not succeeding at something I am neither good at nor care much about. Though, I often wondered what would happen if I got the opportunity to sing rather than dance.

I look at the flyer again. *Musical.* My brain seems to have highlighted that word—colored it in neon yellow. I've only ever sung in a choir. In Nigeria, it was the only outlet available to express my interest in music. Now, with that one word jumping out at me, I briefly entertain the possibility of a new outlet.

My phone vibrates suddenly, and I crumple the flyer. It's a text from Esosa. A GIF of a terrifying clown waving doesn't provide the humor she promised.

ME: I thought you were supposed to send funny GIFs. Not disturbing ones.
ESOSA: Right. Sorry.

The next GIF she sends is of Joey from *Friends* saying, "How you doin'?"

ME: Much better. And I'm okay. What about you?
ESOSA: AMAZING!!!!!

Honestly, that was the response I expected. My little sister, who dives headfirst into any situation, has already adapted to life here, while I'm eating lunch alone, still trying to find my footing. In Nigeria, I always ate lunch with my friends—Tolu, Abby, and Osas. As there was no designated lunchroom, we would eat in the classroom or the courtyard, talking and sharing our food. I miss that. I miss my friends.

Halfway through my sandwich, I install Instagram on my new phone and log into the app. After selecting my chat with Tolu, I click the video call icon. Nigeria is five hours ahead of New York, so I know she's back from school. The phone rings, and when Tolu answers, her face fills one half of the split screen.

"*Americanah!*" she shouts with a wide smile.

I roll my eyes, wishing that wasn't her new nickname for me.

"I've been waiting for this call all day, but I didn't think it would come this early." She squints and leans into the screen to study my background. Most of her face disappears in the process. "Where you *dey*?"

"*Na* school *o*. It's lunchtime."

"Oh." She nods and leans back. Her round face comes into full view again. "Are you with your friends?"

"Which friends? *Abeg*, I don't have any friends . . . yet. I'm trying to get used to everything first."

"Okay. So you haven't replaced me."

"You're one of a kind, T."

She beams with pride. "Eh-heh. That's what I like to hear. Just *dey ginger* me."

I laugh, something that's inevitable whenever I talk to Tolu. She's just that kind of person, the kind with a personality big enough to overshadow my grief and feeling of displacement. She's known for unapologetically speaking her truths, and her truths are potent—a sting if you don't have the repellent of tough skin. Though she's only ever used her skill for good—to shut down the loudmouthed wannabe bad boys with something to prove and the fair-skinned girls with a superiority complex. We cried, holding each other tight the day before I left Nigeria. We promised to stay in touch and always be best friends. So far, we've kept that promise.

"So . . ." She arches an eyebrow. "How far *na*? Tell me everything. How's the school, the people, the boys?" Now she wiggles her eyebrows suggestively. "Give me details. Gist me *na*."

I avoid the topic of boys, particularly Davi, while giving Tolu basic details about the first half of my day. "Okay. Your turn. How your side *dey*?"

"Ah. *Abeg*, what's there to tell? You know it's the same old thing."

But sitting alone on the bleachers, in a school and a country I haven't fully familiarized myself with, makes me crave the same old things. Being my best friend, Tolu senses this. She smiles and bobs her head.

"Okay. Where do I start?" She taps her chin, then snaps her fingers. "*Shebi* you know Franka, that fair Calabar girl that is always talking like she has no sense?"

I nod eagerly, then listen as Tolu tells me about the day we would have otherwise experienced together.

AT HOME, UNCLE DAVIS INSISTS THE WHOLE FAMILY have dinner together. He wants to hear about our first day at school. We're all in the main house, seated around the circular table in the kitchen. Adrian has somehow crammed mashed potatoes, chicken, and green beans into his mouth and is chewing aggressively as he tries to break down the trio. It's a sloppy mess, and Auntie Sara glares at him like she's repulsed.

"Honey," she says, her nose wrinkling. "I know you're a growing

39

boy who needs to eat and all that, but please, for the sake of every-one at this table, conduct yourself with some etiquette."

Adrian stops chewing and looks at his mother. "Sorry." He wipes his mouth with the back of his hand and smiles sheepishly.

Auntie Sara rolls her eyes and turns to me and Esosa, seated side by side. "Girls, why don't you tell us about your day? How was it?"

"It was amazing," Esosa answers. "Everyone loved my makeup. Jen's going to a wedding next week and wants to book me. And Lisa the following week. My client list keeps growing."

"Jen. Lisa," Uncle Davis says. "You've already made friends."

"I've made several."

"That's nice," Mom says, bringing a glass of water to her lips. She takes a sip, then sets the glass down. "I'm happy you're mak-ing friends who support your makeup thing, but how about your classes? Do you like them? Are your teachers good?"

In an instant, Esosa's mood changes. She huffs and sinks into her chair. "Makeup thing?" Her strained tone proves she's holding back the urge to go off.

Esosa hates when Mom reduces her passion to child's play or something she'll eventually grow out of. Esosa's love of makeup and glamour and being in the spotlight isn't a phase. It's who she is. And although that has always been clear to our family and those outside of it, our mother's support has always been halfhearted, measured—a little but never too much. It's as if she fears her full support will nurture something unconventional and impractical in Esosa, something that will produce a whimsical creative rather than a lawyer or a doctor or an engineer.

With me, she doesn't have to worry about that. There is nothing unconventional or impractical to nurture inside of me.

"Enore." Mom completely ignores Esosa and focuses on me. "How about your day? How were your classes and your teachers?"

"Good. Very good."

"And friends?" Uncle Davis asks. "Did you make any?"

Everyone looks at me expectantly, even Adrian, who's stopped chewing. They all want me to say yes. It would prove I'm adapting, no longer the girl declining social invitations and shutting herself in a room to watch old movies. It would prove I'm okay, or at least on the path to being okay.

So I say yes.

I don't tell them I ate lunch alone. I don't tell them I felt so homesick, I spent my lunch period talking to Tolu. I don't mention Davi, a potential friend I plan to avoid.

After lunch, when we met again in AP biology, he asked why I hadn't been in the cafeteria. I told him I got caught up in something. I expected him to look hurt or upset. Instead, he smiled and said, "No worries. There's always tomorrow."

Chapter Six

ON TUESDAY, WHILE EATING LUNCH ON THE BLEACH-
ers, I consider what lie to tell Davi when I see him in biology class
later. Lying isn't my strongest skill, but without direct eye contact,
I can manage. Eventually, he'll stop asking me to have lunch and
probably invite someone else. Maybe a girl who is waiting for him
to notice her. I try to ignore that detail while breaking my meat pie
in half.

One advantage of having lunch out here is eating Nigerian food
without potentially being judged by my peers, who are probably
more accustomed to Western lunches like the macaroni and cheese
I heard the cafeteria is serving today. The flask I filled with rice and
goat stew this morning is empty—every grain of rice scooped into
my mouth. Now I'm enjoying the beef-and-vegetable pastry I baked
last night.

"Enore! There you are!"

I flinch, shocked, then look around and search for the person
who spoke.

"Down here!"

My attention shifts to the bottom of the bleachers, where Davi
waves. He climbs the stairs and jogs toward me. I don't have time to
dwell on my shock. The gears in my head spin as I think of a sensible
and convincing lie.

"What are you doing here?" he asks.

"Um . . ." The gears are still turning, spinning words into the perfect lie. "I needed . . . air. Yes. Air. It's very warm and stuffy inside."

He squints and considers me for a moment. "Were you avoiding me?"

"What?" I shake my head and force out a laugh. Unfortunately, the sound is flat. "No. Of course not."

"You didn't want to have lunch together, did you?"

"Um . . ." I chew on my lip and look from the girls running sluggishly around the field to the coach taking his frustration out on his whistle.

"If you didn't want to, you could've just said no. You didn't have to lie."

Something delicate in his voice makes me look at him, and I sigh. "It's not about you, Davi." Well, it is partially. I fully intend to stay far away from Mr. Popular, but he doesn't have to know that. "It's about the cafeteria."

He frowns. "What about it?"

"Have you ever seen a teen movie? Cafeterias are a notoriously dangerous place for the new kid—trying to find somewhere to sit, wondering if they'll be welcomed or excluded. And then there's the matter of a food fight. How often do those happen? I can't get food stuck in my braids. It would be impossible to take out."

Tension leaves his eyebrows. He tilts his head and watches me from an angle. "How many teen movies have you seen?"

"A lot. I've probably seen every one ever made."

"Wow." He laughs and sits beside me, a respectable amount

of space between us. "Why in the world would you put yourself through that torture?"

"Research. I've never been to an American high school. I didn't know what to expect. I had to prepare."

"And you decided to watch movies?"

"I think they were informative."

He laughs lightly. "Okay. And about the cafeteria. I did ask you to sit with me."

"I know. And that was really nice, but I just wasn't ready to be in there yet. Sorry I lied."

"Don't worry about it." He leans back, rests his elbows on the bench behind us, and stares at the field.

Most of the girls have stopped running; they're hunched over and gasping for air. Today, the sun hides behind clouds, casting shadows on everything below. Dark stripes—a result of the bleachers above us—reflect on Davi's bare arms. I trace the patterns with my eyes, gazing closely at the contrast of golden-brown skin and dark sharp lines. When he looks at me, I turn away quickly and clear my throat.

"Um . . . so you were looking for me?"

"Yeah. Was wondering where you were." He glances at the food in my hands. "What's that?"

"A meat pie."

He looks at me blankly, like my answer did nothing to clear his confusion.

"It's a Nigerian pastry with a beef and vegetable filling." After the explanation, I wait for him to make a face.

"Mmm," he says instead. "Looks and sounds good."

"Um . . . would you like to . . . try it?"

"Nah. It's okay. It's your lunch."

"It's fine. Really." I extend one half of the pastry to him. "Here."

"Okay. Thanks." He takes it, then bites into it, and closes his eyes while chewing. "Mmm. This is good. It kinda reminds me of a *pastel*."

"A *pastel*?" I say. "What's that?"

"It's sort of like this, but a Brazilian version. When I went to Brazil for the first time a few years ago with my parents, they were everywhere—at the beach, at shops, at the farmer's market."

"Are your parents originally from Brazil?"

He nods. "Yeah. They moved to America when they were really young—way before my sister and I were born."

"You have a sister?"

"Yeah. Natalie. She's in elementary school."

"I have a sister too, but she's a sophomore. Her name is Esosa."

"Wait a minute." He squints. "I might know her."

Frankly, I wouldn't be surprised.

"I think I met her at a party during the summer."

"It's likely," I say.

"That means Adrian's your cousin, right?"

"He is. Are you two friends?"

"More like acquaintances. He's cool and all, but he's got his own crowd."

It's strange, but I've never thought of my cousin belonging to a specific clique, and that's because I don't know him well enough to place him as a jock or a nerd or anything else. We've practically been living in the same house for over a month, and in some ways, it's like we're still living on different continents.

"What's his crowd?" I ask Davi.

"The basketball team."

"And I'm guessing yours is the football team?"

He shakes his head. "Not entirely. Just my closest friends—some I've known since middle school and some since kindergarten."

"The same friends you wore a disguise to avoid?"

He laughs. "Yeah. Them."

"And don't you think they're currently wondering where you are? Shouldn't you be having lunch with them?"

"Nah." He looks at me and smiles. "I like it here."

ON WEDNESDAY, I'M SURPRISED TO SEE DAVI ON THE bleachers.

"I brought *pastels*," he says as I approach him.

"Um . . . what are you doing?"

"Eating lunch."

Well, that much is obvious. There's a box of ketchup-coated fries in his hand that likely came from the cafeteria. I'm curious why he isn't eating them there.

"Why are you having your lunch here—outside?"

"It's a beautiful day. Plus, I'm a big fan of fresh air."

I narrow my eyes, and he grins.

"Here. Have some." He extends a plastic container to me. "My grandma made them last night, especially for you."

"Me?"

"I told her there's a girl who has never tried a *pastel*. She felt it was a wrong she had to right."

He mentioned me to his grandmother, who then went to the trouble of cooking for me. A smile I have no control over forms on my face. I sit beside him and pick one of the small pastries. "What's in it?"

"Mostly chicken. Trust me, they're good."

He's right. I practically moan while chewing. "Your grandma can cook."

"Well, I helped." He reads my blank expression and clears his throat. "Okay. I gave her moral support. From a distance."

"Strange enough, that's exactly how I pictured you helping." I grab another *pastel* and bite into it. "So good."

"I'll let my grandma know you approve." He glances at the black reusable lunch bag that looks more like a stylish purse, a gift from Auntie Sara. "What's in there?"

"Some *akaras*. My mom made them this morning." I pull a plastic container from the lunch bag, then flip the lid. "It's basically a Nigerian bean cake or fritter."

"No way." He looks at the round golden-brown puffs in the container. "We have the same thing in Brazil, but call them *acarajé*. That can't be a coincidence." He pulls out his phone, and his fingers move across the screen.

"What are you doing?"

"A little research. I need to know where *acarajés* originated from." He reads through his Google findings, then turns to me with a smile. "West Africa."

"Well." I jut out my chin, grin, and extend the container of *akaras* to him. "Would you like to try the original?"

He laughs and nods. "I would. Thank you very much."

ON THURSDAY, DAVI BRINGS A CONTAINER OF *acarajés*—each golden-brown puff split in the middle and filled with shrimp and caramelized onions.

"How much moral support did you give your grandmother this time?"

"So damn much," he says. "It really helped her pull through."

"You're ridiculous," I say with a laugh, then take another *acarajé*.

"You know, I never get to do this," he says, "bring Brazilian food to school, not since third grade when Adam Jefferson made fun of my *empadão*."

"That's actually one of my fears. I think if I ever work up the nerve to go in the cafeteria, I'll just have fries or whatever they're serving. But until then . . ." I bite into my third *acarajé* and sigh as the flavors come undone in my mouth.

For a few minutes, we watch the gym class without saying a word, then Davi turns to me. "See any teen movies lately?"

"Yeah. Last night, actually. I watched *The DUFF*." It's one of the few movies I've streamed since running through the DVDs Adrian gave me.

"How was it?"

"Um . . . it was nice. I enjoyed it."

Davi squints and studies me. "Really? 'Cause your face says something else."

"Well, it was a good movie. It's just that . . ."

"Yeah?"

I sigh. "It's just that I've noticed people of color rarely play the lead in teen movies. Why is that?"

It's the first time I've used that phrase—people of color—in a sentence. In Nigeria, I heard of it and knew what it meant but never had a reason to use it until now. In America, I am aware of my new identities as a minority, a person of color, Black, *other*. Gradually, I am recognizing all the ways people like myself and Davi are erased or minimized, so we are the comical best friend but never the lead, or we are simply just a spot of color in the background.

"America is supposed to be about diversity, right? Different people from all around the world live here. But when I watch these movies, I don't see that. Mostly, all the leads are white.

"In the rare cases when the lead is a person of color, like in *To All the Boys I've Loved Before*, *The Half of It*, and *Spin*, their love interest is always white. Two people of color are never the romantic leads. The story never revolves around them. Except in two rare cases—*#Realityhigh* and *Love Don't Cost a Thing*."

Davi leans forward and watches me closely. "I know I asked before, but exactly how many teen movies have you watched?"

"A lot. My cousin gave me a box of old DVDs. Once I watched all of those, I started to stream."

"Well, you're dedicated, that's for sure." He huffs and shoves his fingers into his hair, pushing the soft curls backward. "And to answer your question, Hollywood believes one narrative sells better. It's bullshit, but . . ." He shrugs. "It's how things are."

"Well, that isn't fair. You know, in *Confessions of a Teenage Drama Queen*, there's one Black girl. She's friends with the head mean girl. Throughout the whole movie, she says two words: *the baby*. That's it. Someone wrote a script and decided she only gets two words. Two." I groan and rub my forehead. "Sorry if I'm getting worked up."

"Hey." Davi's hand falls on mine, the weight not completely resting on me, just enough that I am acutely aware of the warmth and feel of his skin. "Don't apologize. Trust me. I totally get your frustration. And it's valid."

It occurs to me that while this frustration is new to me, it isn't to him. He's probably had to deal with it all his life. He's probably found a way to live with it, and I suppose I will have to as well.

We turn to the track field. His hand doesn't move; gradually, it relaxes, the weight fully on me. It's nice. A strong breeze breaks through the haze of heat; it fluffs my T-shirt and tousles Davi's hair. My fingers clench, fighting the urge to stroke the displaced curls from his forehead.

"Can I ask you another question?" I say. "It's not about teen movies."

He chuckles. "Sure."

"Wouldn't you rather be having lunch with your friends?"

"I am having lunch with my friend."

I suppose we are friends, even though his popularity status directly conflicts with my goal to go unnoticed. I'm no longer dangerously close to breaking rule number one. I've already broken it. In my head, I cross out the rule and pretend it never existed.

Rule #1: ~~Avoid interacting with or befriending anyone who is popular~~.

"Don't you want to have lunch with your other friends? The ones in the cafeteria?"

"No. I'm good here. With you." He looks at me; his hazel-green eyes are soft but still have an element of intensity. "Honestly, this is the best part of my day."

I smile and nod. "Yeah. Mine too."

As my heart flutters, I wonder if I'll have to draw a line through another rule.

Chapter Seven

ON THURSDAY EVENINGS, I HAVE CHOIR PRACTICE AT Holy Trinity. The church is a fifteen-minute bike ride from home. Typically, practice starts at seven and lasts for an hour and thirty minutes. But sometimes, Ms. Huntington and Ms. Warner—the elderly women in soprano—bicker so much, we hit the two-hour mark. Today is one of those days. I slouch in my seat and roll my eyes as they debate who should take the solo on Sunday.

"Okay, okay," Ms. Silva, the choir director, says. She groans, then mumbles something under her breath in a language I recently identified as Portuguese. The rhythm of that language, almost musical, laces every English word she pronounces, creating the most beautiful accent. "Thank you for your opinions, ladies. It's appreciated." Her fingers comb through her black hair that's streaked with white, and she exhales deeply. "But I already decided who takes the solo."

Ms. Huntington and Ms. Warner sit upright, waiting for the announcement. The other members of the choir, twelve women in total, do the same; they're eager to hear the decision that will put an end to the bickering. My attention is elsewhere, on the curved wooden beams that adorn the ceiling; they make the midsized space seem smaller and more intimate. In Nigeria, many churches aim to be massive, enough that people fill every seat and overflow to the street. My family went to a church like that, and although my father hated the crowd, he pushed through every Sunday to get a seat that had a clear view of the choir. He would have loved this church. I imagine him in a pew, smiling at me as I stand in my blue choir cassock. Here, I wouldn't have to search the crowd for him or squint, trying to catch the nod he always gave me. Here, he would be right in front of me.

"Enore, dear, did you hear a word I said?" Ms. Silva asks.

My head snaps toward her. "Yes. I mean . . . no. Sorry."

"You're taking the solo on Sunday."

"What? Me?" I turn to Ms. Huntington, who, throughout the duration of practice, has basically been running a campaign on why she should get the solo. Now, with a stoic expression, she rubs her pearls and lifts her chin as if unfazed by Ms. Silva's decision. But clearly, the woman is livid; the grip on her necklace makes that obvious.

"Enore, is there a problem?" Ms. Silva asks.

"It's just that I haven't been a part of the choir for long. Shouldn't a more seasoned member take the solo?"

"I completely agree," Ms. Huntington blurts out. "How can we possibly trust her to lead? What if she sings off-key or—"

"Elaine, please," Ms. Silva says, her voice clipped. She huffs, clearly low on patience, and focuses on me. "Enore, honey." Her voice softens. "It doesn't matter if you've been a part of this choir for five years or five days. You're our strongest soprano. Therefore, you're the right choice. Now." She claps her hands and motions for everyone to rise. "Let's run through it." She extends the lead microphone to me, and I take it hesitantly.

The band plays the first notes. The piano comes in and then the guitar and the drums. I know the lyrics to "Believe For It." But when it's my cue to sing, I don't. The instruments run on, fade out, then start from the beginning. Again, I don't sing.

"Enore." Ms. Silva nears me and lowers her voice. "Sweetheart." The creases around her brown eyes overlap as she squints and studies me. "Everything okay?"

I stare at the pews as if I expect him to be there, giving me that nod of encouragement that always relieved the tension in my throat and propelled me to sing.

"Enore?"

I turn to Ms. Silva.

"Honey, I don't mean to put pressure on you. But if you don't do this and basically kill it, Elaine will never let me live it down. And she'll have the license to fight for every solo from now until the Lord calls her home. And I don't have the tolerance for that. Do you?"

I shake my head.

"Okay. Good. Then, sing. I know you can do it." She squeezes my hand tenderly and turns to the rest of the choir.

The band starts again, and I close my eyes and blow out a breath. In my head, I paint a picture, conjure a moment that could have been. He is right here, smiling proudly. The tension built inside me thaws, the flutters at the pit of my stomach stop, and I sing.

My father once described my voice as honey and thunder—sweet and bold, something that could lure you to sleep and jolt you alert, a lullaby and a battle cry. Sometimes, when I sing, I hear that description echo back at me. I hear it right now.

The choir enters at the chorus, their harmony seamless even as the key goes higher and falls again. When I sing the last note, the instruments fade out, and then a single round of applause erupts. My eyes fly open and shift in the direction of the noise.

"Whoa! That. Was. Amazing!" Davi shouts from the back of the church.

Startled, my heart thumps fast. *What in the world is he doing here?*

"That was incredible," he goes on, his eyes on me. "Damn. Those pipes."

"Okay. That's enough," Ms. Silva says, glaring at him. "Settle down. This isn't a concert hall."

"Right." He stops clapping and clears his throat. "Sorry. Go on."

Ms. Silva turns to the choir. "Excellent job, everyone." She smiles in my direction. "That was truly incredible. Now, that's it for today. See you all on Sunday. Please arrive promptly—thirty minutes before the service begins. Enjoy the rest of the week."

The moment we're dismissed, the sopranos, tenors, and altos leave their designated spots and mingle. I say goodbye to the rowdy crowd and meet Davi at the entryway.

"Hey. What are you doing here?"

"I didn't know you could sing." He blinks sharply. "Or sing like that. You were freakin' incredible, Enore."

I love the way he says my name. He's so careful with the syllables, like he's trying to protect them from being mispronounced. He takes extra precaution, catching the rhythm I emphasized in calculus on Monday. The fact that he's careful with my name makes me believe he'll be just as careful and protective with other parts of me.

"I didn't even know you were in the church choir. Why didn't you tell me?"

"It never came up. Besides, I wasn't sure you went to church."

"I do . . . sometimes. Just not lately."

There's more to his response, a lot more. I feel the weight of everything he doesn't say in the air that's suddenly dense. I'm curious, but not brave enough to ask.

"I still don't know what you're doing here. Are you stalking me?"

"First, I'm a burglar and, now, a stalker. Is there a reason you always think the worst of me?"

"Well, the circumstances never seem to be in your favor."

He laughs. "For your information, I'm here to pick up my grandma. My dad usually picks her up, but he's working late tonight."

"Your grandmother is in the choir?"

"Yeah." He nods. "But on another note, I'm still not over your singing. You're incredible."

"Um . . . thank you." I look away and focus on the slight opening in the door. It's difficult to accept his compliment while keeping eye contact, especially since lately my eyes seem set on tracing the shape of his lips.

"You know, Bellwood High has a musical every year," he says. "It's kind of a huge deal. Auditions start on Monday. You should go."

"Yeah. I heard something about that."

"So? Are you going to audition?"

A few days ago, when I saw the flyer, I briefly entertained the idea of the musical—the possibility of a new avenue to sing. But for someone who has only ever sung in a church choir, a musical seems too big, too complex.

"I don't think musicals are my thing," I tell Davi.

"Oh. Okay. Then what is?"

"What do you mean?"

"You said musicals aren't your thing, then what is? What are you into? What's your passion?"

I open my mouth, but the answer doesn't come. The answer doesn't exist, because no one has ever asked me that question, and I have never asked myself. It never occurred to me to ask, to search myself for the same motivation that makes Esosa watch countless makeup tutorials on YouTube and spend hours perfecting techniques and building a client list. Nothing drives me but my mother's expectations. She wants me to become a medical doctor. Preferably, a surgeon. Nothing compares to the title and prestige of a surgeon. The decision she's made for me is so imposing, everything else seems muted, silenced by it, including the answer to Davi's question.

"Hey." He squeezes my arm gently. "You okay?"

"Um . . . yes." I push the wooden door completely open, and we step outside, onto the walkway that's lined with trimmed hedges. The cool night air hits my bare arms, and I unwrap the sweater around my waist and pull it over my head.

"You should really consider auditioning on Monday," Davi says. "I think you would be . . . exceptional."

He searches my eyes in a way that is completely invasive. I should look away. But I don't. Pressure builds in my chest as we stay fixated on each other. Despite the breeze ruffling the hedges, my skin turns warm. When he gently pulls my hair from inside my turtleneck and places it over my shoulders, my spine straightens. His fingers brush my neck while pulling out one last lock, and I inhale sharply.

At this point, I can't say I like Davi as just a friend. A collection of moments—some sweet, some quiet, some filled with laughter—nurtured romantic feelings I can't shake.

In my head, I draw a line through another rule.

~~Rule #2: Control your heart and your hormones. No crushes. And absolutely no boyfriends.~~.

Now my heart, which I've officially lost control of, thumps fast as Davi and I inch closer to each other. Though when someone forcefully clears their throat, we step apart.

"Enore, I see you're getting acquainted with your biggest fan," Ms. Silva says.

I nod and force out a weak chuckle. "Um . . . yeah. Yes."

"The way he was clapping and hooting, you would think he was at a concert." She glares at Davi. "Weren't you supposed to wait in the car?"

He shrugs. "I got bored."

With an arched eyebrow, I look between Ms. Silva and Davi.

"My grandma," he says.

"Really?"

"I know. It's hard to believe someone with my figure is a grandmother." She perches a hand on her slender hip and poses.

With her flattering and stylish clothes, tasteful makeup, and youthful exuberance, it's clear Ms. Silva isn't ready to conform to the stereotypical image of a grandmother. Though it seems like Davi, cringing at her exaggerated poses, would prefer she did.

"You know, I can be a grandma and still be an attractive woman with a vigor for life."

"You gotta stop saying the word *vigor*, Grams. It just sounds dirty."

Ms. Silva rolls her eyes. "Anyway, you two seem friendly. Know each other?"

"Davi and I go to the same school."

Ms. Silva looks from me to her grandson thoughtfully. "You're the girl I've been cooking for all week, aren't you?"

"Yes. That would be me."

"Davi came home on Tuesday and said, 'Grams, there's a pretty girl at school who's never tried a *pastel*. Could you make some?'"

It takes a lot of restraint, but I succeed at not reacting to the word *pretty*. My lips stay firm and straight—not a smile or a giggle or the slightest indication that I'm flattered.

"Well, the *pastels* were delicious," I say. "And so were the *acarajés*. Thank you."

"Don't mention it, dear. Thank you for killing that solo and completely silencing Elaine. Trust me, that is no small accomplishment." She squeezes my shoulder. "Have a good night. See you on Sunday." She walks to a silver Toyota, leaving Davi and me alone.

"Want a ride home?" he asks.

"It's okay." I glance at Adrian's bike that's chained to the bicycle rack steps away. "I've got a ride."

"You could put it in the trunk."

"Don't worry about it. I'll see you at school tomorrow."

"Okay. Cool. Good night." He takes a few steps toward the car, then pauses and turns to me. "So what song are you singing for your audition on Monday?"

"I'm not auditioning, Davi. I already told you."

"What? I didn't get that," he shouts, acting like he can't hear a word I'm saying. "You want to talk about the audition some more? Cool. I'll text you."

"That isn't what I said, and you know it."

"Okay. Talk later." He enters the car, grinning like he's just gotten away with something.

Later that night, while working on my biology homework, my phone buzzes with an incoming text message.

DAVI: I've got an idea for your audition song. Ever seen the movie Frozen?

I laugh, then type a response.

ME: I'm not auditioning. And even if I was, I would never sing Let It Go. NEVER.

DAVI: Wow. All caps. Seems a little harsh. What do you have against it?

ME: I think the entire human race is tired of that song.

DAVI: True. But I wasn't gonna suggest it.

ME: What song then?

I really shouldn't be entertaining him, but I'm curious.

DAVI: Into the Unknown from Frozen 2.

ME: OMG. You've seen the second movie too? LOL

ME: Didn't know you were such a fan of Disney princesses.

DAVI: My sister is eight. I'm a fan by association. Here's the song. Just listen.

I click the link he sends me, and for the rest of the night, I listen to the song on repeat. Not because I'm preparing for the audition, but because the song is surprisingly good.

Chapter Eight

ON SUNDAY MORNING, I STAND IN FRONT OF THE church congregation, the rest of the choir behind me. My hand shakes against the microphone, but I exhale and steady my grip.

Breathe in, breathe out. You can do this.

The band starts, and Ms. Silva gives me a thumbs-up. I turn back to the congregation, glance at my family, who take up the whole fourth pew, then spot Davi at the very back. He wasn't there a moment ago. I'm so startled by his appearance, I miss my cue. The band repeats the intro. This time, I pay attention—breathe in deeply and close my eyes before singing the first note. I don't open them until the song ends, and then my stare shifts to the back. Davi isn't there anymore. I scan the applauding crowd but don't see him.

The moment the service ends, I send him a text.

ME: Hey. You were at church. And then you weren't. Where'd you go?

A minute later, my phone buzzes.

DAVI: Couldn't stay long. There's somewhere I had to be.
ME: Is everything okay?
DAVI: Yeah.

DAVI: But now isn't really a good time to talk.
DAVI: I'll text later.

There's no way to measure later. It could be minutes or hours. Because I don't know when he'll text again, I cling to my phone for the rest of the day—while having lunch with my family, while letting Esosa practice new makeup techniques on me, and while talking to relatives in Nigeria. Sunday is the designated day for calling people back home. Usually, Esosa and I huddle around Mom's phone as she calls her brother and then her sister. We exchange pleasantries with our auntie and uncle, agree to behave and focus on our studies, then let Mom take over. The whole thing usually takes an hour, especially when Esosa and I talk to our cousins. Timothy, my nine-year-old cousin, believes living in America puts me in proximity to celebrities. Our conversations usually start with "Did you see Will Smith today?" and end with "Tell Cardi B I said hi."

After the call with my family, Uncle Davis takes me, Esosa, and Adrian to get frozen yogurt. Sweet Frost is a store decorated in pastels. It's bright and whimsical and always seems to have a crowd. We occupy a table that a family of four vacated, and Adrian immediately starts to devour his extra-large cup of cookie dough swirl. I eat my very berry frozen yogurt at a slower pace, breaking apart the chunks of red velvet cake on top as I think about my dad. Occasionally, he would take Esosa and me to Cold Stone Creamery. Mom, not a fan of sweets, always stayed home. So it was just the three of us. We would sit at a table, talking, laughing, enjoying our first, then second order of ice cream. I miss those days.

"How is it?" Uncle Davis asks me. "Your frozen yogurt."

I smile while licking my spoon. "It's very good."

"I'll be the judge of that." Adrian, without my permission, digs his spoon into my cup and scoops a sizeable portion of my yogurt into his mouth. "Mmmm," he says. "You're right. That is good."

If this was any other day but Sunday, when I'm in a less forgiving mood, I would retaliate by flinging his cup of cookie dough swirl on the floor. It would be an extreme reaction, but nonetheless satisfying.

"Okay." Adrian smacks his lips. "Whose am I sampling next?" He looks at his dad's plain vanilla, then at Esosa's dark chocolate raspberry.

"If you even try it, I promise you'll lose a finger." Esosa holds out her spoon like it's a weapon, and Adrian yields with his hands up.

"Okay. Okay. Relax. I get it."

Uncle Davis watches the scene with a smirk, like he's deriving some sort of entertainment from Adrian's attempt at theft and Esosa's threat of assault. "You guys are hilarious," he says, chuckling. He looks around the table at each of us, and then slowly, his lips fall to a tight-lipped smile. He glances between me and Esosa, and his bright eyes grow dim and sad.

I know immediately, without him expressing it, that he misses my dad. He never imagined it would only be me, my sister, and my mom in America. He imagined his brother as well, perhaps sitting around this lavender-colored table, enjoying frozen yogurt.

After a beat, Uncle Davis blinks sharply and is back to himself. "So," he says. "You guys have been in the States for a while now. Is there anything new you'd like to try—anywhere you'd like to go? We could plan something when I have some time off work."

"I want to go to a concert," Esosa says. "A Megan Thee Stallion concert."

"Who's Megan Thee Stallion?" Uncle Davis asks.

"One of the greatest rappers of our time. You must have heard some of her songs—'Savage,' 'Sweetest Pie,' 'Body.' She's amazing."

The information Esosa offers doesn't clear up Uncle's confusion. He frowns while eating his low-calorie frozen yogurt.

"Looks like my ride is here," Adrian says after glancing at his phone. He drops his spoon into his empty cup and stands. "Jake's outside," he tells his dad.

"Okay. Well, don't stay out late. You have school tomorrow."

Adrian nods, then looks at me. "Wanna come?"

"Come where?" I ask.

"A bunch of us are going to Jake's. It's gonna be fun. You should come—meet some of my friends, hang out."

"Um . . ." I shake my head. "No thanks."

"You sure?"

"Yeah."

"How about you?" Adrian asks Esosa. "You in?"

"I would, but I have homework to finish. Sorry."

"Right." He sighs and shoves his hands in his pockets. "Guess I'll see you guys later."

When he walks out of the shop, Esosa turns to Uncle Davis and starts listing all the places in America she wants to visit. Disneyland makes the cut.

LATER, WHILE I'M IN BED, ABOUT TO SLEEP, MY PHONE buzzes. I sit upright and reach for it on the bedside table. There are two text messages from Davi. I didn't think I'd hear from him today, especially since it's already past ten. It's a relief seeing his name on my phone and even more of a relief reading his messages.

DAVI: You sounded beautiful today.

DAVI: Sorry we didn't get a chance to talk. Long day.

ME: Are you okay?

DAVI: Yeah.

Even though there's no way to confirm it, I'm certain he isn't telling the truth.

DAVI: Are you ready for your audition tomorrow?

ME: Lol. You have to let that go. It's not happening.

DAVI: Why not?

ME: Because . . .

DAVI: Can I call you?

I didn't expect that, but I'm definitely not opposed to it.

ME: Ok.

The phone rings immediately.

"Hi," I whisper, so no one in my house hears me.

"Hey. How's it going?" Davi's voice seems different. There's an absent quality—the lightheartedness in his tone that's warm and contagious. I'm tempted to ask if he's okay again, but don't want to come off annoying. "So," he goes on, "about the audition."

"Yeah. About that. Why does it matter to you so much?"

"I think you have an incredible voice, but . . ." He blows out a breath. "It isn't just about that. When I heard you sing the other day and then today, I felt something."

"Felt something? What?"

"Many things. Everything." He chuckles lightly. "I don't know. But that's rare. A lot of great singers can't make people feel something. You can. That's special, Enore."

For a few moments, the phone line is quiet. I'm not sure what to say, so I hold my breath and wait for him to speak.

"Would you just sleep on it?" he asks. "Maybe you'll feel different tomorrow."

I'm certain I won't, but keep that to myself and say, "Maybe."

Chapter Nine

ON MONDAY, AFTER THE LAST SCHOOL BELL, I SHUFFLE through the crowded hallway and then into the library. Esosa is getting ice cream with friends, while Adrian is attending a computer club meeting and can't drive me home until it ends.

The elderly librarian sitting behind the front desk lowers her glasses and assesses me as if deliberating whether I'm here to be a nuisance or to actually get work done. When I smile, she does the same, then turns to her computer.

I sit by a window with a view of the parking lot, of students and teachers getting into cars and driving off. More people enter the library after a few minutes. Travis, a boy in all of my classes, walks in with a stack of books balanced against his chest. He's the guy who raises his hand before the teacher is finished asking a question. He begs for extra credit assignments even though the semester just began. He is president of the debate team and the robotics club. His entire personality is based on his intense, competitive need to be valedictorian and get into an Ivy League university. By definition, strictly based on the facts mentioned, he is a classic nerd. But other factors, like his incredible style and Drake-esque appearance, make the title *nerd* less applicable to him.

He approaches the table where I'm seated alone. "Hey, Enore," he says. "Mind if I sit here?"

"No. Go ahead."

"Cool." He places his stack of books on the table, slides his leather jacket off, and sits. "What are you working on?"

"Biology. You?"

"Same. Then I'll get started on calculus, then chemistry."

"Wait. We don't have any chemistry homework. Do we?" I glance at my agenda, where I write all my assignments and their due dates.

"No, we don't. I just like to read ahead, in true overachiever fashion."

I laugh, and he does too.

"So, how are you finding it here—at Bellwood High?" Travis asks. "I mean, it's only the second week, but all the AP classes pile on the workload quickly. You handling it?"

I arch an eyebrow. "What are you trying to do—get me to talk so you can find out my weakness, use it to eliminate me as your competition, so your path to valedictorian and an Ivy League university is clear?"

Travis stares at me blankly. "That sounds like the plot of a cliché teen movie."

It is the plot of a teen movie. But *Honor Society*—which I watched last night—turned every cliché on its head for an unexpectedly wholesome movie.

I flip a page in my textbook and shrug. "It is a movie, but it could happen."

"No, it couldn't," Travis counters. "I see you in class—answering questions without having to think twice, solving calculus equations without breaking a sweat. You're smart, but I have valedictorian on lock. Been working for it since my freshman year. You're not my competition. But maybe in another life. And as for Harvard, I've got a glowing letter of recommendation from a very successful, very influential alum." He winks and grins. "Friend of the family." After drinking from his water bottle, he clears his throat. The haughty expression leaves his face. "Besides, I was only asking out of curiosity. Wondering what it's like to start school in a whole new country."

"Well, my school in Nigeria was one of the best in the state. The material was just as advanced and the workload just as much. So the AP classes might be tough, but I'm used to it." I flip another page in my textbook nonchalantly, like I'm unfazed by the complex examination of invasive species. And I am.

"Okay." Travis smirks, impressed. "Noted."

We turn our attention to the questions in our textbooks and work quietly.

In all of our classes, Travis and I make up a tiny percentage of Black students. It's still so strange to look around a room and see only a handful of people who look like me. It's still strange being so hyperaware of my Blackness for the first time in my life, knowing that in a town like Bellwood where there are more artisan coffee shops than Black people, and a country like America where the weight of its history is perpetual and suffocating, my Blackness is usually the first and sometimes the only thing people notice about me.

Since moving to Bellwood, I've learned to search for people who look like me whenever I enter any space, to smile when our eyes connect—a small show of solidarity. Maybe this is why Travis is sitting with me now. Solidarity.

When I'm through with my biology homework, I move on to calculus. Travis does the same, and we continue to work in silence, until the abrupt sound of Davi's voice makes me flinch and sit up.

"Enore," he says, panting. "I've literally looked everywhere for you. I thought you left, but then I ran into Adrian, and he told me you were hanging around, waiting for him."

"Shh," the librarian says, glaring at Davi. "Keep it down. Better yet, don't talk."

"Sorry, Ms. Mulberry," he whispers, then turns back to my table. "Oh, hey, Travis. Didn't see you there."

Travis waves without a word, his lips firmly pressed together. He clearly does not appreciate Davi's interruption.

"I sent you a bunch of texts," Davi goes on in a whisper. "You didn't respond."

"My phone's in my bag," I explain. "On vibrate. Sorry."

"It's fine." There's a sheen of sweat on his forehead, as if his search for me involved some serious exercise.

"Why were you looking for me?"

"The audition."

I roll my eyes. "We already talked about this at lunch. I'm not doing it."

"I thought maybe you changed your mind."

"No. That didn't happen." I look at my textbook and flip a page. "By the way, shouldn't you be at football practice?"

"I told Coach I was sick—lied."

"Why?"

"Thought you might need a little nudge to get you to the auditions."

"Well, you really shouldn't have done that, because I'm not auditioning."

"Hmm." Davi hunches over, rests his arms on the table, and watches me.

"What?" I ask, taken aback by his closeness to my face.

"Want to know what I think?" His stare is fixed on mine. "I think you're scared. And maybe you don't even realize it."

"Scared?" I chuckle. "Of what? I've sung in a choir since I was ten. I'm not scared of singing."

"You've been in a choir for ages, and that's cool. But have you considered that maybe there's more than one way to use your voice? Maybe that's what scares you. The possibility of what you can do."

I don't like it—the way he acts like he, in such a short time, completely understands me, the way he acts like he knows a thought I haven't even admitted to myself. It's infuriating and invasive. And I want to prove him wrong.

"I'm not afraid of anything."

"Seriously, guys," Travis says in a clipped tone. "Can you take this somewhere else?"

"Sorry." I stand and shove my books into my bag. After taking a few steps toward the door, I pause and turn to Davi. He hasn't moved an inch. "Well? Are you going to show me where this audition is?"

His face brightens, and he jogs toward me, then leads the way.

We walk through the theater doors just as someone shouts, "Last call for auditions."

Davi turns to me and smiles. "Looks like we're just in time."

The theater is a massive dimly lit space with spotlights on the immense stage. What in the world was I thinking? I should be studying, not auditioning for a stupid musical. This was a huge, impulsive mistake. I breathe quickly as the gravity of what I'm about to do hits me.

"I can't do this."

"Yeah, you can." Davi closes the gap between us. His gaze is so strong, filled with conviction it seems he's trying to pour into me.

"You were right before. I am scared. Okay? You win, so let's just go."

"Enore, this wasn't a bet. I didn't want to be right. I just wanted you to sing. And I think deep down, you might want that too."

He does it again—pinpoints a thought before I've admitted it to myself. He's right. If I dig deep enough, past obligations and expectations, I will unearth a part of me that wants to get on that stage. And that terrifies me—not only the possibility of what I can do, but who I can be, someone so different from who I'm expected to be.

"Do you want to go up?" Davi asks. "There's nothing to be afraid of."

I'm not sure what it is about him that makes my grip on my apprehensions loosen. There's a quality I can't identify, and I'm okay not knowing what it is. I'm okay with only knowing that with him, I feel safe. "Will you come with me?"

"Yeah. Of course." He takes my hand and leads me to the front of the theater. "One more audition!" he shouts as we climb the stairs that ascend to the stage.

"Well, get on with it," the bald-headed man in the front row says, tapping a pen on a clipboard. "I don't have all day, you know." With his air of authority and slight arrogance, I conclude he's the director of the musical. He looks between me and Davi. "Is this a duet?"

In *High School Musical*, Troy offers to audition with Gabriella. They sing a heartwarming ballad that earns them a callback. For a moment, I hope Davi will offer to audition with me, but he shakes his head.

"No. It's just her." He gives me an encouraging smile. "You'll do great. And don't let Mr. Roland scare you. He's all bark." After squeezing my hand and lingering just a little, he walks to the end of the stage where the curtain falls.

"What song from the musical will you be singing?" Mr. Roland asks.

"Huh? I don't understand."

"Those auditioning are supposed to prepare a song from the selected musical this year. We're doing an original script inspired by Cinderella. With music from Rodgers and Hammerstein's *Cinderella*. I mentioned all this on the PA announcement. It was also on the flyer."

"Um . . ." I glance at Davi, and he gestures for me to stay calm. "Sorry. I must have missed that."

"Great. So you aren't prepared." He rolls his eyes. "Well, what did you plan to sing?"

"'Into the Unknown.'"

"Do you have sheet music for the pianist or a track?"

"I'll sing it a cappella."

"And your name?"

"Enore Adesuwa."

"Spelling."

He scribbles on his clipboard as I spell out my name, then looks at me. "Well, go ahead. We're all waiting."

It's only at that moment I notice the crowd in the theater—the people dispersed all around, looking at me. But when I close my eyes, they aren't there. Only my father is, and I sing.

The first verse is a whisper that echoes in the quiet space. As I repeat the series of *ah*s, my voice gets stronger. The second verse is louder, and then I hit the high keys in the chorus. The lyrics take on a significance they didn't have before; they resonate with me and seem as true as if I wrote them.

"'Are you here to distract me, so I make a big mistake? Or are you someone out there who's a little bit like me? Who knows deep down I'm not where I'm meant to be?'" I sing to this thing inside me that's been silenced by obligation and expectations and dreams that aren't mine—this thing I'm so afraid to claim, to call mine because I don't know where it will lead me and what it will demand from me. I blurt out each note, sing like I've never sung before, and then it's over.

There's a rowdy eruption of whistles and applause. I blink against the sharp stage lights, clearing my eyes until I see people standing, including Mr. Roland, who has traded his aloof expression for a delighted one.

I'm about to faint from the adrenaline rush. My knees wobble, but I manage to hurry backstage. Davi pulls me into a hug, and I wrap my arms around him and hold on tight.

"Enore, you were . . ." He sighs. "Transcendent."

I lift my head from his chest and look at him. "That song."

"What about it?"

I want to tell him it was magic and therapy, a miracle and hope mixed together and poured into me like a potion, stirring something awake. But I say, "Thank you for choosing it. I have never sung like that before."

"Not even in the choir?"

"No. Never. That—out there—was different."

It felt like I accessed another dimension of myself, one I never knew existed.

"Enore?" Mr. Roland calls out. "Is she still here?"

"Yeah! She's right here!" Davi replies and steers me toward the stage.

"You." Mr. Roland taps a pen against his chin and watches me. "You're the lead."

"What?"

"I'm going against protocol here by disregarding the fact that you didn't do a reading and giving you the lead. I mean, with a voice like that, how can I not?" He places a hand on his chest, breathes deeply, and nods as if agreeing with voices in his head. "Yeah. Mhm. You've got the lead role—Cassandra, a.k.a. Cinderella."

My mouth falls open. "Um . . . I . . . I didn't audition for the lead role."

"Then what role did you audition for?"

"Um . . . well, none. I didn't really think past singing."

The crowd in the theater laughs.

"Well, then I did the thinking, and I decided. You're the lead. Rehearsals are Mondays to Thursdays at three o'clock sharp. I suggest you make a lot of room in your schedule. I take my musicals very seriously. See you for the first rehearsal tomorrow." He gathers his things and leaves the theater without another word.

It takes a moment for me to process everything that just happened, to come to terms with it all.

But once I do, I don't regret a thing.

Chapter Ten

I WALK THROUGH THE FRONT DOOR HUMMING MY audition song. In the kitchen, Mom stops scribbling in a notepad and looks at me. Books for her licensing exam are on the countertop, overlapping each other in an untidy pile.

"You're in a good mood." She drops her pen and sets her full attention on me. "What's going on?"

"Nothing. How's studying?"

"Fine." She's tired. Her voice is coarse, and there are dark circles beneath her eyes. She won't ever admit to being exhausted. Or admit the study material is difficult or that she misses Daddy. She just smiles and says, "Everything is fine." But her smile is always strained, like there are invisible staples holding it in place, keeping it from collapsing to a frown. "How was your day? Eh?" she asks. "You seem happy. Did something happen?"

"Um . . . yes. I auditioned for the school—"

"Auditioned?" She sits up straight and crosses her arms. "For what? Is this something that will help you with your studies and get you into a good university?"

"Um . . . no."

"Enore." She sighs and presses a finger to her temple, then mumbles something under her breath in our language, Edo.

I look at the books spread out on the kitchen counter and then at Mom's fatigued eyes and low shoulders that seem weighed down by enough. "I mean, yes," I blurt out. "It will help me with university. It's math club. I auditioned for math club."

"Math club?" She tilts her head. "You have to audition for math club? You can't just join?"

"Um . . . yes. I mean, no. No, you can't just join. Members of the team have to make sure you're really good at math—test you first."

"Okay. So they tested you?"

I nod.

"And? Did they accept you?"

"Yes. They did. I'm a member of the math club now."

"Really?" The tension leaves her face. "Well, that's wonderful. Sara told me that university admissions are very competitive here. I'm happy you're taking initiative so that your application can stand out. Good job."

"Thank you." I struggle to keep a smile on my face.

"But talk to your sister for me, eh? She needs to take her studies more seriously. Because that girl is not serious at all. All she cares about is her makeup nonsense. Now she is talking about starting a YouTube channel. Maybe if she sees how you are behaving, it will help her change and focus on school."

It takes every bit of resolve to stay composed. "Okay. I'll talk to her."

In my room, I fall on the bed and stare at the ceiling. I just lied to my mom, and it's not a little white lie. This one is massive. What exactly will I have to do to maintain this lie—tell more lies, sneak around, ask people to lie for me? I am not equipped to pull all that off. Maybe I should tell her the truth, even though the truth will mean giving up the musical. For a moment, I sit on that option and imagine what it would be like to give up that stage and everything I experienced during the audition. My imagination runs wild, and the loss seems too real, too painful. I can't give it up. Not yet. I'll have to get comfortable with lying.

"So, everyone at school is talking."

I rise to my elbows and watch my sister at the doorway. "Talking about what?"

She enters the room and smirks. "You."

"Esosa," I say, my voice flat. "I'm really not in the mood for whatever this is, so *abeg* just come and be going."

"Well, I have something to show you. Something you will definitely want to see." She extends her phone to me. "Here. Look."

I take it hesitantly, then gawk at the screen. "Oh, my God. That's me! That's my audition!" I jump to my feet and pace around the room. "How? Who did this? Take it down."

"I can't. Someone posted it."

"Why would they do that?"

"Why not? It's a video worth watching."

After tripping on the white rug in the center of the room, I sit on the bed and grunt. "I don't want to be watched. How do I get it taken down?"

"Enore, relax." She sits beside me and pats my back. "It's not that serious. And if you didn't want to be watched, why did you go and audition?"

"I didn't think about this part. Just the singing part."

I didn't realize it before, but I've broken another of my rules—a crucial one.

Rule #3: Don't do anything to draw attention to yourself. Keep a low profile.

"Esosa, how many people have seen this?"

"Close to five thousand views."

"What?" I take deep, controlled breaths and try to stay calm because I'm sure Esosa has made a mistake. "It can't be five thousand."

"You're on the internet, Enore. People like and share. Within an hour of the video being posted, it got almost five thousand views. I'm hoping for viral status by end of day tomorrow."

"This isn't funny."

"And it's also not the end of the world like you're making it out to be." She shoves me playfully. "You know how people say don't read the comments?"

I swallow and nod.

"You should definitely read the comments."

My thumb hovers over the screen, but I don't scroll.

"Trust me."

After a deep exhale, I swipe upward and read.

SKYHIGH99: Damn! Amazing!

REIMAGINEDLOVE: Sis can sing!!

LOLA_LOVE: Who's this girl? I'm obsessed!!

BORNBRAVE2020: Have I watched this 10 times? Yes!

SWEETIEPIE: GOAT

DOSEOFESOSA: That's my big sister!!!! Follow her @EnoreEnchanted

I blink back the tears gathering in my eyes and look at Esosa.

"You saw my comment." She grins. "Didn't you?"

"'Enore Enchanted'?"

"I changed your IG handle. 'Fried Plantain underscore for Life' had to go. I even posted two videos—the one from your audition and the one from Sunday."

"Sunday?" I click on the handle, and I'm directed to a new page. "Esosa, why in the world did you record me singing on Sunday?"

"I needed to mark the moment—your first solo at the new church. Who knew it would come in handy during your rebranding?"

I rub the space between my eyebrows, then squint at something I didn't notice before. "Wait a minute. I have two thousand followers. Yesterday, it was a hundred and ten. How did this happen?"

"Well, people think you're incredible. And you are." Her bright eyes shift across my face. "When I saw that video, I was speechless. I knew you could sing, but not like that." She strokes the watch on my wrist. "Daddy would have been proud."

"You think so?"

"Of course. He loved it when you sang. Do you remember what he used to do whenever we turned on the car radio?"

"How can I forget?"

For every song that came on, for every artist that sang, he would say, "You call this singing? My daughter can sing better than this."

We laugh at the memory, and then I look at my Instagram page. "Why Enore Enchanted?"

"You're the one who sang a Disney princess song. I had to work with what I had. But it sounds nice, don't you think?"

"It does." We're quiet for a moment, and I fidget with my hair while thinking of the lie I told recently. "I didn't tell Mommy about the musical. I lied—told her I joined a math club. If she knew, she would—"

"I know," Esosa says. "Trust me, I know."

In sync, we sigh and our backs hit the bed.

"What if she finds out somehow—sees the video or hears about it?"

"Mommy isn't active on social, so she'll likely never see it. Unless it somehow makes its way to her WhatsApp prayer group. But that's unlikely."

"But what if it does? What if she sees it?"

"Then we'll handle it. We'll figure it out. But in the meantime, I'll tell Adrian to keep his mouth shut and not to say a word about the musical or the video to Auntie Sara or Uncle Davis."

"Okay. Good. Thanks."

I rest my head against hers, and we stay that way for a long while.

"Tomorrow, everyone at school is going to know who you are," Esosa says.

My heart skips as the realization hits me.

She turns to me, studies my expression, and smirks. "Oh, this is going to be interesting."

Chapter Eleven

I HAVE A THEORY. MEAN GIRLS COME IN THREES. THE best proof of this is the witch trio in *The Craft* and the Plastics in *Mean Girls*. Another theory, the girl in the middle is usually the most lethal. Proof: Nancy Downs and Regina George.

While I'm hanging my baseball hat on the hook in my locker, three girls walk toward me—their steps almost in sync. Seconds ago, when I came through the school doors, my hat and oversized hoodie hid my face well enough. No one glanced at me. Esosa called my disguise ridiculous. She wanted me to bask in the attention she predicted I would get today. I wanted to hide from it, and my outfit, inspired by Davi, helped me do that. But the moment I arrived at my locker and flipped the hood off my head, a blond-haired girl looked at me. After whispering to the two girls beside her, they moved in my direction.

Now I'm eager to slam my locker shut and sprint away, but I don't. All three of them have that thing, that quality that compels people to pay attention to them. Esosa has it too. When she walks into a room, people notice. Not because she's the prettiest girl in the room or the best dressed, but because she has the good sense to believe she is. These three girls must believe the same thing, and maybe they aren't wrong.

The blond girl in the middle smiles once she's in front of me. She has big green eyes and a light blush on her cheeks that looks natural, not like something she caked on. Her outfit—tight blue jeans and a cropped T-shirt—is both casual and stylish and flatters her full figure. "Hey," she says. "It's Enore, right?"

"Um . . ." I nod, which is better than the alternative—babble like an awkward fool.

"I'm Bethany."

Again, I nod.

"This is Sybil."

The girl to her right, with straight burgundy hair and an expansive smile, waves at me.

"And this is Ara."

The girl to her left blinks slowly, as if she's both bored and unimpressed. She doesn't smile or wave. Her small face is angular, and with her light brown complexion and dark curls, she bears a striking resemblance to Yara Shahidi.

"We saw your audition," Bethany continues. "Well, everyone's sort of seen it."

"It was amazing," Sybil adds. "You were amazing. Mind if I take a picture of you for the school paper?" She points a camera at my face.

"Whoa." Somehow, I find my voice again and turn away from the long lens. "Please . . . um . . . don't . . . don't do that."

"Stop fangirling, Syb. You're frightening the poor girl," Ara says in a monotone.

"Right. Sorry if I'm coming off too strong." Sybil lowers the camera. "I just think you're totally newsworthy—the new girl, an immigrant from Nigeria, the star of the school play. I could do a whole feature on you. What do you think?"

My stare shifts between all three girls, assessing them, trying to determine their intentions. I don't want my theory to be the deciding factor.

"She's passionate," Bethany says. "Not crazy. I promise."

"Well, let's not lie," Ara mumbles. "Sometimes she can be a little unhinged."

The bell rings the instant Sybil and Bethany glare at Ara. I sigh, relieved this awkward encounter can end.

"Um . . . thank you for the offer," I say, closing my locker. "But I don't want to be in the school paper. I'm just trying to keep a low profile."

"A low profile?" Ara scoffs, and her expression quickly transforms from aloof to livid. She clenches her jaw and scowls. "Then why the hell did you audition for the musical? Were you just looking for something to pass the time—a new hobby?"

I'm confused and taken aback. What in the world is her problem? Instead of trying to figure it out, I turn away and hurry off. It's unclear whether I'm running from Bethany, Sybil, and Ara, or if I'm running to class. I try not to dwell on the distinction while moving through the active crowd.

Quickly, I step into the classroom, and then I flinch, startled by the abrupt sound of applause.

There's a scene in *Clueless* where the whole student body applauds Cher for playing matchmaker and getting two strict teachers together, an act that eventually makes the lovebirds more lenient about grades and homework. I've done nothing that brilliant, but the moment I walk into AP Calculus, everyone claps. Instead of smiling and curtseying like Cher did in *Clueless*, I shuffle to my seat in the back.

"Hey," Davi says. "Everyone saw your audition."

"Oh." I shrink in my seat, wishing I could disappear.

"You hate this, don't you?"

"It's uncomfortable. Can you make it stop?" I thought Mr. Mitchell would bring the room to order, but he's clapping too.

"Okay," Davi calls out. "She gets it! Let's give it a rest!"

Gradually, the clapping stops. Wild Curls, whose name is actually Miles, stops whistling with his fingers. When the noise dies down completely, I mouth, *Thanks*, to Davi, then turn to the rest of the class.

"Thank you," I whisper, flattered and embarrassed.

"No, thank you for blessing my feeds with those vocals," Tamara, a girl with a perfectly rounded Afro, says. "And for knocking Queen Ara off her musical theater throne. She reigned for far too long."

I squint and consider Tamara's words. At the same time, I revisit and examine my recent interaction with Ara, connect all the dots, and then everything makes perfect sense.

WHEN THE LUNCH BELL SOUNDS, I MEET DAVI AT HIS locker.

"Hey," he says, fastening the lock. "Was just heading to the bleachers."

"About that. I thought we could have lunch somewhere else today."

"Okay. Where do you have in mind?" Davi leans into me, searching my eyes and smirking as if he knows what's coming.

"The cafeteria."

"Ahh." He nods. "And you think you're ready for the terror that's the cafeteria?"

I laugh and shove him playfully. "Yeah. I do."

After surviving the morning being the center of attention, I'm better equipped to handle the cafeteria. In each of my classes, people I never spoke to knew my name. They referenced my audition and raved about it. The same thing happened as I walked down the hallway. At first, the attention was overwhelming. Gradually, I got used to it. I started having conversations with people and accepting invitations to parties, knowing I was already past the point of no return.

"After the morning I've had, I can handle the cafeteria. Also, I think I've kept you from your friends long enough."

"I wasn't complaining. But if you say you're up for it, let's do it."

Davi and I aren't holding hands, but we walk considerably close as we enter the cafeteria. I'm not surprised by the layout of the room; it's like what I've seen in movies—crowded tables, the school's signature colors on the walls, and a range of food tended by lunch ladies. Honestly, it's an intimidating place. I'm tempted to take Davi's hand and turn back. We could go to the bleachers, just the two of us. Already I miss the simplicity of that equation, especially when he directs me to a crowded rectangular table.

There are five people at the table, but three familiar faces. Bethany, Sybil, and Ara. I freeze, and Davi turns to me.

"Everything okay?" he asks.

"Um . . . are those your friends?"

"Yeah."

"The same ones you've known since kindergarten?"

"That's them."

Should I call this a coincidence or a severe case of bad luck? I mean, even coincidences don't hit this hard. This, right here, is pure bad luck. My luck.

"Come on. I'll introduce you." He takes my hand before I can escape. "They're cool. You'll see."

We approach them, and when all five focus on us, I clench Davi's hand. The window that extends behind their table is so large; sunlight pours through it and hits all of them just right. This is it—the table everyone wants a seat at, the people everyone wants to befriend. No one needs to tell me this. It goes without saying.

"Guys, this is—"

"Enore," a boy with a topknot of dreadlocks says, cutting Davi off. "Yeah. I know you. Or know of you. Dope audition." He moves his hands as he speaks, and the rings on his fingers catch the light and glint. "I'm Zane, by the way."

Is it strange to say someone looks like art—the sort of unintentional art where a painter splashes colors on a canvas, and somehow, through the graceful chaos of it all, the piece comes out stunning and emotive and captivating? That's Zane—unintentional art, gracefully chaotic. There are too many colors and patterns on his kimono, but the white T-shirt he wears inside creates the perfect balance. There are tattoos on his arm—five symbols that look ancient—etched on his light brown skin. His vibe is tranquil, soothing, and enigmatic. He speaks slow and calm like he's savoring syllables, truly appreciating them. And I feel what every person at this school probably feels when they look at him—fascination.

"So." The muscular guy sitting beside Zane smirks, and his blue eyes narrow. "Are you the reason Davi's been avoiding us during lunch?"

Davi laughs and shoves him. "Shut up, Blake."

"What? She's cute. I totally get why you've been hiding her, keeping her away from the competition." He pulls off the square-shaped glasses that make him look studious and winks at me.

"Ignore him," Davi says. "He has a massive ego. We all thought he'd grow out of it by now, but no such luck." He turns away from Blake and toward the girls. "This is—"

"We've already met," Bethany interrupts.

"Yeah," Sybil adds with a smile. "This morning."

"Oh. Cool." Davi nods, and because it's too late to run, I sit beside him.

"Sorry about earlier," Bethany says to me.

"What happened earlier?" Davi asks.

Bethany and Sybil glance at Ara, who moves a fork through a bowl of fruit. When she stabs a strawberry, she puts it in her mouth and chews while watching me blankly.

Somehow, Davi understands. Under the table, he squeezes my hand. This isn't the first time we've held hands. The newness is gone, but the thrill isn't. When he touches me—skin to skin—I feel so much at once, strong emotions that make self-control seem unattainable. I like Davi, and that scares me as much as standing on that theater stage did. I worry what liking him will make me do. Will I sneak around to see him? Lie some more to my mother? Ask people to lie for me?

In every teen movie I've watched, teenagers don't think twice about dating. They're allowed to without question. Well, except in *10 Things I Hate About You*, when Bianca's father bans her from dating until her older sister does. But eventually, both Bianca and her sister have boyfriends, and their father accepts it. In Nigeria, teenagers don't date. It isn't just a rule within distinct families. It's more like a cultural rule—a norm. How is a girl like me—who has never been on a date, whose first and only kiss happened in a school stairway with a boy whose tongue wagged too much—supposed to navigate having a crush that could be reciprocated?

I'm in America now. I like a boy. I think he might like me too. But what now?

"Enore," Sybil says. "I meant what I said this morning. I would love to feature you in the school newspaper. I promise to be less confrontational with my camera."

I laugh. "Yeah. The lens in my face was a bit much."

"Sorry about that." She twirls a lock of her hair and watches me through long, dark lashes. "Would you maybe reconsider?"

It's hard to say no when she watches me with a doe-eyed expression. I sigh and nod. "Okay. I'll do it."

"Yay!" She claps and squeals. "Thank you!"

"It's that look," Zane says. "Beware of it. Works every time."

Sybil sticks out her tongue at him, then turns to me. "So, I'll meet you after you're done with rehearsal today. I'll only ask you a few questions. It won't take long."

"Okay." I look around the table and clear my throat. "So, um . . . Davi told me you've all been friends since kindergarten and middle school. That's amazing."

"It is, isn't it?" Bethany says, beaming. "And it's our last year together." She huffs and shakes her head, no longer smiling. "I don't even wanna think about that."

"You gotta sometime," Blake says. "Last prom. Last homecoming. Last chance to kick Fairview's ass. I swear this is the year. Right, Davi?"

"Damn right!" Davi's enthusiasm seems forced, but I doubt Blake notices.

"Are you all on the football team?" I ask.

"Just me and Blake," Davi answers. "Zane doesn't do sports."

"Wrong. I prefer sports that involve less grunting and more . . . pep." He throws a grape in the air and catches it in his mouth. "Cheerleading, for example."

"Really?" Bethany says. "Then how come you've never tried out for the team, especially since you know I've been trying to recruit more guys for years?"

"The uniforms. Polyester doesn't agree with my skin or my lifestyle."

Bethany rolls her eyes. "I honestly can't even deal with you sometimes." She turns away from him and looks through her phone. "Enore, interested in trying out for the cheerleading team?"

"I don't think so. I'm not the most coordinated person. Are you guys all on the team?"

"Just me. Sybil's editor of the school newspaper. And Ara—"

"Can speak for herself, thank you very much." Ara's harsh tone stuns everyone at the table.

We're quiet, the atmosphere suddenly tense and awkward.

"Um . . . I . . ." Sybil mutters, shifting anxiously in her chair. "Enore, since we have time right now, I could ask you some of the interview questions." She's likely trying to defuse the tension, fill the awkward silence with words.

"Sure. Go ahead," I tell her.

She flips open a small notepad. "So, you're new to Bellwood. How do you like it so far?"

"It's good. Great."

"And what inspired you to audition for the musical?"

"I actually didn't plan on it. Davi pushed me to do it. He was very persistent."

"Really," Ara says. "Davi pushed you." She looks at him, nods thoughtfully, then shoves her chair back and storms off.

Everyone at the table, aside from myself, shares a knowing look.

"Give me a minute." Davi lets go of my hand and stands. "I'll be right back." He smiles apologetically at me, then walks away.

"Um . . . is everything okay?" I ask no one specific.

"Nope," Blake says before biting into a taco. "Not by a long shot."

"Ara's been the lead in the school musical since freshman year," Zane explains. "She isn't taking this well."

"Yeah, so bring the fangirling down a notch," Bethany tells Sybil.

"Right. Sorry."

I don't understand how someone can be so upset about not getting a role. I'm excited about the musical, but maybe it doesn't mean that much to me yet. It clearly means a lot to Ara. I feel guilty suddenly, for having something she values more.

Davi doesn't return to the cafeteria, but his friends are good company, and Bethany and Sybil seem genuinely nice. When the bell rings, I say goodbye to them and make my way to class. Just as I attempt to turn down a hallway, I see Davi and Ara. They're having what seems like an intense conversation, so I duck back and give them some privacy. However, as people enter classrooms and the chaos in the hallway dies down, I hear their conversation.

"Honestly, I don't understand why you're mad at me," Davi says. "I didn't do anything."

"You didn't do anything? Seriously? You made her audition. You basically pitted her against me."

"Come on, Ara. You know it's not like that. I heard Enore singing and thought she was good, so I told her to audition—that's it."

"Yeah, but she got the goddamn lead. The lead. And I'm the understudy." Her voice cracks and shakes. "I have never, ever been an understudy in my life."

Davi sighs. "I don't know what you want me to say. And I don't know why you're so upset about the musical, especially since you don't even . . ." He pauses.

"Especially since I don't even what?" she asks. "Go ahead. Say it."

He doesn't say a thing.

"You know, I get we're not dating anymore, but I didn't think you'd stop having my back."

The second bell rings. The hallway is quiet. At some point, they both likely walked away, but I haven't moved an inch. My heart pounds. My stomach tightens. Ara's last sentence repeats in my head.

There's a word I've never said, finding it almost too heavy to pronounce. Now, however, my lips shape the word easily and I spit it out.

"Fuck."

Chapter Twelve

THE SCRIPT IN MY HANDS TRANSLATES TO ONE THING—commitment, one I might not meet. I think of the lie I'll have to tell my mom today and tomorrow and the days and months ahead. I think of the lead role, the weight of it, the expectation, and my huge lack of experience. I filter through the crowd onstage until I see Ara, the bitter understudy and Davi's *ex-girlfriend*, who definitely hates me. She deserves this more than I do, and she knows it. Her eyes meet mine; they narrow as if sizing me up, noting all the ways I don't compare to her.

And then it occurs to me. I am dangerously close to having an enemy—a rival. And that is the last thing I want. In fact, it's a rule on my list of high school dos and don'ts.

Rule #4: Don't make any enemies or start a rivalry.

This rule is so important, I took an extra measure and created subrules.

a. *Don't brag about your grades.*

b. *Don't be competitive.*

c. *Avoid conflict/drama.*

But these extra steps were pointless because in the end, all I did was sing on a stage and like a boy—things that somehow led to Ara glaring at me and probably plotting my demise.

"Okay," Mr. Roland says, clapping his hands. "Welcome to the production of *Cinders and Embers*, Bellwood's modern retelling of

Cinderella, set in New York City. I love that social media is a big part of this story, and that in the end, Cassandra—a.k.a. Cinderella—takes things into her own hands. I cowrote it, and I will admit, it's brilliant. Opening night is scheduled for Friday, December eighth. That's in three months. So let's get started. We have lots to do."

It's a little past three. The last school bell rang thirty minutes ago. After dodging Davi, I sprinted to the theater for rehearsal. Since overhearing his conversation with Ara this afternoon, I've avoided speaking and making eye contact with him. Getting that information about his past changed things between us. He isn't aware of this change, but I am, and it's affecting how I interact with him. I'm more cautious now—careful not to hold his stare for too long or return his smile or walk too close to him. Careful not to feel too much or feel anything at all, because Davi is the complication I hoped to avoid in high school.

"Let's take twenty minutes to go through the script. Use this time to highlight your lines. But I expect everyone to know their lines by next week."

Mr. Roland's instruction brings the theater to silence as everyone looks through the script and starts highlighting. His production assistant, a slim blond woman likely in her twenties, collects everyone's email and phone number on a clipboard. After scribbling down mine, I look up and see Ara casually scanning the script, looking unfazed by its length. Maybe by the end of rehearsal, she'll know every word, every action, every song. After all, she is a pro—Bellwood's reigning musical theater queen. And I am . . .

I sigh.

I don't know what I'm doing here. The script in my hand has too many neon-colored lines, indicating where I speak and sing. It's too much. I haven't acted a day in my life. I'm not even sure I can act. The weight of the role hits me again—the expectation, the commitment, my huge lack of experience. Suddenly, my heart thumps fast, and my breaths are short.

While I'm trying to manage my growing anxiety, Mr. Roland assembles the actors in the first scene. I stand with them onstage, the bulky script squeezed in my grip. Cole, the student playing the millionaire playboy—a.k.a. the prince—glances at the script in my hand and laughs lightly.

"Are you nervous or just annoyed and planning to whack Mr. Roland over the head with that?"

I loosen my grip on the bundle of paper and shrug. "A little of both, but more of the latter."

He laughs again, louder this time. Mr. Roland stops speaking to the group and spins to us. "I'm sorry." His impeccably shaped eyebrow, thick and the perfect contrast to his bald head, arches. "Am I amusing you?"

Cole and I shake our heads.

His hard stare remains on us for a moment, then shifts to the rest of the group. He continues speaking, elaborating on his incredibly high expectations and his very low tolerance for mediocrity and imperfection.

A knot forms in my stomach. Does this man know we're high school students and not professionals? Well, everyone but Ara.

"Hey," Cole whispers. "You okay?" He scans my face. Clearly, signs of my discomfort are on it.

"Just a little nervous." I exhale. "Really nervous. I haven't done anything like this before."

"Well, I was here. In the theater. During your audition." Cole's eyes follow Mr. Roland as he marches across the stage and makes exaggerated hand gestures. "You weren't nervous then."

"I was. At first, but then I felt . . ."

"You felt what?"

I search my mind for the right words, the best way to explain the emotion that pushed me to sing like I did yesterday but come up with nothing. "I don't know."

"You don't have to fully understand that feeling or even know where it comes from. Just go with it. Trust me. It helps." He turns to me, and the corners of his lips lift. A deep blush warms his white skin. As if he's aware of the change in his complexion, he looks away quickly and tilts his head down, enough that his brown hair dangles and covers part of his face.

"Okay!" Mr. Roland claps. "Let's begin! We don't have all day."

After a long sigh, I turn my crumpled script to the first act.

Ayana, who is playing the celebrity stylist—a.k.a. the fairy godmother—starts reading. "Once upon a New York minute," she begins. The only sound in the theater is her voice—solid but soft because of the acoustics. When she stops speaking, she and everyone else turn to me.

I'm supposed to say or do something. I glance at my script for direction, then look at Mr. Roland. "It says Cassandra enters beneath the moon. And then it says she runs to a post light." I look around the stage. "What post light? There isn't one."

After a second of silence, everyone laughs, including Ara, who's sitting in the front row of the theater.

"Obviously, there is no set design yet." Mr. Roland sighs. "Just use your imagination, Enore."

"Oh." My cheeks turn hot, burning with embarrassment.

"Go ahead," Mr. Roland urges. "Carry on."

Everyone watches, waiting for me to say something stupid again. Cole's kind eyes encourage me, and I run to a spot where I imagine there's a post light. I'm supposed to cry now while leaning against the post light. I clear my throat, then release a shrill sound that's meant to be a whimper. People chuckle. It's difficult, but I ignore them and focus on the script. The one line I'm supposed to say in this scene has only six words, but my mouth dries as I try to say them, and I stutter like a malfunctioning robot.

"Okay. That's enough," Mr. Roland says. "It's only the first rehearsal."

"Maybe it should be her last," Ara retorts. She meets my stare and smirks, enjoying my humiliation.

"Let's call it a day."

I haven't known Mr. Roland for long, but I'm surprised those words came out of his mouth, surprised he isn't using every minute of the two-hour rehearsal to whip every cast member, especially me, into shape. Everyone looks just as surprised; they gawk at him with wide eyes as if he's sprouted a second head.

"We'll continue tomorrow. Make sure to learn your lines and musical numbers. We'll start rehearsing with the band in a few weeks. And watch your emails for any announcements." He claps twice. "You're dismissed."

People gather their things. Ara gives me one last condescending smirk, then struts off.

"Enore." Mr. Roland says. "Stay back. I would like to talk to you in private."

"Oh. Okay." After my pathetic attempt at acting, I'm sure he regrets making me the lead. He likely wants to strip me of the title. And maybe that wouldn't be such a bad thing.

I glance at Cole, who's beside me, sliding his arms into his jean jacket. He looks from Mr. Roland to me, offers a sympathetic smile, and then walks offstage.

I fidget with my bag strap while watching Mr. Roland.

"Have you ever been in a play?" he asks when we're alone and the theater doors are closed, blocking off the noise in the hallway. "You're awkward onstage, so I'm guessing you haven't." He taps his chin and considers me deeply, like he did after my audition. "Actually, I'm not sure if you're awkward, clueless, or just lack a great deal of confidence. Maybe it's a combination of all three. What do you think?"

I frown. Does he really expect me to answer that?

"I would like an answer, especially since I'm trying to understand what's going on here?"

He's rude and very casual about his rudeness as if he expects everyone to just deal with it. I'm tempted to grab the script in my bag and smack him with it. Cole put the image in my head, and now it's playing on a loop.

"I'm trying to help you, Enore."

"Then maybe you should change your approach a little." I bite my lip, stunned by my snappy tone.

Culturally, I've been taught to respect my elders. In the movies

I've watched, teenagers are often rude to their teachers. They play pranks on them, insult them, and have outbursts that disrupt the class. None of that would happen in a Nigerian school, not with teachers who have access to canes and the authority to use them on any badly behaved student. The fear of being flogged is enough to keep most in line. It always kept me in line, but with that element—the threat of a firm wooden stick hitting my palm—gone, I've suddenly become uninhibited. Still, what I've been taught culturally— by my parents and so many others—resounds in my head. *Always respect your elders.* Respect elders who sometimes don't deserve respect. That obligation is tangled with many others I can't seem to untether myself from.

"Sorry," I say, looking at my feet. "I shouldn't have . . ." After blowing out a breath, I lift my head. "I should go."

"Excuse me?" Mr. Roland scowls. "We're having a conversation."

"I quit," I blurt out. Tears settle at the rims of my eyes. "I can't do this. I . . . I don't know how."

His face is impassive. His lips are pressed in a tight line like he's holding back a lot of words.

I get off the stage and rush down the aisle and then through the door, trying to convince myself, as I get further away, that I did the right thing.

Chapter Thirteen

I STEP OUT OF THE SCHOOL BUILDING AND SEE ESOSA sitting on the steps, exactly where her text said she would be. She's with a dark-haired girl, who's blowing air into a piece of pink bubble gum. After a closer look, I realize it's Jade from Tech and Techies. They're sharing a phone screen and laughing at whatever has their attention.

"Hey," I say.

Esosa looks up from the phone and smiles. "How was rehearsal?"

"Um . . . okay." Thanks to the restroom trip I made before coming outside, there's no evidence of the disastrous rehearsal. My eyes are dry—no trace of the tears that fell as I left the theater. "Ready to go?"

"Yeah." She stands and shoves the phone into her pocket. "By the way, this is Jade. Jade, my sister. Enore."

"We've met," Jade says with a straight face. "Is that piece of junk still functioning?" Her lips, coated with black lipstick to match her hair, twist upward. "I would be surprised if it didn't fall apart on the way home."

Honestly, I don't see the appeal of being friends with Jade, but I'll leave that to my sister.

"Let's go. Where's Adrian?"

"He left," Esosa answers. "He said he had something important to do."

"How are we supposed to get home?"

She shrugs, and I sigh.

"I guess we're walking."

Esosa says bye to Jade, and we start the walk home. Trees line both sides of the small street; their branches curve, creating an arch of leaves that shields us from the sun.

"I signed up to do makeup for the musical," Esosa says.

"Oh?"

"Yeah. It will be good experience. And I'll get to do your makeup. And you know you can trust me to make you look amazing."

I don't tell her the truth—about today's terrible rehearsal that confirmed I am not a performer. I'm only fit to sing in a choir.

A minute into our walk, a silver Toyota pulls up to the curb.

"Hey, Enore." Davi's face appears in the open car window. "Want a ride?"

"Um . . ." I'm so caught off guard, I can't find the words to politely say no.

"Yes!" Esosa answers without a second thought. She attempts to move toward the car, and I grab her wrist.

"No. Thank you. We're fine." The smile on my face is strained and I'm sure very unconvincing.

"What are you doing?" Esosa whispers in my ear. "A cute boy is offering us a ride home. What's the issue?"

"Nothing. I'd just rather walk," I whisper back.

"Why? Isn't he your friend? Haven't you two been sneaking off to have lunch together since school started?"

"Wait. How do you know that?"

"Everyone knows. Everyone also thinks you two are secretly dating."

"What?" Shocked, I forget to whisper.

Davi frowns, and his eyes shift between my sister and me. "Everything okay?"

"Everything's perfect," Esosa answers, then turns to me. Her firm, no-nonsense expression is a little intimidating. "Look. If this is you making *shakara*, don't. It's not the time. I'm wearing wedges, and I'd rather have a ten-minute ride home than a thirty-minute walk." She pulls her arm from my grip, opens the car door, and enters the backseat.

Both she and Davi look at me, and because I don't want to look like a complete idiot, I walk to the car. When I try to enter the backseat, Esosa holds the door handle and motions for me to sit in front. I roll my eyes but relent.

"Hi." I don't look at Davi while pulling the seat belt over my chest. "Thanks for the ride."

"Yeah. Sure. Where to?"

I give him the address, and he drives. His grip on the steering wheel is tight, his back erect as he looks straight ahead. If he wasn't aware of the change between us before, he must be now. There's tension, heavy like a weighted blanket. In the back, Esosa hums along to the song playing on the radio, blissful and carefree. I, however, look out the window as if the trees we drive past are the most interesting things in the world. I want to speak, start a conversation to lighten the mood, but it seems like too much effort.

The car enters the driveway and stops in front of the main house.

"Thanks for the ride!" Esosa says before rushing out of the car. It's obvious what she's trying to do.

"Whoa." Davi gapes out the window. "This is your house?"

"It's my uncle's."

He nods.

Davi knows nothing about my family situation. I planned on telling him about my dad, but it's pointless now. I'm trying to put some distance between us, not create intimacy.

"I'll see you tomorrow. Thank you again." I step out of the car and breathe in the tension-free air. As I walk toward the path that leads to the guesthouse, Davi steps out of the car.

"Hey." He jogs toward me, then stuffs his hands in his pockets. "Did I do something?" His eyes shift from my face to the ground and then up again. "'Cause you seem a little off . . . like I did something. Like you're mad at me."

I'm not mad at him. I'm just trying to navigate high school without being sucked into the chaos and the politics, without being overwhelmed by it all. And being with Davi, even as friends, is making that impossible. Because he is more than just the complication I hoped to avoid in high school. He's the reason I've broken four of my rules. But truthfully, that's my fault. Not his. I should have done exactly what I was supposed to do, exactly what was expected of me.

"You didn't do anything, Davi. And I'm not angry at you."

"Okay. Then what is it? You've been acting weird all afternoon. Did something happen at lunch? Did Blake say something when I left?"

I shake my head. "No. Blake didn't say anything. He and everyone else were nice."

"So what is it?" He takes a step toward me, and then another, until we're close. "What's going on?"

Davi and Ara's conversation plays back in my head—the tense

exchange and the bomb dropped right at the end. "You used to date Ara."

He exhales, and his eyes gradually turn from concerned to apologetic. "I wanted to tell you."

"I really wish you had."

"We started dating back in January. We ended things by March. It honestly seems like so long ago now. It doesn't even matter."

"But it does," I say.

I watch his eyes, the striking blend of hazel and green, and warmth bursts in the pit of my stomach. With Davi, my body always reacts in ways it never has before. I have analyzed each reaction and found they're triggered by infatuation and feelings of a romantic nature. When we first met, it was strictly infatuation—something crazed inside me, fueled by teenage hormones. But lately, the pace of my heart, the moisture that gathers in my palms, and the sensations in my gut are all triggered by romantic feelings.

"I like you, Davi. Not just as a friend." I'm shocked by my bluntness. If Esosa was here, she would scold me for not making *shakara*. I really should have . . . even a little. But I've made a mistake and lost grip on my emotions and self-control. I'm so embarrassed but surprised when Davi's lips expand into a smile.

"I like you too," he says. "A lot."

Well, there it is—a confession from both of us. I huff, deeply relieved he reciprocates my feelings.

If things were different, if there wasn't the complication of an ex-girlfriend or a set of rules that give me a sense of security, we would inch closer. Our heads would tilt slightly—one falling to the right and the other to the left. We would pucker our lips, and just before they touched, just before we kissed, I would warn him. I would tell him I might be bad at it, at kissing just like Jamie said to Landon in *A Walk to Remember*. But he would kiss me anyway, and it would be sensational. And there would be a moment when our lips stopped moving, but we stayed close, reluctant to step apart.

But none of these things can happen. And while I already know that, Davi realizes it slowly. His wide smile falls, and his brows furrow as he squints and searches my eyes.

"Enore, Ara and I are over. Our breakup was mutual. We realized we were better off as friends. That's all we are now—friends."

If there's any truth to what he says, it doesn't matter. I can't let it matter.

"I'm sorry. But it just seems like a lot. I don't want any drama or issues with anyone, you know? I just want to keep my head down and mind my business. So maybe it's best we just . . ." The words that complete that sentence hang in my throat—stuck, resisting release. I exhale, clear my throat, and push them out. "Keep our distance."

"I'm really confused right now. We went from saying we like each other to . . . this." Davi shakes his head. "Honestly, I don't even know what this is. Are you saying you don't want to be friends anymore?"

Slowly, I nod. "I think that might be best."

He laughs lightly. Though it's missing the element of humor that makes a laugh a laugh. It sounds, instead, empty. "Are you"—another empty chuckle—"joking?"

I say nothing, but there's a clear answer, even with my lips sealed.

"Oh." He nods. "Is that really what you want—for us to just stop being friends? Just like that?"

"My life is complicated right now, Davi. It's a mess." Tears sting my eyes. I blink, willing them to stay back for a while longer, until I'm alone. "I'm a mess, and I'm trying to survive this country and this town and school. If I can do that—if I can just survive this one year with no issues, with nothing else getting out of my control, I think I'll be okay."

He watches me, then takes a tentative step forward. When he reaches out to touch me, I rush down the path that leads to the guesthouse. Thankfully, he doesn't follow.

At the front door, I rub the tears from my eyes and breathe deeply. I force myself to smile—to put on a mask—before turning the knob and stepping into the house.

Inside, there's the savory aroma of home cooking. It doesn't take much guessing to know Mom has made jollof rice. I pull my shoes off on the doormat and drop my bag on the salmon-colored couch that's topped with white throw pillows. When I step into the kitchen, I'm surprised it's full. Uncle Davis, Auntie Sara, and Adrian sit at the counter, all with a plate of jollof rice in front of them.

"Hey!" Adrian says while chewing. "Where've you been?"

"At school. Where you left us," I reply, annoyed. "I thought you left because you had something important to do."

"That's what he told me," Esosa says, searching the refrigerator.

"I did have something important to do—eat jollof rice. Dad told me Auntie made some. You guys were taking forever, so I left."

"And how exactly did you expect us to get home?"

"Didn't really think that part through. You know, I had j rice on the brain."

Uncle Davis drops a heavy hand on Adrian's shoulder. "Stop

running your mouth and apologize to your cousins for being inconsiderate."

"But what's the big deal? They got home all right."

"Adrian."

"Okay. Fine. Sorry. It won't happen again."

Uncle Davis shakes his head disapprovingly at his son, then turns to me. "So, how did you guys get home?"

"We got a ride from a . . . um . . ." I think for a moment, and the word I land on stings. "Classmate." That's what Davi is now. No longer a friend.

"Why don't you sit down," Auntie Sara says. "I'll fix you a plate, and you can tell us about your day."

"No. That's fine. I'm not hungry. Where's my mom?"

"In her room, taking a call."

I nod and join Esosa by the refrigerator.

"Classmate," she says to me while pulling out a container of sliced pineapples. "Is that really all Davi is? Are you sure he isn't something else?"

"What?"

"You know." She turns to me and wiggles her eyebrows. "A love interest?"

I glance at the packed counter, ensuring no one heard my sister. "Would you please stop?" I whisper back at her. "Davi and I aren't . . . you know. Dating." I grab a bottle of water and twist the lid open. "We aren't even friends . . . anymore."

"Well, the tension I sensed in the car seemed like friends-on-the-verge-of-lovers tension and not friends-on-the-verge-of-enemies tension."

"Well, I didn't say we were enemies."

She shuts the refrigerator and smirks. "Exactly."

I roll my eyes, and just as I'm about to gulp down the water, I freeze and focus on my mom as she enters the kitchen. After gawking at her for a moment, I turn to my sister, whose shocked expression must mirror mine.

"Well? What do you think?" Mom smiles and spins around. "Do you like it?"

"Your . . . your hair," Esosa stammers. "You cut it."

No, our mother didn't cut her hair. She shaved it, every strand gone. Our mom has a buzz cut.

The water bottle in my hand suddenly feels heavy. I drop it on the counter and it splatters, but I don't care about the mess I've made or about Adrian's grumbling. I walk to my mom and get a closer look. "You shaved your hair. Why?"

She runs a hand over her head and shrugs. "I wanted something different."

"But . . . Daddy. He loved your hair."

Whenever she got it braided, he would take his time to oil her scalp, ensuring the blend of peppermint and coconut oil reached each row of plait. And when new growth caused the braids to loosen at their roots, he would help unravel the attachment from her hair. He would wash it whenever she was too lazy to visit the salon. He would comb the tight coils whenever she couldn't summon the energy to, working a wide-tooth comb through her hair in a way my sister and I never could. And whenever she winced, even the slightest, he would soothe her in a way that made me cringe and also smile. My father loved her hair. He took care of it, and now it's gone.

"I don't understand," I tell my mother. "How could you just . . ."

"Shave it!" Esosa finishes for me. "All of it. Gone!"

"Don't be dramatic. I still have a little."

"Well, I like it," Adrian says.

"She definitely has the face to pull it off," Auntie Sara adds.

"She looks fresh," Uncle Davis says. "Young."

Their opinions—whether they're the truth or just a cushion to soften the blow of this situation—do not help.

"You shaved your head." I can't stop repeating the words. "You shaved your head. Your head. How could you do that . . . to Daddy?"

My mother sighs and walks to the sink. She squeezes soap on a sponge and starts washing dishes, fully concentrating on the plate in her hand.

"He loved your hair—just the way it was."

"Yes. But it's my hair." Her tone hardens. She pronounces her words pointedly. "I can do whatever I want with it."

"I know . . . but . . . but he's—"

"Gone. Dead!" She drops the plate into the sink, and it cracks. "And every time I look in the mirror—every time I see my hair, every time I touch it—I think of him, and I hate it!"

I flinch and shrink back. The room goes quiet. Tears come down Esosa's eyes. I want to go to her and hold her, but I'm too stunned to move.

I don't understand. He's been gone for three months. We left our home and our country—so much of him behind. Why isn't she trying to hold on to more of him—more of what he loved, more of what he can be remembered by? I wear his watch every day just to hold on. I envision him everywhere I go and play out scenes that could have been. Why is she so quick to let go of him and in such a drastic way? Why doesn't she want to remember him?

The grief I usually manage so well, the one I wrap up like something breakable and secure in a box, comes undone. I can't contain it anymore. It's all too much, and when I release the cry that's been building in me all day, my body shakes. Uncle Davis wraps his arms around me, rubbing my back, telling me to breathe deep and slow. But I can't. Breathing suddenly requires too much effort and concentration, and so does standing. My knees wobble, and I push away from Uncle Davis and race down the hall and into my room.

After shutting the door and turning the lock, I open my closet and push hangers aside until I see a series of T-shirts. I drag down a gray one and slip it on. My legs finally give out, and I drop to the floor, curl into a ball, and cling to the cotton fabric that smells like old books and aftershave, inhaling vigorously and trying with all my strength to keep fragments of my father alive.

Chapter Fourteen

MY RED, PUFFY EYES ARE LOW AS I WALK DOWN THE
school hallway. I slept little last night. I watched the sunrise and got
dressed before Mom and Esosa woke up. Auntie Sara, also up early,
let me into the main house through the kitchen door. She gave me a
long hug, then made pancakes—comfort food, I assume. I only ate
a little.

The ride to school was unusually quiet, with no excessive talking
from Esosa or loud music from Adrian. He drove with caution, staying too long at stop signs while his eyes rose to the rearview mirror
to peek at Esosa and me, sitting apart in the back. We haven't talked
about last night. What's there to say? What's the magic word that
can make everything okay? There isn't one.

The first bell rings as I open my locker. I should rush at this
point—grab my things and race to class before I'm late. But I'm not
motivated to do any of that. I stand still and stare into my locker
without blinking. Slowly, my vision goes out of focus and blurs.

"Enore?"

I flinch. Davi is beside me, though I'm not sure how long he's
been standing there. I close my locker and force a smile that doesn't
extend far. "Hi."

"Are you okay?" He squints and searches my eyes, which definitely
hold the answer to his question. "What's wrong?"

"It's not . . . Nothing."

"Enore." He takes my hand in his and grips it gently. "You can talk to me."

It seemed like I squeezed every single tear out last night, but there's still more; they fill my eyes just as something heavy settles on my chest and my breaths shorten.

"My dad," I tell him. "He's dead."

The wrongness of those words doesn't make them any less true. He's dead. Still, I'm trying to reconcile how someone I saw every day of my life is no longer with me. One moment, everything was perfect, my life shaped by the routine of early morning rooster crows, loud neighbors, a jovial mother, and a playful father. And then in another moment, a somber doctor says all the wrong things and breaks the routine. Now my reality is distorted, the entirety of it reshaped by loss. No matter how much I try to contain my grief, it fights its way out of the box I've placed it in. But sometimes it's more skillful. It slips out of the box and slithers with a slickness that makes it obscure. It leaves its residue everywhere and on everything. It hangs in the air like humidity, and I can't help but breathe it and push it into myself. It stays with me, luring me to sleep and then shocking me awake. And it's here again, pressing against my chest as I stand in a hallway full of students who rush to class.

"Enore." Davi holds me. "I'm so sorry. When . . ."

"Three months ago." I cry against his chest, caring very little about the attention we might attract. When the second bell goes off, I pull back and wipe my eyes. "We should go . . . to class."

"Hey." He holds my shoulders and stops me from moving. "Maybe you should take a minute."

"We're going to be late."

"It doesn't matter." His hands move along my arms—up and down in a slow motion that relaxes me slightly. "Just take a minute. Okay?"

Briefly, I stop worrying about going to class. I remember my coping technique.

With my eyes shut, I breathe with intention.

In and out.

Slow and steady.

Then I imagine my breaths as a tide of cool blue water flowing through me—dousing the flares of emotions and then soothing the disquiet. When I open my eyes, Davi and I are the only people in the hallway.

"Do you want to get out of here?" he asks.

"Go to class?"

"No. Not class." He scans the hallway, then looks at me. "Do you want to skip school?"

I frown. "You want to leave school?"

He nods.

"Can we do that—just leave?"

"Well, technically no. But if we run before any teachers see us, we could get away with it."

"Oh. Um . . . I don't know about that."

"Enore." Davi lowers his head and meets my stare. "Do you want to be here today?"

I shake my head. "No. I don't."

"Okay. Then let's get out of here." Davi extends his open hand to me.

I look at it, knowing that once I place my hand in his, we'll race down the empty hallway and toward the doors. I have never skipped school before. Of course, I've always wanted to but never had the opportunity. In Nigeria, a tall gate surrounded my school and a no-nonsense security guard tended to the gate. But here, there is no gate or security guard. There's nothing stopping me.

I breathe in deeply, place my hand in Davi's, and we run.

Chapter Fifteen

NIGERIAN TEENAGERS LIVE IN THE CLUTCHES OF their parents and answer to them well into adulthood. For American teenagers, the age of eighteen is a line that separates them from their parents and marks them as adults. But in the movies I've seen, before most teenagers hit that milestone, they enjoy the perks of adulthood like having a driver's license and a car, a privilege the average Nigerian teenager doesn't have.

Today, I am an American teenager.

I leave school. I get into a boy's silver Toyota, and we drive down winding roads with the windows down and warm air fanning our faces. We are free, and I bask in it—in this false adulthood.

We are several miles away from school, surrounded by thick, green forestry on either side of the road. Everything that should matter suddenly seems so far away—out of sight and all that. I don't ask where we're going. There's no need because I'm strangely unbothered by our destination. I think Davi likes this—the fact that I don't ask, that I'm not worried. He might interpret it as trust. As me trusting him. He might be right.

When he glances at me, his stare lingers, and I shove him playfully.

"Pay attention to the road, Ferris Bueller."

"Huh?" He chuckles and looks ahead. "Ferris who?"

"Bueller. A character. From a movie."

"Let me guess. One of your teen movies?"

"Mm-hmm."

"Of course," he says with a smile.

After driving further, Davi pulls into a driveway. The gravel pavement leads to a white two-story cottage that's surrounded by clusters of trees and shrubs. When I step out of the car, I catch the shimmer of blue water behind the house—a lake that extends in the distance. It's the kind of setting that draws every source of tension from you like splinters, plucks you free of them until you exhale. I turn to Davi while pushing out a long breath.

"Nice, right?" he asks.

I nod. "Is this your house?" We're about an hour from school, so I doubt it.

"It's my family's summer home . . . Well, it is for a little while."

"What do you mean?"

"My dad, the man right there." He points at the FOR SALE sign wedged in the groomed lawn. The suited man on it is handsome— his dark hair slicked backward, his smile wide, his arms folded in a typical Realtor pose. "He's selling it."

I scan the serene setting again, trying to understand why anyone would give it up.

"We need the money," Davi says. "For my college and . . ." He clears his throat. "Other stuff."

Other stuff. It's obvious those two words are loaded with meaning. His lips part like he's about to elaborate, but then they flatten to a firm line. He takes my hand and gently nudges me toward the house.

We walk along the cobblestone pathway, and then Davi turns

the lock on the door. The entryway is spacious and extends to an all-white living room. It's a cozy space with an accent of wooden furniture—a table, a dresser, and a rocking chair. The large white couch is topped with a blanket and throw pillows, and the shaggy white rug beneath it has specks of silver.

"Don't look so impressed," Davi laughs. "Dad had it staged."

"Staged?"

"Yeah. Fixed up, so it looks nicer for potential buyers. Trust me, it never looks this put together."

"Oh." I look around the room again. "Well. It's a nice house, either way." The large window behind the couch reveals the stretch of water in the backyard; a boat drifts in the distance. "I'm sorry you have to sell it."

"My family has come here for years. We've got a lot of memories. As long as we can keep those . . ." He shrugs. "It's fine . . . I guess." He smiles faintly, then squints and watches me as a moment of silence passes between us. "Enore." His voice is gentle. "Why didn't you tell me about your dad?"

"Well . . . I . . . um . . ." I sink into the couch, and I'm greeted by the plush blanket and pillows. "We were just getting to know each other, and . . ." My fingers fidget. "It wasn't something I was ready to share yet."

"Yeah. I get that." He sits beside me. "I'm really sorry."

"He was sick," I explain. "It all happened so fast, and then two months after the funeral, we moved here, and I'm still trying to hold it together. He meant everything to me. My dad. He meant everything."

Davi takes my hands in his, and I feel comfortable enough to say more.

"He was a professor. He loved teaching. Sometimes, after school, I would take a bus to the university where he worked and sit in on his lesson. Then after, we would go home together. We would talk during the entire ride—talk about nothing and everything." I smile at the memory, but then my lips tighten to a frown. "My mom isn't like him. We've never been close. She's always been my mom. A good mom. But just my mom. He was my friend. He understood me, saw me. I could tell him anything. And now he's gone. And there's a big hole in my life. In my family."

Even though I try to fight it, tears fill my eyes. Davi holds me tight as moisture settles into his shirt. He doesn't let go, doesn't flinch even when I sob.

I'm not sure how long we stay like this, but then I settle down, soothed by the fresh scent of soap on his T-shirt, the circles he draws slowly on my back, and our proximity. I rub the tears away, then look up and meet his eyes—hazel-green and kind and full of warmth and other emotions that are so clearly directed at me.

I like you too. A lot, he said yesterday, right before I told him we couldn't be friends anymore. And even with that, with me dismissing his explanation about Ara and ending our friendship so abruptly, he looked at me this morning and knew I wasn't okay. And he cared enough to bring me here. Whatever fog clouded my judgment yesterday clears.

"I'm sorry," I tell him. "About yesterday."

He frowns, though I suspect it's not because he's angry but because of the memory of yesterday—the confusion and frustration he must have felt.

I sit up, so our eyes level. "The truth is, I have these rules."

Davi's eyebrows dip even lower. A few more words, and I'll look like a complete fool—the girl who boxes herself in with rules because she's scared any tiny misstep will make her a little less in control. It's pathetic, but it's the truth. And even if my explanation makes me appear completely unhinged, Davi deserves to hear it. After yesterday, I owe it to him.

"Losing my dad and then moving to a new country has been . . . hard." I swallow the lump in my throat. "In the past three months, a lot has been out of my control. With school, I thought understanding what I was getting myself into and then controlling the outcome would make things more tolerable. I thought if I could get through this one year with no issues, with nothing else going out of my control, I would be okay. Hence the rules." I chuckle nervously. "It's ridiculous. I know."

"It isn't," he says. "How you choose to cope is your choice. It's not ridiculous, okay?"

There's no judgment in his eyes, so I push away my initial embarrassment.

"The thing is, I've been breaking a lot of my rules because of . . ." After biting my lip, I release my grip and exhale. "You."

"Me?" Davi points to himself, confirming what I've just said.

"Not intentionally. But yes."

My answer doesn't clear the confusion on his face.

"Being with you forces me out of my comfort zone. Like when I auditioned for the musical."

"What rule did you break by auditioning?"

"Rule number three. Don't draw attention to yourself. Keep a low profile."

He laughs. "You would have broken that with or without auditioning. You're not the hide-in-the-shadows type, Enore. You had my attention the moment I saw you."

I want to kiss him so badly. How could I not when he says things like that? How could I not when he's Davi—the first friend I made in America, the boy I fall asleep thinking about, the boy who makes me draw lines through the rules I promised to follow? I inch closer to him, not thinking to warn him first—to tell him I might really be bad at kissing.

He watches the space between us shrink and mimics my movement, shifting toward me.

"What's your first rule?" he whispers.

"Avoid interacting with or befriending anyone who's popular. I broke that one on the first day of school or, actually . . ." I think for a moment and shake my head. "That day at Tech and Techies."

"I'm not popular."

"Um . . . the parade of heys and fist bumps that greet you whenever you walk down the hallway proves otherwise."

He doesn't dispute that solid evidence. Instead, he leans closer to my face. "What's your second rule?"

My heart thumps too fast; I breathe quickly to catch up with the pace. "No crushes," I say, my voice barely audible. "And absolutely no boyfriends."

Davi's eyes sweep over my face. His hand cups my cheek and then slides along the slope of my neck. "Is that why you said those things yesterday—why you pushed me away?"

"Yeah. And because of rule number four."

He waits for me to elaborate.

"Don't make any enemies."

He nods. "Ara."

"Yeah. She—"

"Isn't a problem," he adds. "We're friends—that's it. And I . . ." He sighs, then smiles. "I like you, Enore. A lot."

"I know. I like you too, Davi. A lot."

I don't tell him about the other rules I haven't broken yet, about my small grasp at control in a world where I have none. I don't think too much or try to talk myself out of having this moment with him. I don't include rationality in this equation of emotions and wild teenage hormones. And I don't warn him about my lack of kissing experience.

I just do it.

I kiss him.

He kisses me.

His lips are soft on mine; they move in a slow, gentle rhythm that I match. Everything comes easy—strangely natural, like we've been doing this since the day we met. There isn't an awkward moment where we shift our bodies or reshape our pursed lips so we fit better.

We just fit.

Seamlessly.

The taste of his mouth—sweet peppermint—laces mine. Everywhere he touches—my lips, my waist, my neck—tingles and heats and pulses and aches. Eager for more, I lean in greedily. I forget to be reserved and patient as my tongue skims over his. I forget to question everything I'm doing—the rightness of my technique. It feels too good to question, and the moment is too heated to interrupt for notes or affirmation. Davi's lips trail down my neck, then cover my mouth again. He kisses me deeper, and I melt into him as we recline on the couch, my body over his.

I'm not sure how much time passes, but we eventually break apart. Laughing, we sit upright. I straighten my T-shirt, while Davi runs his fingers through his hair.

"Hungry?" he asks.

"A little."

"I think we've got some pizza in the freezer. Don't worry. It's not store-bought." He takes my hand and leads me into the kitchen, a part of the open-concept space. "My grams makes it from scratch and stocks the freezer full of them."

"I'll eat anything your grandmother makes."

He opens the stainless steel door and looks through the freezer. "We've got veggie and pepperoni. Got a preference?"

"Pepperoni, please."

The pizza heats in the oven while I sit on the counter and eat an apple.

"How you doing?" Davi asks, arranging plates and napkins on the dining table.

"Good." Definitely better than I was at school.

"Happy to hear it."

"You can take credit for it if you want. For me, being good . . . being happy."

He turns to me with napkins in his hands. "Only if you want to give me credit."

I bite into the apple and smile while chewing. "I'm good because of you."

"Same," he says, watching me deeply. "I'm good because of you."

He says nothing else—doesn't explain why he wasn't good to begin with. I want details, but sense he's guarded and reel in my curiosity. Maybe it's for the best. Maybe there's been enough emotions and heaviness today. Maybe we've had our fill. Maybe now we only deserve the distraction of each other's company.

After we eat the pizza, one of the best I've ever had, he puts on a movie. We watch halfheartedly, alternating between kissing and talking as it plays. Davi goes on about his little sister, who he's obviously obsessed with. It's really adorable.

"Watch any princess movies with her recently?" I ask, giggling.

"Ha ha. Funny." He rolls his eyes. "For your information, these days she equally appreciates princesses and spies. She's currently obsessed with watching *Totally Spies!*"

"I love that show."

"Yeah . . . well, she claims to be a Clover, and I think I should be worried."

We both laugh.

"So," I say between giggles. "Your grandmother is retired. Your dad's a Realtor. What about your mom? What does she do?"

"Um . . ." Slowly, his smile drops. "She's a teacher."

"Oh. Cool. Where does she—"

"It's really not that interesting." He clears his throat. "Um . . . how was rehearsal yesterday? We never got a chance to talk about it."

The abrupt and bumpy subject change basically gives me whiplash. I study Davi, whose eyes are too busy darting around the room to meet mine. What in the world was that? I'm tempted to say something, but I'm not sure what. Instead, I carry on with the subject he brought up.

"Um . . . rehearsal was . . . okay. I guess."

"Enore?" He watches me suspiciously. "What happened?"

"Well, I . . . I quit."

"What? You quit? Why?"

"It was overwhelming—more than I expected. I don't know how to act. And I think, at some point, I'm expected to act and dance and sing. All at the same time. That, my friend, is a recipe for disaster."

"You don't think you could have learned during rehearsals?" he asks softly.

"With everyone looking at me, judging me, and laughing at me?" I fear one person doing that more than anyone else, but don't mention it. I can't bring up his ex-girlfriend, not when we've spent the past few hours kissing. "Also, Mr. Roland is really mean."

"He's all bark. Remember, I told you that."

"Well, could he not bark? I really could do without his bark. I hate his bark. Yesterday, I was very close to whacking him over his head with my script. This close." I bring two fingers together, leaving a sliver of space between them.

Davi bursts out laughing. "I'm not gonna lie. I would pay to see that."

"Well, how much are you thinking, and do you think others will pay too? Because for the right price, I would really put on a show."

He laughs harder, and I can't help laughing too.

"Seriously, Davi. He's infuriating and so condescending. As if it's not hard enough standing up there with everyone looking at me."

"I know, I know." He stops laughing and hugs me. "But you have to tolerate him. If you want to be on that stage, forget about everyone else, especially Mr. Roland. Just focus on you, on perfecting your part."

"But what if . . ." I pull away from him. "What if I'm not good enough to be up there or to be the lead?"

He holds my face between his hands and stares boldly into my eyes. "You are. Trust me, you are."

Why does he have more confidence in me than I have in myself? Maybe it will take me time to believe I deserve a place on that stage. Until that day comes, I'm happy I have Davi.

When I kiss him, it's for a moment, and then he pulls away.

"We should go," he says.

"Go? Where?"

"Back to school. I have football practice, and you have rehearsals."

"But I quit."

"But you still want to be in the play, don't you?"

I think briefly, then nod.

"Then tell Mr. Roland you've changed your mind."

"What if it doesn't make a difference?"

"Then convince him. Don't take no for an answer."

I sigh. "Okay."

"Come on. It's gonna take us an hour to get back." He extends his hand to me, and I take it.

"You know, you're really good at the whole tough-love-pep-talk combo," I say when we're inside the car.

"Well, I've had lots of practice being part of a football team that has never won a championship."

I laugh. "Well, you might need to put your skill to use with me. A lot."

He takes my hand and presses it to his lips as he speeds up on the open road.

"Anytime. Just say when. I got you."

Chapter Sixteen

I RUSH THROUGH THE THEATER DOOR FIFTEEN minutes past three, fifteen minutes after rehearsal begins. When the door thuds closed, everyone onstage turns to me. Mr. Roland must have announced I quit. That would explain the silence in the room, the stares following me as I rush onstage. Or maybe everyone is staring because I had the audacity to walk into rehearsal fifteen minutes late. As Mr. Roland explained during the first rehearsal, he has a low tolerance for people who waste his time.

I stand beside Cole and then ruffle through my bag quickly, my hands shaking. I pull out the script and meet Mr. Roland's intimidating gaze. Taking in a deep breath, I muster the confidence to hold his stare. After a moment, he arches his eyebrow and tilts his head slightly, a clear question I answer by nodding. He lowers his single brow, straightens his head, then turns to the rest of the group, who were quiet throughout our wordless exchange.

"Let's run through the first scene!"

Everyone scurries to take their rightful positions.

"I thought he ran you off yesterday," Cole says, nudging me with his elbow. "Glad he didn't."

"Thanks." I smile, then frown while considering something. "Did everyone think that too—that Mr. Roland ran me off?"

"Not me." Ara appears suddenly, her arms folded over her chest. "I just thought you were smart enough to realize you can't pull this off." Her eyes shift over me—up and down, then up again. "Guess you weren't."

At this point, I can cross out the one rule I really thought I could keep.

~~Rule #4: Don't make any enemies or start a rivalry.~~

I have an enemy. It's a fact, but it's hard to accept because I've never been the kind of person to go looking for trouble. Some people feed off drama and tension and just plain madness. I don't have the nerve to throw up my fists or the skill to select the right words and structure the perfect insult. But for the first time in my life, because I am so irritated by Ara, I wish I had both the nerve and skill and even an appetite for drama. A combination of all three would definitely shut her up. But since that isn't the case, I do what I did to every mean girl back in Nigeria—act like they're insignificant. Nothing upsets a mean girl more than making them feel irrelevant—like their words and actions left no dent in your self-esteem . . . even if it does. It's all about perception.

I turn to Cole and force what is hopefully a believable smile. "Let's get started on this musical."

If Ara had a reaction to me being dismissive, I don't notice. I only hear the quick patter of her shoes as she rushes off stage.

During rehearsal, I complete the first scene without embarrassing myself. Studying the script on the drive back to school helped a lot. I remember some lines and glance at the script for a quick reference when I don't. No one laughs. Mr. Roland only watches quietly, his hand cupping his chin, one finger tapping his lips. He keeps that position as we move on to the next scene. He gives Cole and the other actors instructions or criticism but says nothing to me. I'd be stupid to mistake his silence as a good sign. I didn't become a brilliant actor overnight. My acting is . . . well, tragic. It was yesterday, and it still is today. If I'm going to improve, I'll need his direction. But I get nothing from him.

When rehearsal ends, everyone gathers their things and leaves.

"You coming?" Cole asks, with his bag hanging from his shoulder.

"Um . . ." I look from him to Mr. Roland, who is talking to his assistant, Cheryl. "No. You go ahead."

"Okay. Cool. See you around."

Once he climbs off the stage, I take in a deep breath and walk toward Mr. Roland. My heart pounds as I get closer.

"Um . . . Mr. Roland. Hi."

Slowly, he turns away from Cheryl. "Enore. Hello." After the dry, clipped greeting, he turns to Cheryl again, continuing his conversation as if I'm not standing by, waiting for his attention.

Not only is this man arrogant, but he's petty too. Yes, he let me back into the musical without calling me out for quitting in front of the cast. But he's clearly still upset about yesterday. He probably expects me to grovel. And I'm seriously considering falling on my knees and kissing his velvet loafers. Who would have thought I would trade my dignity for a high school musical? It's a steep price. But maybe the end justifies the painful, demeaning means.

"Enore."

Mr. Roland's voice breaks through my thoughts.

"You're still here. Why?" He waves goodbye to Cheryl, who's walking away, then turns to me.

"Well . . . um . . . um." I sigh, unsure of what to say.

Just wondering why you didn't give me any feedback during rehearsal. I could really use it. In fact, I need it.

The words make perfect sense in my head, but I can't get them out as I squirm under his daunting stare.

"Yes, Enore?" He arches an eyebrow. "Can I help you?"

"I'm sorry about yesterday," I blurt out. Maybe this, a simple apology, will suffice. To some degree, he deserves it. I was rude to him. But in that case, I deserve an apology too. "I shouldn't have spoken to you like that or quit."

And you shouldn't have been so blunt and insensitive.

Rather than say what's in my head, I wait and hope he sees how he messed up, too. The wait is long. The tension doesn't leave that one arched eyebrow. It looks like he's both petty and stubborn.

"If you're going to be a part of this musical, you must take it seriously," he says. "You can't quit on a whim because of one bad rehearsal. You must be committed. Because next time, I won't be so forgiving."

I intend to walk away and move on from this conversation, but the word *forgiving* makes me pause. He just had to throw that in there. And because I've recently become a little uninhibited, I just have to respond.

"Forgiving?" I say. "You completely ignored me during rehearsal. You didn't give me any feedback. It's like you were punishing me."

"Well, as I recall, yesterday you mentioned not liking my approach. And now you need it. Which is it, Enore?"

I'm tempted to really give him a piece of my mind. But it's pointless.

Mr. Roland is who he is. I can't control how he acts, only how I react. That's what I imagine my father would tell me at this very moment. He would likely throw in a Nigerian proverb for good measure too—just so his advice really hit my core. I imagine he would say something like, he who beats the drum for the madman to dance is no better than the madman himself.

I inhale a deep breath and release it. "I would appreciate your feedback during rehearsal, Mr. Roland. And of course, carry on with any method you think is suitable for high school students who are likely dealing with anxiety, peer pressure, and a hundred other things you couldn't possibly know or understand."

Slowly, his high eyebrow drops. I doubt I've gotten through to him, but it feels good to get a slight reaction out of him.

"Well, bye. See you tomorrow." I grip the bag strap on my shoulder and climb down the steps, grinning.

I'll count that as a small victory.

WHEN I WALK THROUGH THE THEATER DOOR AND into the hallway, I see Sybil leaning against a locker and looking through pictures on her camera. When the door clicks closed, she looks up and beams at me.

"Enore. Hey. I've been hanging around, waiting for rehearsal to be done."

I frown, confused. "Um . . . why?"

"The interview for the school paper. I was supposed to interview you yesterday after rehearsal. You were supposed to meet me in the newsroom but never showed."

"Oh. Right." I rub my forehead. "That completely slipped my mind. Yesterday was . . ." I sigh when the memory materializes in my head. "Sorry about that."

"No worries. You're here now. Got twenty minutes to spare?"

Esosa and Adrian already left; neither of them had after-school activities to keep them back. Adrian offered to wait for me. After his dad reprimanded him for leaving us yesterday, it was the sensible move. But I told him to go ahead. Davi already offered to take me home, and I'm looking forward to the drive, to being alone with him again.

"I have some time," I tell Sybil. "I'm riding home with Davi, and he should be done with football practice in a few minutes, so we can talk."

"Cool." Her lips, coated in a cherry red gloss, stretch in a broad smile. "Where would you like to do this? Any preference?"

"Well, I would love some fresh air."

"Okay. Outside, then."

When we step out of the school building, we sit on a wooden bench that's below the flight of stairs.

"Okay." Sybil pulls her phone out and opens a voice recording app. "Let's do this."

The interview feels conversational, and I suppose that's because Sybil is good at her job. While asking about preparations for the musical, she lifts her camera to my face. The long lens isn't intimidating like it was yesterday. I don't shy away when she snaps multiple pictures. After, she extends the camera to me and shows the portraits she captured.

"These are really good," I say.

"The camera loves you."

I look at Sybil closely, suspiciously. Something about this doesn't make sense. Sybil and Ara are friends. Ara hates me. But here Sybil is, being nice to me. In fact, all Ara's friends have been nothing but nice to me. I'm not familiar with this dynamic. If I didn't like someone, for whatever reason, Tolu wouldn't like that person either. It's petty, yes. But she's my best friend, and it's a matter of loyalty. So, it's either Ara's friends have no loyalty to her or they're up to something—maybe a ploy to befriend me while secretly scheming to subject me to a major public humiliation. I've seen *Carrie*—the original and the 2013 remake. There's no way I'm getting doused in pig's blood.

"You okay?" Sybil asks while searching my narrowed eyes.

"Um . . ." How do I resolve my suspicion without sounding like a paranoid idiot? Honestly, there might be no way around that. "I'm just wondering. You're Ara's friend."

"Yeah. So?"

"Well, I'm sure she hates me because I got the lead in the musical, but here you are interviewing me for the paper, further promoting the fact I got the role instead of her. Shouldn't you be siding with your friend, hating me right along with her?"

Sybil watches me blankly—no written expression on her face. And then, gradually, her red lips tilt into a smile, and she bursts out laughing. "Okay. First, I'm a journalist." She stops laughing, but a smile stays on her face. "I gotta keep my readers informed, no matter what. That's why I'm interviewing you. Second, Ara is one of my best friends. And if it was serious, a life-or-death situation, I would have her back."

It was my understanding that in high school, everything is life or death.

"Besides," Sybil goes on, "Ara didn't even want the lead role, so she can't possibly hate you for getting it."

I frown, remembering what Davi said during his conversation with Ara yesterday.

I don't know why you're so upset about the musical, especially since you don't even . . .

He hadn't finished the sentence, even when Ara pushed him to. While I listened to their conversation a few feet away, I tried to fill in the blanks without success. But now, it's clear. From everything Sybil said, I select the words that perfectly complete Davi's sentence.

I don't know why you're so upset about the musical, especially since you don't even want the lead role.

I suppose I have solved that mystery, but I'm still confused. Ara's actions continuously prove she's upset about not getting the lead role.

"Look." Sybil touches my arm. "If my best friend fought tooth and nail for this role, wanted it more than anything in the world, and you got it instead, this interview might happen, but I wouldn't be the ray of sunshine I currently am. But she didn't want it. And we all know that—me, Bethany, Davi, Zane, and Blake. All of us.

"You got the lead role because your audition was incredible. I can't tell you how many times I've watched that audition video. You deserve this, Enore."

Okay. I'm starting to believe there might *not* be a ploy to publicly humiliate me in the works. Sybil's genuine smile pushes that suspicion out of my mind.

"So," I say, determined to solve a new mystery—the one about the girl who fights for something even though she doesn't want it. "If Ara doesn't want the lead, why is she acting like she does?"

"Well, it's . . . complicated. Can't really say much about it."

"Oh. Okay." I guess that mystery will remain unsolved.

"Hey."

My head snaps up when I hear the distinct bass of Davi's low voice. He's standing in front of Sybil and me, but I'm not sure when he showed up. His hair is damp from the shower I guess he might have taken in the locker room. There's a fresh spicy scent coming off him. I breathe it in and exhale.

"Hi."

For a few seconds, our eyes remain on each other. I'm tempted to leap up and kiss him, though Sybil's presence holds me back.

"Hey, Syb," Davi says, finally looking at her.

"Hey, yourself." She stands with her phone and camera in her hands. "We're all done here."

"Are you sure?" I ask. "We could speak for a few more minutes if you have more questions."

"Nah. I've got everything I need. It's gonna be a great piece. Thanks again." She waves and turns toward the school. "I'll see you guys tomorrow."

Davi and I walk to his car in the parking lot. When our seat belts are fastened, he drives out of the school premises with low music playing on the radio.

"So," he says once we're on the road. "How was rehearsal?"

"Good. Definitely better than yesterday."

"Did Mr. Roland give you a hard time?"

"Nothing I couldn't handle."

He glances at me, smiles, then takes my hand. He doesn't let go as he drives the short distance to my house. When he stops the car in the driveway, he looks at our joined hands.

"Would you like to go out with me?" he asks. "On a date? This weekend?"

I stare at him with wide eyes, grinning with all my teeth. It's possible I look like an idiot, but I don't know how to hide my excitement.

"So . . ." He laughs. "Is that a yes?"

I nod until I find my voice. "Yes. That's a yes. I would love to."

"Cool. Great."

When he leans into me, I pull back.

"Everything okay?" he asks.

"It's just . . ." I sigh. "My mom. She could be around here some-where." If she caught me kissing a boy, all hell would break loose.

"Right." Davi nods. "Got it."

"I'll see you tomorrow?"

"Yeah," he says. "And I'll call you later."

"Okay." This is my cue to step out of the car, but I'm not ready to let go of his hand and leave him yet. "Thank you for today. For . . ." Something tight builds in my chest, a heaviness that forms when-ever I think about my father. "Yesterday was really hard. I woke up this morning unsure of how I would get through the day. But you made today bearable. You made everything better. Thank you." And because I feel prompted to express my gratitude more deeply, I dis-regard the possibility of my mother lurking somewhere in the back-ground, and I lean forward and kiss him. He's surprised at first, but then he recovers from the shock and pulls my face closer to his. We break away from each other, breathing deeply.

"Okay." This time, I don't linger. I have to go before our lips smash together again. "See you tomorrow. Bye."

I rush out of the car, and as I walk toward the pathway that leads to the guesthouse, Davi calls me. Gripping the strap of my bag, I spin around. His face is visible through the lowered passenger window.

"I had the same thought this morning," he says. "I wondered how I would get through the day. But you made everything better." He smiles; it's the kind that brightens his whole face. "Thank you."

Even though I want to, I don't ask questions. I don't pry into the parts of his life he clearly isn't ready to reveal.

Today it's okay if we end things just like this.

With a smile.

Chapter Seventeen

IT'S FUNNY HOW SPENDING THE DAY WITH DAVI PUT mental distance between myself and my mother and her shaved head and her insensitive outburst yesterday. When I step through the front door, all these things, once blurred by distance, come into focus again. Everything becomes vivid and blinding like a piercing light coming at me in full force.

I sigh while pulling off my white sneakers. The house is quiet. But in the silence, I hear everything my mom said yesterday; her words echo.

I don't want to be here—in this house that isn't really my house, my home. I want to run away again with the boy I like—get into his car and be a carefree American teenager with the means to enjoy temporary adulthood. But because that isn't an option, I walk toward my room, the only place in this house I can stand to be right now. I'm shocked to see my mom standing in the corridor.

She still has a shaved head. But what did I really expect—that her hair would miraculously grow overnight because Esosa and I expressed our disapproval? Yeah. That did not happen. She is still very much bald. I have to squint a little and force my eyes to adjust to this new version of my mother that might, unfortunately, be permanent.

"Eh-no-ray." She breaks down my name and enunciates each syllable. That is the first sign I'm in trouble. That and the fact she's glaring at me. "Where are you coming from, and where have you been?"

That's the thing about being reckless and uninhibited. When you act and damn the consequences, you forget they'll come eventually. I sigh and prepare myself for them, while also piecing together a lie in my head. What would be convincing? What would pacify my mom's anger and curiosity?

"I received a call from your school," she says. "They reported you absent. You were not at school today." She props her hands on her hips. "Where were you?"

I chew on my bottom lip. The gears in my head turn, working hard, trying to forge a believable explanation.

"Enore, I asked you a question."

She's low on patience, and I'm out of time.

"Um . . . I went to the . . . movie theater. Yes. The movie theater," I say the words slowly, as if getting a real feel for them, testing them, ensuring they sound plausible. They do. "I spent the whole day alone, watching movies." Alone is a critical part of the lie.

"You went to the movie theater rather than school?" She tilts her head from side to side like she's tossing the thought around, trying to make sense of it. Because whether or not it's a plausible lie, it is still very ridiculous. "Enore. Is something wrong with you? Éwin lògò wè?"

My eyes lower. I don't say a word.

"You spent the day watching movies. Movies." She claps her hands slowly, though not giving me a round of applause. It's more a Nigerian gesture of disbelief that pairs well with tight, pouty lips and a series of huffs.

"I just—"

"You just what? Eh?" Her hands stop moving.

140

"Needed a break," I say.

"A break. From what?" She arches one eyebrow. "What do you need a break from?"

My life, this one I no longer recognize as mine. Of course, I don't say that. But she waits for the answer, her eyebrow still high and inquiring.

"Enore."

"Ma?" I say.

"What do you need a break from?"

I shrug and whisper, "Everything." And because I can't help it, because this thought is always on my mind, I say, "I miss him."

Her eyebrow drops. The tension that's been straining her features lessens. She exhales—deep and slow. She sucks in air and does another deep, slow release. "I miss him too. But . . . but I can't just abandon everything and go to the movie theater for the day. That is not how things work."

"You miss him?" I ask.

"Of course I do."

"You shaved your head so you wouldn't have to think about him."

My words, even though they're exactly what she said yesterday, are harsh. I'm accusing her of something even though I don't voice it.

Her face falls flat. Then slowly, her features alter to reflect her confusion. She watches me the way I watched her minutes ago, like she's trying to recognize me, reconcile two versions of me.

The Enore in Nigeria, the one who had a living father, did not lie. She had no reason to. She didn't skip school with a boy. She had no reason to. She didn't say hateful things to her mother. Again, she had no reason to. This Enore, the fatherless one, who is constantly trying to suppress her grief, who is always grasping at control—something to keep her grounded—is tired.

I am tired.

And in pain.

And angry.

And suffocating under the weight of grief and change.

Nothing is the same, and neither am I. And I think my mother sees that clearly. And I don't think she likes it.

When she tells me to go to my room, I don't say another word.

Five minutes into some well-deserved alone time, Esosa steps into my room with a mischievous grin.

"Rebel with a cause. I *dey* hail you," she says, saluting me.

I roll my eyes.

"I heard you skipped school and went to the movies."

Of course she heard. She most likely had an ear pressed to her bedroom door, eavesdropping on my conversation with Mom. We don't call her *tatafo*—gossip—for nothing.

"I'm not going to lie. I was shocked and even impressed that you, Miss Goody Goody, had the balls to do something so daring, so out of character." She lifts her chin and watches me. "But you know what's even more surprising? The fact that you weren't at the movies *alone* like you claimed."

My eyes expand and shift to the doorway, checking if our mother is standing there by any chance.

"Oh, relax." Esosa closes the door and turns to me. "So? Where were you?" My sister is really living up to her title as *tatafo*. "'Cause word on the street is, you and Davi Santiago left school together. In a rush."

"Who told—"

"People talk," she interrupts. "And for some reason, they really love talking about you. Must be that viral video of yours."

"Viral?"

"Mm-hmm. Just as I predicted. Last time I checked, one million views."

I sit on the edge of my bed and breathe deeply. "One million people have watched me sing?"

"Isn't it incredible?"

"Um . . ." It's not the first word I would use, but it might be the second.

"Also, I gave your TikTok account an upgrade," Esosa says as she sits beside me. "I changed your handle to match your Insta handle. Also, I'll be coming into rehearsals to get some footage of you for your socials. Don't worry. You won't even know I'm there."

I press my fingers to my forehead and rub the tension away.

"A star has been born, Enore. We must nurture it, so it doesn't wither away and die. This is me nurturing it. Consider me your social media manager and publicist."

"I thought your area of expertise was makeup."

"I'm a girl of many talents. You should know that by now."

"Yeah. Sure." My eyelids, suddenly feeling heavy, fall closed. It must be the effect of not sleeping last night and the excessive crying and then my eventful day.

"Are you okay?" Esosa asks.

"Just tired."

A moment passes without my sister saying a word, then she shuffles on the bed until our knees touch. "Are you . . ." She inhales deeply, her breath shaky. "Are you going to forgive her?"

I look at Esosa. Tears gather in her eyes, but she blinks rapidly, her long false lashes fanning the moisture away. "Forgive who?" I ask.

"Mommy. I'm going to forgive her because . . . because . . . we just have to."

As my sister rubs the tears that escaped her eyes, I realize she has broken character—the one she assumed when we moved. Her American accent is gone. The pretense and facade are stripped away, and she sounds like herself, like me. I'm sure our accents will change at some point, become more American or maybe a unique blend of Nigerian and American, but I don't want to force the transformation. And maybe Esosa doesn't want to anymore either.

I wrap an arm around her, and her head falls on my shoulder.

"You have to forgive her, Enore," she says, sniffing. "Or this family, what's left of it, will fall apart."

What's left of it. Esosa, Mom, and I.

Can a body function with one major organ missing? Is forgiveness enough to make this family fully functional when one major member is gone? Are we—Esosa, Mom, and I—capable of living, of celebrating birthdays, holidays, milestones without him? Or will things fall apart?

Have they already started to?

Chapter Eighteen

FOR THE FIRST TIME SINCE I JOINED THE CHURCH choir, I'm late for rehearsal. Struggling with my bag straps and the books in my hand, I rush down the aisle and meet the rest of the choir at the altar.

"Rehearsal started twenty minutes ago. You're late," Ms. Huntington states the obvious before I can apologize and give an explanation.

The explanation, in my opinion, is very reasonable. Rehearsals for the musical ran late. Mr. Roland insists on perfection even though today was only the third day of rehearsals. Cole sang slightly off-key during the number "Do I Love You Because You're Beautiful," and Mr. Roland demanded he sing his verse until he perfected it, and even then, his pursed lips proved he was unsatisfied.

"Something isn't right," he said, tapping his chin with a pen and idly strolling around the stage.

For a moment, I was positive I was the problem. After all, I missed a dance step and stumbled into Cole, who stumbled into a set designer, who then dropped a pail of paint that destroyed what would have been the backdrop of New York City. I did all that, but when Mr. Roland stopped pacing around the stage, he didn't call me out as the problem. He simply said, "I can't put my finger on it just yet. But I will."

But I will.

Those words—the possibility that any day now, I'll be singled out as the problem—make me wince.

"Enore?" Ms. Silva whispers. "Everything all right, dear?"

"Um . . . yes." I shake my head and push aside my concerns about the musical. "Sorry I'm late. I got held up at school."

"No problem, sweetheart. Take a seat."

For once, practice doesn't drag on. Missing the first twenty minutes definitely sped things up. In the end, after Ms. Huntington has somehow wrestled Sunday's solo from a fellow soprano, I gather my things and head for the door. Uncle Davis promised to pick me up, but his black Mercedes isn't in the parking lot yet. Instead, I see Davi leaning against his Toyota. The little girl beside him looks eight. She has his complexion and wavy dark hair, though hers extends to her back. She's likely his sister.

"Um . . . hi," I say, approaching them.

"Enore. Hey." Davi's eyes light up when they meet mine. He stands up straight. "What are you doing here? Your text—you said rehearsal for the musical was running late and you couldn't make it to choir."

"Yeah. It's what I thought, but Mr. Roland finally let us go, so I took an Uber down."

"Oh," he says, nodding. "Cool. I'm here to pick up my grams."

"We're here to pick her up." The sharp, no-nonsense correction comes from the little girl. She frowns at Davi, obviously annoyed her presence has gone ignored.

"Hi," I say to her. "You must be Natalie."

A flush of red hits her cheeks as her eyes expand. "You know my name?"

"Yeah. Davi talks about you a lot."

She glances at her brother, then faces me again. "I know who you are," she says. And just when I think Davi has been talking nonstop about me at home, Natalie says, "You're the girl from that video—the one who sings 'Into the Unknown.'" She tugs Davi's hand. "Right? She is. Right?"

"Yep," he answers. "That's her."

Natalie bounces on her toes and squeals at a high pitch that rings in my ears.

"Didn't I mention my sister is a fan of yours?"

"No," I say, laughing. "You did not."

"You also didn't tell me you know her." Natalie smacks her brother's arm, then gawks at me. "Whoa. I can't believe I'm meeting Enore Enchanted."

My mouth drops. I'm shocked to hear the social media name Esosa coined for me. I look from Natalie to Davi; his lips are pressed together like he's holding back a laugh.

"Will you sing at my birthday party?" Natalie asks. "Please."

"Um . . . what?"

"It's my birthday. Next week. I'm having a party. A princess party. All my friends are dressing like any princess they want—Ariel, Jasmine, Tiana. I'm gonna be Elena of Avalor." Natalie beams with pride, her chin lifted. "She's badass."

"Language, Nat," Davi scolds with a frown and a firm tone.

"What? She is." Her brother's attempt at intimidation clearly didn't work. "Anyway, will you come to my party? It would be so cool if you performed. My friends would lose their minds." She pouts and flaps her long, dark lashes.

There is a firm *no* moving through the channel of my throat, on its way out of my mouth, but then Natalie's doe-eyed expression stops it. "Um . . ." I look at Davi for help, but he just shrugs, and I know it's hopeless. My resolve, flimsy as it was to begin with, dissolves completely. "Okay. I'll come."

"And sing?" She doesn't miss the most crucial detail of our agreement.

"Yes, and sing."

Again, she bounces and squeals. I'm taken aback when she rushes forward and wraps her arms around me.

"Thank you! Thank you! Thank you! You can have as many cupcakes as you want at the party."

"Is that supposed to be my payment?"

"Yeah." She pulls back and watches me with apprehension. "Is that okay?"

I tap a finger on my chin and think. "Will there be carrot cake cupcakes?"

"I'll make a note to my grandma."

"A note for what?" Ms. Silva asks, stepping through the church doors.

"My birthday," Natalie replies. "We're gonna need carrot cake cupcakes. A bargain has been made."

Ms. Silva chuckles. "Noted." She walks to the car and opens the passenger door. "Good night, Enore."

"Good night, Ms. Silva."

"Bye, Enore," Natalie says, moving toward the car. "See you at my party. And don't forget to dress up."

"Dress up?"

"Yeah. See ya." She enters the backseat and shuts the door.

"Wait. What?" I look at Davi. "What does that mean?"

"I think you know exactly what it means." He grins knowingly. "You gotta look the part."

"Oh, my gosh." I drop my face in my palm and groan. "What in the world have I gotten myself into?"

"Relax." Gently, he pulls my hands from my face. "It'll be fun."

"I'm not sure about that. She wants me to dress up like a princess. Where am I supposed to find a princess dress?"

"Don't worry about it. I know someone."

"You know someone?" Despite the slight anxiety I'm experiencing, I'm tempted to laugh. "You know someone who happens to have a princess dress fit for a teenage girl? Who?"

"Zane."

I tilt my head, think for a moment, and then nod. "Yeah, that doesn't surprise me."

We laugh as my anxiety disappears.

"Natalie is adorable, by the way. Adorable and feisty. She reminds me of my sister."

"Is your sister also annoying?"

"Oh, very," I say.

"Maybe all little sisters have the same personality traits."

"Until proven otherwise, I'm going to believe that theory."

We laugh until Natalie pokes her head through the break in the car window and shouts, "Come on! Wrap it up!"

Davi sighs and rolls his eyes. "Anyway, do you want a ride?"

"No, thanks. My uncle should be here soon."

As if on cue, Uncle Davis pulls into the parking lot; his headlights shine a spotlight on me and Davi, and quickly, I step away from him. I certainly don't want our proximity to spark any suspicions in my uncle's mind, especially since he might feel inclined to share those suspicions with my mom.

"I'll see you at school tomorrow," I tell Davi, moving toward my ride.

"Yeah, tomorrow. And don't forget about Saturday."

How could I possibly forget Saturday? It's the day we go out—on our first date.

Chapter Nineteen

WHEN I LIVED IN NIGERIA, I OFTEN FANTASIZED ABOUT my first date, but it always seemed so out of reach, like something only possible once I was in university and away from my parents. I imagined a cute boy in one of my classes would invite me to have drinks at a cool café with live music and art on the wall. We would talk about literature and politics, and maybe after our lengthy and engaging conversation, we would stop at a *suya* stand. After, he would drive me home or maybe we would share a taxi, and just before I stepped out of the car, he would kiss me.

Since coming to America, my idea of a first date has changed based on the movies I've watched. Now, waiting to date until I'm in university seems absurd. I want to experience walking down the stairs in a sundress, a cute boy, who my father has intimidated, waiting for me below. I want him to drive us to a restaurant for dinner, and then to the theater for a movie. Then at the end of the night, when he brings me home, I want a good night kiss on my front porch. But all those things seem more like a fantasy.

On Saturday evening, I sit on my bed and stare at my open closet. My date with Davi is in two hours. I have the perfect outfit—a sunflower-yellow mini dress, white flats, and a jean jacket. Cute and casual. But I can't possibly wear said outfit, nonchalantly wave goodbye to my mom, and get into Davi's car. Unlike the all-American girls in the movies, I don't have a lenient mother who gives her teenage daughter the liberty to date. I have a strict and traditional Nigerian mother. That's a factor I really should have considered before agreeing to this date.

A few minutes ago, when I spoke to Tolu about the situation, she reminded me what most American teenagers do when restricted from leaving the house. Sneak out.

"It seems risky," I told her. "I won't get away with it."

"Says the girl who spontaneously auditioned for the school musical, sang her heart out, became a viral sensation, lied to her mother about said audition, and got away with it. Or who skipped school with a boy, lied about her whereabouts, and again, got away with it. *Abeg.*" She hissed. "You're more than capable of sneaking out and going on this date. All you have to do is use the pillow-under-the-blanket trick."

"No. Absolutely not. It's too risky."

She sighed. "So, what are you going to do? Cancel?"

I considered that option. It seemed like the only one.

"Come on, Enore. You were so excited about this date, and now you're just not going to go? You aren't even going to try? Maybe give the pillow idea more thought?"

I ended my call with Tolu with no clarity on what to do. Now my phone buzzes, and I instantly believe it's her messaging me a better idea. But it's only my cousin Naomi. She came across my audition video and hasn't stopped raving about it. I read her new message.

NAOMI: Let's all do something fun when I come home for Thanksgiving. I miss you guys.
ME: Okay. That would be nice.

She responds with a series of emojis that all translate to love. I do the same, and the conversation ends while my first-date issue is still very much an issue. Frustrated, I flop on my bed and groan.

"What's wrong with you?"

When I hear Esosa's voice, I spring upright. "Nothing. I'm fine."

"I'm not even a little convinced."

I roll my eyes.

"So? Are you going to tell me or what? I mean, if this thing, whatever it is, is making you this miserable, I'm sure you're dying to get it off your chest."

Well, she isn't wrong. Talking to Tolu didn't help much. Maybe I need another set of ears.

"Close the door," I say before going into the details.

Esosa, being the true *tatafo* that she is, rushes to the door, shuts it, and sits beside me. "Yeeesss." She draws out the word as a grin appears on her face.

"Well . . ."

"Yeah . . ."

I sigh. "I have a date with Davi tonight."

One of Esosa's eyebrows curves up slowly. "As you should."

"'As you should.' That is your reaction? Did you hear what I just said?"

"I heard you perfectly." She crosses her legs. "And I stand by my statement. You two make a cute couple. And you obviously like each other. I was in the car the other day. The chemistry between you guys was intense. So yay for the date. Have fun."

My sister is either delusional or has simply forgotten one major factor that would prevent me from going on my date: our mother. I grunt again and fall on my back.

"Wait. Am I missing something?" Esosa asks. "What's the problem? Don't you want to go?"

"Of course I do. But it's not like I can just get dressed, walk out of the house, get into his car, and leave. What am I going to tell Mommy?"

"Oh. Right." Esosa falls on her back and exhales. "I see the issue now."

"Yeah. I did not think this through. I'll have to text Davi and cancel." Maybe I shouldn't have been so quick to let go of my original idea of a first date. After all, university is only a year away. I can wait till then. The thought is painful, but I accept it.

"I have an idea!" Esosa says, sitting up. "Do you have friends?"

"What?"

"From school. I'm assuming you've made at least one friend you trust to some degree."

I sit up and think. Davi and I have had lunch with his friends all week. Apart from the bad vibes I get from Ara, I'm cool with the rest of the group. Though, since the interview, I've gravitated more toward Sybil. She seems to be a genuinely nice person, and I hope my instincts aren't off on that.

"Yeah. I have someone," I tell Esosa.

"Great. And you have her number?"

I nod.

"Good. Text her. Ask if she's home. If she says yes, tell her you need her help with something, and then ask if you can come over."

"What? Why?"

"Just do it, Enore."

For once, just this once, I follow my little sister's instructions without asking too many questions. Because I'll admit, if there's one person who can resolve this situation, it's Esosa.

I grab my phone and send Sybil the first text.

ME: Hey Sybil. You home?

Seconds pass as we wait for a response. When it comes, I hold my breath and read it.

SYBIL: Hey. Yeah I am. What's up?
ME: Need your help with something. Mind if I come over?

I tap my foot, waiting anxiously for the reply. When my phone buzzes, Esosa and I look at the screen and I exhale.

"Excellent. Now we have a cover story." Esosa stands—her posture straight and her shoulders squared like a general elaborating on the details of a mission. "Next, you're going to throw your date outfit into your school bag. And I'll throw my makeup kit into mine. We'll tell Mom we're going to your friend's to study. A group study session and on a Saturday night?" Esosa chuckles. "Mom will love it. Then we'll ask Auntie Sara for a ride to your friend's—she never asks questions. Then you'll ask Davi to pick you up there and bring you back at the end of the night. I'll ask Auntie Sara to pick us up twenty minutes after your drop-off time, giving you enough time to change out of your date clothes. And that's that." She releases a deep breath and smiles. "Do you get?"

It's a detailed and expansive plan that really should do the trick, leaving very little room for suspicion. I'm tempted to give my sister a round of applause, but I'm confused about one detail.

"Why exactly are you coming?" I ask.

"Look. I'm taking any opportunity there is to get out of this house. Also, I think you might require my makeup skills tonight."

I suppose I wouldn't mind putting the extra effort into my appearance, considering the occasion.

"So?" Esosa sways with her hands behind her back, looking innocent, like she hasn't just devised a brilliant exit plan. "Are you up for this?"

I watch my twiddling fingers and consider. If I go through with this, it will be the biggest lie I've ever told my mom. And worst of all, I will be bringing my little sister along for the ride. She might have come up with the plan, but I should be the one setting a good example, steering her on a straight and narrow path paved with practicality and obligation. As the oldest, it's my responsibility. It's what I've always tried to do. But these days, what I used to do just doesn't come as naturally as it once did.

I look at Esosa and nod. "Yeah. Let's do it."

Chapter Twenty

ESOSA AND I STAND ON SYBIL'S FRONT PORCH AND wave at Auntie Sara as she drives away. When the car disappears from our view, Esosa nudges me with her elbow.

"Looks like we got away with it."

I don't want to speak too soon, but she might be right. I release a long, loud breath. The tension that formed in my chest when we approached our mom with the lie finally loosens. Okay. I think we actually did get away with it. Esosa and I smile at each other, and then she presses the doorbell.

Within seconds, the door opens. Sybil's big, bright eyes shift between Esosa and me.

"Hey, Enore. Come in." She opens the door wider and allows us to step in.

The house, although it isn't as expansive and grand as my uncle's, is beautiful—a classic American ranch-style house with a cozy interior. I look at the collection of family pictures on the powder blue walls, squinting to get a better view of the faces in the frames. When Sybil clears her throat, I turn to her.

"You said you needed my help with something. What's up? Everything okay?"

I take in a deep breath and gather the nerve to explain her role in Esosa's plan. But what if she doesn't agree to be an accomplice? That would create a huge dent in the plan. Anxious about Sybil's reaction, I glance at my sister, and she instantly comes to my rescue.

"So here's the thing," she begins without the slightest tremor in her voice. Honestly, I want just a fraction of Esosa's audacity. "Enore has a date with Davi in . . ." She pulls out her phone from her pocket and glances at the screen. "In about an hour."

Sybil claps while bouncing on her toes; her lips part like she's about to let out a squeal, but Esosa doesn't give her a chance to react to the news.

"Put a cap on your excitement for a minute," she says, holding up her hand.

Sybil's thrilled expression flattens.

Okay. Maybe my sister has a little too much audacity.

"There's one tiny problem," she goes on. "Our mom would never let her go on a date. Well, not until she's in her final year of university. FYI, our mom is really strict." She huffs and rolls her eyes. "Anyway, so we . . . actually, I came up with a plan." She grins proudly. "Basically, we told our mom we were coming over to yours for a study session. But the truth is, Enore is going to get dressed here, then Davi is gonna pick her up. They'll go on their date, he'll bring her back, and our aunt will be here to drive us home at about ten thirty. And that will be that. The world keeps turning, and our mom won't know a thing." Her proud grin expands.

Meanwhile, Sybil's eyes are wide as she soaks in the information Esosa has just thrown at her. "So you want me to be your accomplice?"

"I actually prefer *partner in crime*. It has a more dramatic flair. But yes, accomplice works too."

Sybil's head bobs slowly and then fast. "Okay. Accomplice, partner in crime, whatever it is, I'm in." She grabs my hand, she pulls me up the stairs.

"Wait," I say, my first word since letting Esosa take the lead. "You're okay with this—with helping us?"

"Well, yeah. You're my girl."

That answer, the confirmation of our friendship from Sybil, makes me halt on a step. I smile.

"Besides," she goes on, "it's a Saturday night, and Bethany and I are bored out of our minds. But here's some fun. Right at my doorstep. As if I placed an order on Uber Eats." She laughs.

"Wait. Bethany is here?" I ask.

"Yeah. We were just hanging out when you texted. Come on." She pulls me up the stairs again, and I follow with Esosa behind me.

When we walk into Sybil's room, Bethany is on the bed, swiping through her phone with a blank expression. She sits up when she notices us and tosses her phone aside.

"Hey, Enore and . . ." She looks at Esosa and frowns.

"I'm Esosa. Enore's little sister. Bethany, right?"

"Yeah."

"I follow you on Insta and TikTok. Love your content."

Without a second thought, I know Esosa is networking. If she believed in business cards, she would pull one out and hand it to the body-positive social media influencer who is also our school's cheer captain and say, "For all your makeup needs." But business cards aren't her thing. She believes they're too direct. So instead, she says, "Enore has a date and we're gonna help her get ready. I'm doing her makeup. Wanna help?"

That's more her style of networking and advertising—subtle. Tasteful and unintrusive, as she once described it.

"Hell yes." Bethany jumps to her feet. "It's not like I have anything else to do."

"Excellent." Esosa rolls her bag straps off her shoulder, undoes the zipper, pulls out her makeup case, and places it on Sybil's white dresser. When she presses a button, the case unfolds, unveiling trays filled with makeup.

Sybil and Bethany look between the extensive collection of makeup and Esosa, their eyes wide and amazed.

This, right here, is part of Esosa's tasteful and unintrusive advertising.

I sit in front of the vanity, and Sybil and Bethany gather around as Esosa works a makeup brush against my face. Whenever I imagined my first date, I always overlooked the preparation. Instead, I focused on the date itself—the biggest part of the night. But it occurs to me this moment holds more significance than I ever thought. But maybe the added value has more to do with the company. All three of them dote over me; their voices and the music Sybil put on fill the room.

"We should probably keep it down," I say. "Just so we don't bother your parents."

"They're not here," Sybil says. "They're away for the night—seeing some show in the city."

And she isn't throwing a party? It's the norm in the movies I've watched, the only course of action when parents are away and a teenager is home alone. It's what Jules did in *Superbad*.

"Let's go with a soft lip," Bethany says. "Matte or glossy?"

Esosa taps a finger to her chin and ponders briefly. "Glossy," she concludes.

"Yeah. My thoughts exactly," Sybil adds.

I'm not part of the decision-making process. Even the outfit I planned to wear has changed—the yellow sundress swapped for a red one.

"You want to make a statement," Esosa said as she folded the spaghetti strap number into my bag before we left home. "Trust me, this is the dress."

When I step out of Sybil's en suite bathroom and look in the full-length mirror, I don't regret allowing my sister to steer this operation. I'm in red slingbacks and the red minidress—truly the ideal combination of cute, sexy, and elegant. I look incredible because of her. I'm about to go on my first date because of her. She just might be my version of a fairy godmother.

"Oh my gosh," Bethany gasps with one hand over her mouth. "You look freakin' amazing."

"Right?" Sybil adds. "Like, drop-dead gorgeous. Red is definitely your color."

Esosa watches me with her arms folded, smirking. "I think I might add stylist to my credentials."

I roll my eyes and laugh, and then the doorbell chimes. My heart races. That must be Davi.

Esosa glances at her phone. "Seven on the dot. Right on time." She looks at me. "You stay here. Let him wait a little. I'll get the door."

"I'll come with," Sybil says, trailing after Esosa.

When they leave, Bethany examines me again and nods. "Yeah. If he's not blown away, he doesn't have a functioning brain."

I chuckle softly—awkwardly, actually. My shaking hands ball up as I breathe deeply and try to contain my nerves. Being left alone with Bethany doesn't do much to alleviate the flutters in the pit of my stomach. We've sat at the same lunch table before, talked, laughed. Though the group always created some sort of distance between us. We've never talked intimately—one-on-one—like Sybil and I have. Because of that, I'm still trying to pinpoint her intentions. More and more, I'm convinced she isn't a mean girl concocting a plan to humiliate me. But I still haven't figured her out completely.

"Isn't this a little strange for you?" I ask, watching her through narrowed eyes.

"What do you mean?"

"Well, you know, I'm about to go on a date with your best friend's ex-boyfriend."

She chuckles. "Honestly, sometimes I forget that ever happened."

"They only broke up in March. How can you possibly forget that?"

"Trust me, we've all tried to forget it." Her green eyes wander for a moment, then she cringes. "Them dating was the worst. They weren't even, like . . . compatible or whatever."

"Then why did they date?"

"A miscalculation. They mistook their connection as friends for a romantic connection. It happens. When two people are lonely and in pain and going through shit. That was them at the time. So yeah . . . they started dating."

There's a lot to unpack from Bethany's statement. There are questions I want to ask and details I need to clarify. It takes a lot of restraint not to probe.

"Anyway, them dating was the worst thing that could have happened to us. They fought all the time. They were miserable, we were all stressed, and Zane's chakra was all out of sorts. To this day, he claims he's not fully recovered." She rolls her eyes. "But he's a major drama queen. Anyway, it was, like, the worst couple of months ever. When it finally ended, it was the biggest relief." She sighs deeply. "Trust me, no one's mourning that loss. Not even Ara."

A moment of silence passes between us. I absorb everything Bethany said while still watching her through narrowed eyes.

"Look. If you think I'm harboring some sort of bitterness 'cause you're into Davi, I'm not. He's one of my best friends. He was miserable with Ara. But he lights up with you. It's goofy as hell, but it's cute. So, yeah. This works for me."

Slowly, I nod. My narrowed eyes return to their normal size. Maybe it's time I let go of my paranoia, the fear that the prettiest girls in school are out to get me. Well, maybe Ara is. But Sybil and Bethany definitely pass the vibe check.

"Come on." She hooks her arm into mine and leads me to the door. "Let's not keep him waiting any longer."

Chapter Twenty-One

AS I WALK DOWN THE STAIRS, MY HAND SHAKES against the railing. Below, Davi watches me. When our eyes connect, my heart thumps hard.

In the movie *She's All That*, Laney Boggs, the awkward and unpopular art nerd, receives a makeover for her date with the school's hotshot, Zach Siler. Her reveal as she comes down a flight of stairs is gradual. First, her shoes appear—red, chunky-heeled peep toes—and then her bare legs that move in a slow stride. "Kiss Me" by Sixpence None the Richer, one of the most beautiful songs I have ever heard, plays in the background; it complements the sweet moment perfectly. When Zach, eagerly waiting at the base of the stairs, finally sees the full reveal—Laney in a little red dress—he inhales deeply, and his mouth falls open just a little.

This moment, the one I am somehow experiencing, feels strangely similar to that scene. In my head, the perfect soundtrack, "Somebody's Son" by Tiwa Savage and Brandy, plays. The chorus is on repeat as I come down the stairs. Everything is cinematic; it's a movie-perfect moment where I—a dark-skinned girl with box braids and a non-American accent—am the star, alongside a boy with hazel-green eyes and a golden-brown complexion.

Air gathers in my chest when I come face-to-face with Davi.

"Enore, you look . . ." He sucks in a deep breath. "Incredible."

I beam as heat sneaks up my cheeks. "Thank you. So do you."

After glancing at his outfit—dark blue jeans and a white T-shirt—he shrugs. "Nothing compared to you."

"I'd say," Bethany adds, glaring at Davi's casual yet well-coordinated outfit.

"You guys should probably head out," Sybil says as she opens the front door.

"Are you ready?" Davi asks.

I nod but hesitate before walking through the door with him. "Esosa, what are you going to do while I'm gone?"

"I think I'll chill here with Sybil and Bethany. Play around with some makeup." She glances at the two girls. "That's if they don't mind."

"Hell no we don't," Bethany shouts. "Like, your makeup skills are next level. Please let my face be your canvas. I'm going live on TikTok in a bit. I'll totally give you a shout-out."

There you have it. Esosa's unintrusive advertising, paying off.

She smiles sweetly at Bethany, then turns to me with a smirk. "Have fun. And you . . ." She scowls at Davi. "Remember what I said." Her tone is serious, threatening even. "Remember every word."

"Trust me," Davi says, chuckling nervously. "I'll never forget."

As we walk through the door, I turn around to look at Sybil, Bethany, and my sister. They're smiling like proud parents sending their child off to college. *Thank you*, I mouth to them. Because they all played a part in making tonight happen.

At the curb, Davi opens the passenger door for me. Inside the car, I glance at him.

"What did my sister say to you?"

"Don't worry about it. Just know she loves you very much."

I nod, satisfied with that answer.

"By the way, I was surprised when you texted me to pick you up at Sybil's. Why not your place?"

"Oh." I clear my throat. "That." Telling the boy I like I'm not allowed to date is a little embarrassing, especially when said boy has a car and far more freedom than me. Regardless, I muster the nerve. "My mom. She's sort of against me dating while in high school. Basically, I'm not allowed to." I chuckle awkwardly. "But I really didn't want to miss our date, so I had to be a little creative."

He nods thoughtfully, then watches me with a playful glint in his eyes. "And exactly how creative were you?"

Davi starts the car, and as he speeds up the road, I tell him all about Esosa's brilliant plan.

Chapter Twenty-Two

I SIP MY STRAWBERRY MILKSHAKE AND LOOK AT THE expanse of trees and hills stretched out beyond me. I'm sitting near the edge of a cliff, and it should be terrifying. But Davi's presence erases the angst I would have otherwise felt. The heat emitting from his body, the soft fragrance of laundry detergent on his shirt, and his firm hold on my waist all make me calm.

"Wanna swap?" he asks, extending his chocolate milkshake to me.

"Okay."

We exchange cups and turn back to the exceptional view.

Before Davi told me what he had planned for our date, I imagined dinner and a movie. A classic American date. And while his plan was similar to that, it varied a little. After leaving Sybil's, he drove to Shakers, a retro diner. He placed our order in the drive-thru, and a waitress rolled out of the restaurant on roller-skates, our large order balanced in her hands. Then Davi drove to Bayer's Cliff ten minutes away, a spot he explained has a great view.

He was right.

The lush trees spread over hills and the stream that runs through the valleys create the most stunning scenery. When we arrived, I gaped at the view while he laid a checkered blanket on a patch of grass. Then he arranged our order from Shakers—two burgers, curly fries, chicken strips, a corn dog, and two milkshakes.

"It's good," I say after a long sip. "But I like the strawberry one better."

We swap milkshakes again, and I watch him through my lashes while sipping. And then a smile I can't control forms on my lips.

"What?" he asks, matching my smile. "What's so funny?"

I shrug. "Nothing, really. I suppose I'm just . . . happy."

And I am. I didn't think I would feel happy for a long time. And I was okay with that. I was content with my grief. What else is a girl supposed to feel when she loses her father and her life suddenly becomes a tragic before and after? My sadness was justified, and I was okay to carry it with me for a long time—years, maybe even forever. Because I couldn't imagine ever feeling true happiness without him. But here I am, fatherless, yet sitting with a boy at the edge of a cliff—happy. The grief is still there, but it's less potent. Maybe it will never completely go away, but maybe it will recede a little and give me room to feel other things, like the happiness I'm experiencing in this moment.

My head falls on Davi's shoulder as the sun dips lower beneath the horizon and casts a reddish-golden hue on everything.

"Can I ask you something?" he says.

"Okay."

After a long pause, he clears his throat. "I've noticed whenever you sing, you close your eyes. Why do you do that?"

My posture instantly goes rigid.

"Um . . . I . . . I'm sorry." He must notice the way my body tenses up. "You don't have to answer that. It's just something I noticed at your audition and at church and when I sit in on rehearsals."

Slowly, I lift my head from his shoulder. "You sit in on rehearsals?"

He nods.

"Why? Shouldn't you be at football practice during that time?"

He shrugs, and his eyes wander. "Well, I don't do it all the time. Maybe once . . . twice. But only for a few minutes. Then I rush off to practice or debate club, depending on the day." He rubs the back of his neck. "Is that weird?"

I shake my head. "No. It's sweet."

He slowly releases a breath.

"I picture my father in the audience," I say. "When I close my eyes, I picture him there. It helps. Though it really annoys Mr. Roland. He's complained a few times. He says singing with my eyes closed is a hazard, since I have to move around while I sing. So unless I want to fall off the stage, I have to stop."

"And you can't?"

"Sing without picturing him there?" I think for a moment, then shake my head. "Back in Nigeria, I only used to sing in the choir. And he was right there, in the congregation, smiling like he couldn't be prouder. Every time, he was right there." Tears sting my eyes, and I blink sharply. "He isn't in the congregation anymore. And I need him to be there. So I imagine he is. I don't know if I can sing without doing that."

Davi watches me closely. "Would you like to try?" he asks. "With me? You could sing to me. Eyes wide open."

The idea is both terrifying and enticing. To sing without being grounded by the image of my father. Indisputably petrifying. But then to sing to a boy I like, whose sweet, easy smile always unwinds something taut inside me. Tempting, without a doubt.

On the more practical side, if I don't start singing with my eyes open, Mr. Roland is going to snap. Or even worse, I'll miscalculate my steps and fall off the stage—face flat on the floor, right in front of the first row. I might not chip a tooth, but I'll definitely lose my dignity.

I exhale deeply and face Davi. "Okay. I'll try."

"Yeah?"

I nod. "Yeah. What should I sing?"

"How about your favorite song."

"Okay." I draw in a deep breath, then expel it slowly. On instinct, my eyes fall shut, then fly open when Davi clears his throat. "Right. Sorry."

The first words of Paloma Faith's "Only Love Can Hurt Like This" are a whisper. My stare is aimless, darting to the trees in the distance as I force the lyrics out. What I'm doing definitely can't be considered singing. Maybe mumbling. Along with some slight humming. Frankly, I'm embarrassing myself, and I'm set to quit, but then Davi's skin comes in contact with mine unexpectedly. He holds my hand, caresses it with the light movement of his thumb, and my stare shifts to meet his. He doesn't say a thing. But his eyes, those hazel greens layered with sincerity and kindness, convey something reassuring, something that's vital at this moment, something that's needed to thaw the blockage in my throat.

After a sharp breath, I sing—project every note with clarity and conviction and in perfect pitch while never breaking focus from him. I smile, stunned I'm doing something that, minutes ago, seemed impossible.

Davi helped me get here. I'm grateful, but also a little confused by him. How can someone say nothing and at the same time say just enough? How can he, without an extensive speech or a spirited pep talk, help me overcome a hurdle that seemed huge? I try to understand it, but I'm at a loss. This connection between Davi and me is a mystery. One that doesn't need to be poked and dissected by curiosity. It's best left alone.

"That was . . ." He beams after I sing the last note. His mouth hangs open like he's waiting for the right word to fall into it. "Incredible," he says finally.

"Thank you." I look him over and chuckle. "You know, nearly every teen movie paints you as an asshole."

"What? Me?"

"Well, not you exactly. Just guys like you. You know, the handsome jock. Mr. Popular."

He laughs.

"Seriously. Your kind are hardly ever nice. And when they are nice, it's because they have an ulterior motive."

"Ulterior motive?"

"Yeah. Like in *Never Been Kissed* and *Carrie*."

He watches me blankly, clueless about my references.

"Never mind. The point I'm trying to make is, there's a lot more to you than meets the eye. Debate club, for example. Not a very cliché jock move."

He laughs again. "Well, I want to get into politics down the road. So debate makes sense."

"You? A politician?" I squint and study him for a moment. "Okay. Yes. I see it."

"And is that because of the whole Mr. Popular thing?"

"Yes. And other attributes too. Good attributes. You could be one of those rare politicians that is actually honest."

"That's the dream. But Blake won't want to hear none of that." He sighs. "He wants us to pursue a football career—play college football, get drafted into the NFL and all that."

"You don't love football as much as he does, do you?" It was easy to spot that the first time I had lunch with Davi and his friends—Blake's passion for the sport and Davi's lukewarm excitement that Blake didn't notice.

"I mean, I loved football at first—during freshman and sophomore year. But I have other interests now."

"Then why are you still on the team?"

"For Blake. It means a lot to him we're both on the team. But after this year, I'm done with football." He shakes his head and huffs. "Anyway, I could totally see you becoming some kind of singer."

I snort. "There's no way that is ever going to happen."

"Why not?"

"I'm going to be a doctor."

Now he squints and studies me. "Yeah. I don't see that at all."

"Well, my mom sees it perfectly."

"So, she wants you to become a doctor?"

I nod.

"Well, what about you? What do you want to be?"

"A doctor."

"No. You only want to be a doctor because it's what your mom wants."

"And what's wrong with that?"

"What if doing what your mom wants doesn't make you happy?"

I think about that possibility, but it doesn't faze me. The only thing that could faze me is disappointing my mother.

"Enore." Davi stares brazenly into my eyes. "What makes you happy?"

I bite my lip and think. "Singing, I guess. In the choir. And especially onstage during rehearsals."

"Well, there you go." He claps his hands. "That's what you've gotta do."

"Sing?"

"Well, yeah. You could make an entire career from being a singer."

"Like Olivia Rodrigo?"

"Yeah. Sure. Like Olivia. But you could consider a career in musical theater too. Like on Broadway."

"My mom doesn't even know I'm in the school musical. If she finds out, she'll be livid. And I'll definitely have to quit. So a career in musical theater?" I scoff. "That isn't an option."

"And being a doctor is?"

I nod. "It's the only option."

"But it isn't what you really want. Can't you just tell your mom no?"

"Nigerian kids can't just tell their parents no."

"Why not?"

"It's considered disrespectful."

"Oh," he says.

It's clear Davi doesn't understand how, in my culture, disobedience is tied to being disrespectful. Skipping school or going on a secret date is nothing compared to looking my mom in the eyes and telling her I won't be a doctor. That blatant level of defiance isn't something I'm equipped for. But Davi doesn't understand this, and for the first time since we met, I see how different we are and how our backgrounds have made us expect different things out of life.

He was born in America, the land of dreams, where happiness means following your bliss, and the path to success can mean becoming an actress or a singer or even a dancer. But Nigeria is all about hustling, starting a business, or having a solid career that ensures you are fed and housed. In Nigeria, if you fail, you go hungry and become homeless. Most Nigerians have a survival mindset that doesn't permit them to follow their bliss. They choose careers in medicine or law—practical options that presents no risk and guarantees financial stability. A career in the arts is not only impractical, but it doesn't always provide security or guarantee success. Therefore, it can never be an option for me, especially when I have a mother who is determined to see me become a doctor.

"Enore, listen," Davi says. "You're amazing. Your voice. Every single time you sing, I just . . . I just . . ." He smiles and watches me with so much admiration, my heart flutters.

I want to disregard the major difference I just spotted between Davi and myself. I want to disregard the fact that he might never truly understand me. If I can do that, being with him will be easy. This first date I lied to make happen will end on a good note. So I disregard everything. I push my discovery aside, lean forward, and press my lips to his.

Chapter Twenty-Three

ON MONDAY, MR. ROLAND STANDS IN FRONT OF THE cast and crew.

"It took some time," he says, "but I figured out the problem with this musical. And luckily for all of you, I know exactly how to fix it." He grins like he's cooking up an equally devious and genius plan.

No one speaks. They all wait to hear the issue and the solution. I, however, have a feeling the problem is me and my lack of musical theater experience. When Mr. Roland looks at me, I get confirmation. Simultaneously, everyone turns to me.

I'm used to this by now. This morning, my walk through the hallway involved the same dose of attention. Eyes shifted to me and Davi as we walked side by side. News of our date had gotten out, and I suspect by means of Esosa.

On Saturday night, after my date, shortly before Auntie Sara picked us up, Esosa squealed when she heard how things went.

"Only two weeks into the school year and you've already gone on a date with one of the hottest guys in school." She beamed with pride. "He'll probably ask you to be his girlfriend any day now. Then you'll join the cheerleading squad, and you guys will be a power couple." She sighed, starry-eyed. "It's the American teenage dream."

"Oh my gosh. Yeah," Bethany added. "You should join the cheer squad."

"No. Absolutely not," I said.

I wonder, though, if that's still a thing—the romantic pairing of a jock and a cheerleader. I've seen it enough in the movies, but I choose not to fixate on that cliché. Davi hasn't asked me to be his girlfriend yet. He probably wants to take things slow. I can respect that, but if he had asked me to be his girlfriend on Saturday night while we sat on Bayer's Cliff swapping milkshakes, I would have said yes.

But whether we are officially a couple or not, going on a date with Davi Santiago, a.k.a. Mr. Popular, has put a spotlight on me. Though when I mentioned this to him earlier today, he strongly disagreed and handed me a copy of the school's biweekly newspaper. The first thing I did when I looked at it was gasp. Then I wanted to cry strictly out of terror because, to my utter surprise, my face was on the front cover.

"Looks like you're famous." Davi chuckled. "First you go viral and now you make the front page of the school paper. I think it's safe to say I'm getting all this attention today because of you."

I gawked at the newspaper, mortified. When Sybil asked to write a story about me, I thought it would be a small article on the last page. I never, ever expected my face in print with the headline COMING TO AMERICA. Clever? Yes. Fitting? Absolutely. But why? Why? Why? Why? The article talked about my move to America, my audition, and the viral video. It's a well-written article. Sybil is both a talented photographer and writer. But again, why?

"Enore," Mr. Roland says now. "Are you with us?" He squints, leans forward, and examines me. "You seem a little spacy."

"Um . . . I'm fine." The tepid smile on my face is likely telling a different story.

"Right." He taps his chin slowly, a gesture he does too often. "Anyway, the issue with this musical, as I was saying, is—"

"Me! It's me!" I finish his sentence before he has the chance to. It's better this way. If I'm the one calling out my shortcomings, it's less embarrassing.

"You?" Mr. Roland presses a hand to his chest and laughs. "Honey, no. My goodness, you're the solution."

"Huh?" I tilt my head, so his words go in from another angle.

"Well, as I was saying before you interrupted, the issue with this musical is that it's boring. We all know the Cinderella story; we know how it begins and ends. It's a classic and a goodie and always a crowd-pleaser. With our original script, the story is fresh—modern. But it could be better . . . so much better. Enough to really wow the crowd." He arches his eyebrow. "That's where you come in, Enore."

"Me?" I gesture to myself for confirmation.

"Yes, you." With his hands behind his back, he strolls toward me. Cheryl follows him with a clipboard. "I read the school newspaper today. Well, it was especially hard to miss with your face on it."

I cringe.

"An interesting article. 'Coming to America.' It was . . ." He looks up at a spot in the air and stares at it for a long while. "Inspiring," he says finally. "It certainly sparked some ideas."

"Ideas?" I ask, then glance at Cole, who shrugs, equally clueless.

"I spent the day rewriting parts of our original script—making it even more original. Now, here's what's going to happen. This play is going to focus on you, Enore."

"Um . . . but didn't it always?" Cole says, echoing my confusion and likely everyone else's. "She's Cassandra—the star of the play."

"Yes. But now it's going to reflect her reality—a life-imitating-art situation," Mr. Roland explains. "Cassandra, a recent orphan, moves to America from Nigeria to live with her aunt and cousins. We infuse culture and diversity into this version. I can see it now." He stares into space again; his eyes are wide and dreamy. After blinking sharply and shaking his head, he turns to me. "Of course, Enore, I would need your help to incorporate the Nigerian culture into the script. Is this something you'll be up for?" He watches me closely, and I'm not really sure what to say.

The concept is interesting. In every teen movie I've watched, people of color were eliminated or reduced to secondary or background characters and sometimes caricatures. But here I am, not only a Black girl but a Nigerian immigrant, starring in the school play with the chance for my culture to play an equal part in the lead.

I smile and nod. "I think it's a cool idea. I'd love to help you."

"Oh, wonderful." He sighs, relieved. "Now, for the new script. It isn't finished quite yet. So let's take today off and meet tomorrow. Enore and I will take today's rehearsal time to go through the script and incorporate parts of the Nigerian culture. Sounds good?" He frowns and looks around, daring an objection. When none comes, not even from a very displeased Ara, he turns to me. "Shall we get started, then?"

I nod, and the rest of the cast and crew leave the auditorium.

It's certainly strange, sitting beside Mr. Roland and having him ask about my culture—the food, the clothes, the customs. It's not a position I ever thought I would be in.

Thirty minutes into what I call a culture consultation, I squint as a thought occurs to me. "Um . . . Mr. Roland, I was wondering . . ."

He stops typing on his laptop and turns to me. "Yes?"

"It's about my character. She just emigrated from Nigeria, so I'm guessing she'll have an accent like I do?"

"Well, yes. I thought that was obvious."

I exhale. To do justice to Cassandra, the main character who was originally an American girl, I've been privately working on adapting a believable American accent, as advised by Mr. Roland on the third day of rehearsals. It hasn't been easy to resist what comes naturally to me. I don't know how Esosa does it. I basically break a sweat in my pathetic attempt. But now, with this new setup, I don't have to twist and bend my tongue to get into character. This art-imitating-life situation certainly has its perks.

Chapter Twenty-Four

DAVI WASN'T JOKING WHEN HE SAID ZANE COULD provide a princess dress fit for a teenage girl. On Friday evening, when Esosa, Bethany, and I walk into Tabitha's Wardrobe, the costume shop Zane's parents own, it all becomes clear. The massive space has a goth vibe and is mostly separated by eras. Within seconds, I go from an eyeful of regency fashion to 1950s circle skirts. Then the masquerade masks on the red wall capture my attention, until I'm looking at the heads of stuffed animals on another wall.

"Oh my gosh," Esosa says. Her mouth drops open and doesn't snap shut.

"I know. Cool, right?" Bethany says, grabbing a Victorian bonnet and placing it over her blond curls. "I love this place."

"I can see why," I say. "It's amazing."

According to Davi, my very own informant, Zane's parents are costume designers who provide wardrobe for theater productions across the country and even a few television shows. They have a Tabitha's Wardrobe in Brooklyn that's much larger than this location. I look around again, finding it hard to believe anything could outdo this space.

"Enore." Zane steps out of the back room and into the shop. The fringe on his black suede jacket sways as he walks toward me. "I've been expecting you." He looks from Bethany to Esosa. "And you brought an entourage."

"Ha. Funny." Bethany smacks his arm playfully. "For your information, we're here to help Enore pick a dress."

"The only help she needs when she's in this emporium is from me." He smirks, and Bethany rolls her eyes.

"Are your parents here?" I ask, while extending my head toward the back room. "I would like to say hello to them."

"My folks are in the city till Monday. Holding down the fort till then." He pushes his fingers through his long dreadlocks and they fall backward. It's as if the movement happens in slow motion, like in the movies when music plays in the background and girls look on in awe.

Because my heart only ever flutters for Davi, and Bethany has, on multiple occasions, described Zane as the brother she loves but never wanted, I know there's one person left in the room who might be in a state of awe.

"Your outfit." Esosa's eyes shift over Zane's lean physique—slowly down and then slowly up until she meets his gaze. "Love it." She runs her fingers through the fringe on his jacket and smiles just a little. "You have great style. Anyone ever told you that?" Her tone is soft, low, and slightly hoarse.

I'm not exactly sure what's going on, but it's definitely strange and uncomfortable to watch. Is Esosa flirting? With Zane, my friend? Yeah. I can say that now. Zane is my friend. I spent every lunch period this week eating and talking with him, Blake, Sybil, and Bethany. Of course, Ara was there too, but she doesn't fall under the category of friend. Zane, though, is a friend, a friend who is grinning at my little sister encouragingly, like he's receptive to whatever she's giving.

What in the world is happening?

"Um . . ." I clear the knot in my throat. "Could we get started?" Hopefully, my interruption will snap them out of their momentary insanity.

"Yeah. Right." Zane blinks sharply and turns to me. "A princess dress, right?"

"Yes."

"We've got plenty of those. You thinking medieval princess or Disney princess?"

"A combination of both would be ideal," Esosa answers. "Like Princess Tiana meets Anne Boleyn. Jodie Turner-Smith's Anne Boleyn, of course."

"Obviously," Zane agrees. "I'm thinking something like the iconic emerald gown."

Esosa smirks. "Perfect."

He turns toward a rack and sorts through the clothes. Colorful, detailed fabrics sway against each other as he riffles through the extensive collection. Esosa watches his every move. Basically, checking him out.

What is happening?

"Hey," Bethany whispers in my ear. "Are you seeing this?" She gestures at Zane and my sister.

"How could I miss it?"

"Yeah, that's some serious eye humping."

At those words, that really shouldn't go together but somehow make perfect sense, I choke on my spit and start coughing. Zane and Esosa turn to me, frowning, and Bethany waves them off.

"She's fine. It's all good." She taps my back. "Carry on. Nothing to see here."

They both continue with their previous activity—Zane sorting through the costumes and Esosa ogling him.

"Chill. It's nothing," Bethany says. "She probably just has a little crush on him."

"Yeah?" I get out after clearing my throat. "And what does he have?"

"Likely a brief infatuation with the only person who has ever complimented his bizarre style. Seriously, it's probably nothing to worry about."

I really hope she's right.

Zane hangs four green dresses in the fitting room, and as I enter the small space, I worry what my absence will prompt Esosa to do. Has my newly found dating life inspired my sister to pursue her own American teenage dream? Is she following the example of her big sister? Ideally, I should be on a straight and narrow path and should ensure Esosa is on that path with me. It's what my mother expects from me—to be a shining example for my sister. But as someone who, in the past few days, has lied, skipped school, and gone through with an elaborate scheme, I can't say that I am.

Lately, I find myself somewhat detached from the person I used to be, slowly being shaped by my new environment and new desires.

I don't want to be a hypocrite, dating while depriving my sister of the same. But the difference between Esosa and me is that I'm still dipping my toes into these new experiences, enjoying them with some sort of caution that's tied to obligation. Esosa has never operated with that same sense of caution. But she's always had me—the blueprint to making our parents proud. And to some degree, I think that has restricted her wild, carefree, make-my-own-path nature. But if she no longer has me to be that example, my sister will be everything my mother doesn't want her to be. Forget the possibility of her being a lawyer or a doctor or an engineer or having a nine-to-five career with a steady and hefty paycheck. Esosa will be herself—the whimsical creative who so naturally gravitates to another whimsical creative.

And you know who would take the blame for that?

Me.

Chapter Twenty-Five

ON SATURDAY AFTERNOON, ESOSA, SYBIL, AND I WALK into Davi's massive backyard. Children—some dressed like princesses, others like princes, and a few like dragons—run around. Colorful balloons and paper lanterns hang from trees and the wooden fence. With a clown, a magician, a face painting station, and a bouncy castle, it's the perfect playground for any child. There are at least twenty of them dressed to suit the theme of the party. And unfortunately, so am I.

With two hands, I lift the full skirt of the emerald-green gown. Embarrassment aside, it's a stunning dress with a sweetheart neckline and small puff sleeves. There's an embroidered corset that makes my waist look smaller than it really is, and somehow, I manage to breathe in it. Last night, Zane styled the gown with a small tiara and lace gloves. A few hours ago, Esosa secured the tiara on my braids as I got dressed at Sybil's house. I certainly couldn't leave my house looking like a Victorian-era princess. What would I have said to my mom—that I'm the musical entertainment at my almost boyfriend's little sister's birthday party? No. Another lie about studying at a friend's got Esosa and me out of the house. And Sybil, who takes great pleasure in being an accomplice, welcomed us with open hands and a pitcher of sangria—nonalcoholic, to Esosa's major disappointment.

Since school started, I've crossed out a few rules on my list. But there's one rule I haven't broken.

Rule #6: Choose your friends wisely.

Despite my initial reservations, Sybil and Bethany have turned out to be good people and even better friends. I've connected with them more than anyone else in the group. Well, except for Davi. I'm comfortable around them, comfortable enough to be myself. To date, neither of them has given me a reason to believe they plan to douse me in pig's blood.

Rule #6: choose your friends wisely. ✓

"Oh, my gosh!" The abrupt high-pitched scream overrides the music blasting through the speakers. Natalie pushes past a clown twisting a balloon and races toward me. Her red gown rubs the grass as she moves.

Last Thursday, when she mentioned dressing up like Elena of Avalor, I looked up the character out of curiosity, and I have to admit Natalie's dress is near identical to Elena's.

"You came! You really came!" She claps while bouncing and squealing. "Look, everyone! It's Enore Enchanted! Enore Enchanted is here, and she looks . . ." Her wide eyes take in my appearance. "Amazing!"

I'm still trying to connect the dots—trying to understand how a simple, last-minute audition for the school musical made me a viral sensation, branded me Enore Enchanted, and led to me being the musical entertainment at an nine-year-old girl's princess-themed birthday party. It's moments like these that can make a person question their life decisions, mounting up regrets and trying to figure out what they could have done differently. And I'm really tempted to do that, but the look of absolute glee on Natalie's little face melts my heart. The gratitude and happiness of a child hits different, so much that I'm okay the dots connected the way they did.

"Will you sing?" she asks.

"Yeah," the kids gathered around me all say together.

"The song from the video," a little girl dressed like Princess Tiana screams.

"No, do 'A Whole New World,'" a Princess Jasmine look-alike says. "It's my favorite."

Soon, disagreeing little voices overpower each other.

"Damn," Sybil whispers to me. "You've got fans."

"Cute, little ones," Esosa adds. "But they're kind of terrifying too."

When a voice calls for everyone's attention, my head snaps up. Davi is on the small stage, beneath a balloon arch. He's holding a microphone and dressed as if he just stepped out of a fairy tale. His dark hair is slicked back, no wavy lock dangling in front of his face as usual. His coat and pants are white, while the sash across his chest and his tassel shoulder pads are gold. He looks like a legit Prince Charming, and I'm caught between gasping, laughing, and just gawking at him.

"Well, damn. He looks hot." Esosa takes the words right out of my mouth.

Right now, I could really use one of those hand fans to cool my heating cheeks. Zane definitely should have included it as an accessory.

"I know there are a lot of opinions about what we should hear first," Davi says to the crowd. "But why don't we let the birthday girl decide?" He looks at his little sister. "Nat?"

Without much thought, she says, "'Into the Unknown.'"

"All right." Davi looks at me and smiles, the kind of smile that signals my heart to thump fast. "Everyone, let's welcome Enore Enchanted."

The crowd of kids and supervising parents clap.

I lift my dress and walk to Davi. "Hi," I say.

"Hey." He glances at my outfit, then moves the microphone from his mouth. "You look incredible. Gorgeous."

"Thanks." At this point, after Davi and I have shared many kisses and held hands multiple times, my heart shouldn't go offbeat whenever he's around, but it still does—every single time. "You look gorgeous, too. Um . . . I mean . . . handsome. You didn't tell me you were wearing that."

"I know asking you to dress like a princess was a big ask. I couldn't possibly let you go through the embarrassment alone." He laughs. "We can both look ridiculous together."

I giggle. "That was very sweet of you. Thanks."

Totally captivated by my Prince Charming come to life, I forget about everyone else. I lean forward, fully prepared to kiss him. But then a loud voice, my sister's in fact, brings me back to my senses.

"Let's get on with the show!" she says with her hands cupped around her mouth. "The real show!"

"Right." Davi hands me the microphone, gently brushing my fingers as he does. "Good luck."

I sing three songs, starting with Natalie's request. The kids sit on the grass and watch attentively as if I descended from heaven with wings and a halo. Esosa, my PR person by force, holds a phone toward me the entire time, getting footage for social media. My session ends with a round of applause from the audience.

"That was . . . was amazing!" Natalie says once I'm done posing for pictures with her and her friends. She hugs my legs, or at least the layers of fabric covering my legs. "Thank you."

"You're welcome." Restricted by my corset and unable to reach down to hug her back, I extend my hand and tap her head.

"Your payment of carrot cake cupcakes is available at the dessert table. You can have as many as you like. You've earned it." She pulls away from me and trots off to her friends.

"She's right. You earned it."

When I turn around to face the person talking to me, I see a man who looks familiar. I've seen him before, on the FOR SALE sign in front of Davi's summerhouse. But even without that connection, it would be easy to identify the man as Davi's father. They look alike— the same dark wavy hair, the same complexion, and the same smile.

"Hi." He extends his hand. "I'm Marc. Davi's dad."

I knew coming to Davi's house would mean meeting his parents. This week at school, he told me he planned on introducing me to his dad during Natalie's party. I wanted to place a hand on his forehead and ask if he was sick. Really, I was concerned. In Nigeria, people don't introduce their parents to their romantic interest. Usually, people bring a potential husband or wife home. Unless a relationship will end in a marriage, it doesn't warrant the attention of parents. Because Davi and I are a long way from a lifelong commitment—in fact, we aren't even officially a couple yet—I thought the idea of meeting his parents was ridiculous. But then I remembered that in America, things are a lot different.

"It's nice to meet you, Mr. Santiago." I shake his hand.

"Likewise. Davi actually wanted to introduce us himself, but I can't seem to find him anywhere, and I couldn't wait another minute. You were incredible. My God. That voice. Those pipes."

Again, I could really use that hand fan to hide my embarrassment.

"Thank you so much for doing this for Natalie. Trust me, it means the world to her."

"It was no problem. Really." Well, at first it was. But I got into it later.

"Dad." Davi steps out of the house and runs toward his father. "You're here." He presses his lips into a tight smile. "Talking to Enore. Alone."

"Just couldn't wait. Plus, I didn't know where you were."

"Was in the kitchen, helping Grams."

"Ah. Well, no worries. Enore and I have gotten acquainted. I was just telling her how amazing she sounded."

"Yeah." The tension holding his lips in a strained smile disappears. "She's pretty amazing."

"Mm-hmm." With the way Davi is looking at me, it's likely his dad is a little uncomfortable. He takes a small step away from us. "I think I'm gonna help Grandma in the kitchen—see if she needs anything. Enore, it was a pleasure meeting you, and thanks again." He turns away from us and walks into the house.

"Your dad is nice. Where's your mom? I'd like to meet her too."

Davi frowns and looks at me like I've said something wrong—a word that has the power to disrupt a moment and ruin a mood. I study his demeanor that changed from happy to guarded so quickly. I don't understand it, but it's happened before. Last week, at his family's summerhouse, he had the same reaction when I asked about his mom. There was a split second when he wasn't himself, when he didn't meet my stare. This time, the split second where he isn't himself drags on. I shift my weight from one leg to another while his eyes wander around the yard.

"Um . . . she isn't . . . here," he finally answers.

"Oh." His response does nothing for my curiosity or concern. "Then where is she?"

He looks at me; his mouth falls open, but nothing comes out. He shuts it and sighs. "I think it's time for Natalie to cut her cake," he says. "I need to go set that up. I'll find you after, okay?" He marches off before I can say a word.

I'm not a presumptuous person—jumping to conclusions before facts are presented. Usually, I prefer to see all the evidence laid out. But this time, I'll make an exception. I don't have the facts. I only have one simple observation—Davi is uncomfortable every time I mention his mom. He avoids answering my questions about her. This observation leads me to one conclusion: Davi is keeping something from me.

Why? Maybe he doesn't feel comfortable sharing some aspects of his life with me yet. I understand that, but it hurts regardless. I've been so vulnerable with Davi. I've told him about my father, about my rules, about my fears. I've even cried in front of him. I wish he felt as comfortable with me as I do with him, enough to let his guard down.

Chapter Twenty-Six

IN 2018, THE NIGERIAN RAPPER FALZ RELEASED A song called "This Is Nigeria," a cover of Childish Gambino's "This Is America." The song highlighted many of the socioeconomic issues in Nigeria. It called out corrupt leadership, SARS brutality, criminal activities of radical groups, and so much more. I remember nodding with complete understanding while Tolu and I watched the music video. But I didn't have the same understanding of Childish Gambino's original—"This Is America." The lyrics and the symbolism in the video made no sense to me, even after watching several YouTubers' thorough explanations. The harsh depiction of America in the video contradicted my image of America, what I'm now realizing was a curated image.

When I lived in Nigeria, shows like *Friends*, *The Fresh Prince of Bel-Air*, and *Gossip Girl* (the original, not the remake) painted a sparkling, pristine picture of America. Along with the grass-is-greener-on-the-other-side ideology most foreigners have, America seemed like a utopia to me. But the more my stay extends, the more that pristine image is distorted by the realities of living in a town where I am a minority.

I look over my shoulder and glance at the middle-aged white man who has consistently been six feet from me since I walked into Pick-a-Book. There are other customers in the store, but he left his post at the cash register and has been stalking me under the guise of arranging books on the shelves. I know what's happening. It's happened before—a few weeks ago when Mom and I went to the beauty store. A saleswoman followed us as we moved through the aisles, looking for products suitable for our hair. We ignored her at first, but it became increasingly difficult. When my mom completely lost her patience, she spun around and said, "Is there a reason you have been following us around this store?"

In response, the saleswoman folded her arms and said, "Look. I don't want any trouble."

With one glance, she had branded us troublemakers, peace disrupters, and thieves. She only needed one fact to come to that conclusion, and so does the man who's been trailing me for the last five minutes. There is already a book in my hand, and I intend to pay for it. Though now, I wish I'd listened to Tamara's advice to avoid this bookstore.

Today in English class, after protesting the assigned reading material to no avail, she fell quiet for the rest of the period. I caught her in the hallway after the bell rang.

"You were right," I told her. "This semester's reading list should include books by African American authors. I should have said something too."

She shook her head, but her perfectly rounded Afro stayed intact. "It wouldn't have made a difference. Mr. Erin is small-minded and inflexible. There's not much we can do." She sighed, and her shoulders slumped.

"Well, I haven't read a lot of African American literature. Would you mind recommending some?"

She smiled immediately. "*Their Eyes Were Watching God* by Zora

Neale Hurston is one of my absolute favorites. Also, anything by Toni Morrison and James Baldwin. But for something more contemporary, I recommend *Long Way Down* by Jason Reynolds."

I pulled out my phone and typed out the books and authors she motioned. "Okay. Thanks. I'll drop by the bookstore today."

"Yeah. Just make sure you avoid Pick-a-Book. Cute name, I know. But the manager, some balding white man with thick-framed glasses and coffee-stained teeth—is a dick. Go to Hazel's Books instead. It's Black-owned, and you'll likely find all the books there, anyway."

The ten-mile distance between my house and Hazel's Books eliminated it as an option. Pick-a-Book was only three miles from home, on the same shopping strip as Tech and Techies. Though I now regret basing my decision on convenience. The man Tamara described is definitely the man who has been following me. He pushes his thick-framed glasses along the bridge of his nose, glances at the book in my hand, then meets my gaze.

"Are you going to pay for that?" he asks, grimacing.

I clench my jaw and grind my teeth. My heart pounds even though I haven't physically exerted myself. This interaction is enough to get me worked up.

"We don't tolerate shoplifting here."

"Shoplifting?" I spit out the word, and my voice shakes with rage. "I am not a thief, but you've been treating me like one—following me around since I entered this store."

"I'm just doing my job."

"And what exactly is your job?" I'm not the one who asks that question. The disembodied voice comes from behind me. When I turn around, I see Blake. He's scowling, and for the first time since I've known him, his muscular physique is imposing and threatening. "Is it your job to be a dick who harasses customers?"

The store manager takes a step back but sticks to his defense. "I was just doing my job."

"Then maybe I should give Mrs. Wallace a call and tell her about the job you're doing at her bookstore."

"Mrs. Wallace?" The manager's voice quivers.

"Yeah. She's a friend of my dad's. They go way back."

The manager rubs his forearm, pushing the sleeve of his plaid shirt upward. After clearing his throat several times, he turns on his heels and rushes away like a coward.

"Hey," Blake says to me, his voice gentle. "You okay?"

I stare at the carpeted floor, unable to look at him. The worst part about incidents like these isn't the anger that inflames my whole body or the shocking realization that people can be willfully ignorant. It's the shame that comes after the scene ends.

I never felt ashamed of my skin until I moved to America. After every interaction like the one I just experienced or every intentional coincidence where people like me are erased, shame settles on me like dust. I feel dirty, a less shiny version of myself.

Since my move to America, "Brown Skin Girl" by Beyoncé and "Brown Skin" by India Arie have become sacred, holding more significance to me than they did before. In my head, I repeat the lyrics of the two songs like a mantra—*she need an Oscar for that pretty dark skin; beautiful mahogany, you make me feel like a queen*—until they polish the shame off.

"Enore." Blake puts his hand on my shoulder. "Are you okay?"

"I just want to get out of here." I drop the book I'm holding on the floor and walk toward the exit.

Outside, I breathe deeply. It's the last week of September, and there's a chill in the air. I pull up the zipper on my hoodie and wrap my arms around myself, rocking slightly.

"Hey." Blake is beside me. "I'm sorry that happened to you."

"It's fine."

"No, it's not. Shit like this used to happen to my mom all the time. It still does sometimes."

I frown and look at him.

"My mom's from Kenya."

My frown deepens as I examine Blake's flushed white skin, honey-yellow blond hair, and pale blue eyes.

"My stepmom," he says, laughing.

"Oh."

"Yeah. My birth mom left when I was five—something about wanting to be a singer on a cruise ship." He rolls his eyes like he's more annoyed at the thought of his birth mom than hurt. "Anyway, my dad met Hiari in New York City. They fell in love, and she moved to Bellwood."

"And it was hard for her?" I ask. "Being here?"

"Well, Bellwood isn't exactly New York City, so it took some adjusting. But not to say New York City is perfect and Bellwood is a shit town. There are a lot of good people here."

"Yeah. I know that. I just wish my uncle had told us how things can sometimes be here—in this country."

I think of a lifetime of more incidents, of situations where I will have to speak out—like Tamara did in class—and fight to insert myself in places where I am marginalized. I think of instances where my voice will be ignored—again, like Tamara's—and instances where the only option will be to walk away, to leave things unchanged, and to leave narrow-minded people just as they are. It's sickening. Terrifying.

"Maybe your uncle wanted to protect you from it somehow. Even if it was only for a little while."

I shrug. "Yeah. Maybe."

It's dark now. Most of the stores on the strip are already closed. Blake and I are among the few people on the street. I pull my phone from my pocket and glance at the time: 7:30 p.m. It's strange that a town is this quiet on a Friday night. I look at Blake, who's watching me closely, clearly still concerned.

"Thank you," I say. "For what you did in there."

"It was nothing."

"Were you looking for a book? Is that why you were there?"

"Yeah. For my little brother. His birthday's on Sunday. But I'll just drop by Hazel's Books tomorrow—better selection, anyway." He pulls a bunch of keys from his pocket and jiggles them. "Are you still up for the bonfire tonight, or would you like me to give you a ride home?"

"Yeah. I still want to go. I could use the distraction. My cousin was actually supposed to pick me up here and then take me to the bonfire."

Yesterday, Adrian somehow convinced my mom to let me and Esosa attend a party on the beach on a Friday night. He said something about us having new experiences, then ranted about the importance of us participating in a Bellwood High tradition. As he explained, the bonfire, which always happens a week before the homecoming game, is symbolic, an act of solidarity that shows each student's team spirit and commitment to the school. I never thought the truth—the exaggerated truth—would work on my mom. But it did.

"Well, we could just go together," Blake says.

"Okay. Sure. I'll text my cousin and tell him I have a ride."

"Sounds good."

We walk to the curb, and Blake opens the passenger door of his blue Jeep Wrangler. I step inside and fasten my seat belt.

"I have to make a stop before we head to the beach," Blake says after starting the car. "Gotta get Zane."

"All right."

The ride to Tabitha's Wardrobe is short. Zane is already standing outside the store; the streetlight shines a spotlight on him. His eyes are closed. He sways, likely to music coming from his AirPods. Tonight, he's wearing baggy overalls over a multicolored sweater, and his dreads are in a messy topknot.

"Get in, man!" Blake shouts, sticking his head out the window. "We don't have all night!"

After Zane's eyes fly wide open, he crosses the street and approaches the Jeep. He's clearly surprised to see me sitting in front, but smiles and gets in the back. "What's up, guys?" he asks.

"Just ready to get this night started," Blake answers.

"Wait. Before this car moves, I need to know what we're listening to because I've been on an Ayra Starr binge all day, and I'm not ready for it to end.

I spin to the backseat, forgetting I'm strapped in by the seat belt.

"You listen to Ayra Starr?" I can't contain my excitement when I hear the name of my favorite Afrobeat artist.

"Of course," Zane says. "She's fire."

"I know, right?"

"Who are you guys talking about?"

Zane and I turn to Blake and glare at him like he's insane.

"What? Just asking."

"Zane," I say, "please enlighten him."

"Done." His thumb moves against his phone screen, and within seconds, "Rush" is playing on the stereo.

When Zane starts singing, effortlessly spitting the pidgin English lyrics like a true Naija boy, I lose my cool, undo my seat belt, and turn around. At first, I just watch him, completely impressed. And then I start singing, and soon, we're in each other's faces, screaming the lyrics.

"Okay," Blake says, laughing. "It's a vibe." He turns the volume up and drives.

The music, the laughter, and the company are everything I need right now—a good memory to suppress the memory of the bookstore.

Chapter Twenty-Seven

THE FIRE CRACKLING AGAINST THE CLUSTER OF wood releases embers that float like fireflies in the night air. Zane's arm is around my shoulders as he, Blake, and I maneuver through the crowd of Bellwood High students gathered at Deep Water Beach. With the brightness the assembled tiki torches provide, I notice mostly seniors are in attendance, but there's my sister, laughing with a group of sophomores. We wave at each other when our eyes meet, and then she turns to her friends and starts dancing to the music blasting through undetectable speakers.

"Enore!" Adrian jogs toward me, his curls falling over his face. "You made it."

"Yeah. Blake was at the bookstore, so he offered to give me a ride. Then we picked up Zane and stopped at Shakers for some food."

As we drove away from Tabitha's Wardrobe, Blake announced a detour. We ended up in a booth with a large order of sweet potato curly fries, cheeseburgers, milkshakes, and a large s'mores sundae. We spent almost an hour eating and talking about music, which basically involved convincing Blake that Afrobeat went beyond Burna Boy. Then, just as I was stealing some of Zane's fries and raving about the talented and underrated artist Simi, my phone buzzed with an incoming text.

DAVI: Hey. You still coming to the bonfire? I'm here. Can't find you anywhere.

ME: With Zane and Blake. On our way.

If Davi had not texted, we might still be in that booth at Shakers.

Adrian nods at Blake and Zane, a wordless *hey*, before turning to me again. "So you ready to meet my boys from the basketball team? Remember I was gonna introduce you?"

"Yeah." I look between Zane and Blake, recalling how they cheered me up after the bookstore ordeal. The last thing I want to do right now is meet new people and spend energy carrying conversations and forging new relationships when I feel safe and seen in the relationships I've already formed. "I think I'm going to hang out with my friends for now, but I'll catch up with you later."

"Um . . . okay." Adrian sighs and bobs his head. "Sure. Do you."

"Later, man," Zane adds before turning me away from my cousin.

Sand crunches beneath my sneakers as we near the driftwood logs that enclose the firepit. Bethany, Sybil, and Davi are a few of the people seated on the logs. I'm surprised to see Travis as well, drinking from a red plastic cup. He's sitting beside Misty from biology; his arm is around her shoulders. He nods at me, then continues sipping his drink.

"Finally," Bethany says, standing. "You guys are here." She hugs me but sticks her tongue out at the boys, then takes my hand and pulls me to sit between her and Sybil.

"What took you so long?" Sybil whispers in my ear. "This one"—she tilts her head toward Davi, who's sitting beside her—"has been moping around, waiting for you to show up."

I shift on the driftwood and look over Sybil's shoulder. Davi meets my eyes and smiles.

"Hey," he says.

"Hi," I reply.

He opens his mouth to say something else, but Blake speaks first, addressing the group with his orotund voice.

"Where's Ara?" he asks.

"Couldn't make it," Bethany answers. "She's seeing a play in the city with her mom."

"Yikes." He cringes. "She's gonna be in a shitty mood on Monday."

"Yeah." Bethany huffs and shakes her head. "Don't I know it."

"Hey," Davi calls for my attention. "Wanna get out of here?" He clears his throat. "With me?"

"Yeah. Okay."

As we walk away from the firepit, I'm surprised and relieved no one in the group makes any juvenile comments alluding to us hooking up. We stroll away from the party and move to an area of the beach not lit by tiki torches or the firepit. Here, the full moon is the only light; its silver glow shimmers on the expanse of water lapping the shore.

I glance at Davi as we walk. Tomorrow, Saturday, will mark a week since his sister's birthday party—since that awkward conversation where he avoided talking about his mom. When we saw each other at school on Monday, it took some effort to get back into our normal flow—to talk without pausing and stuttering, to sit beside each other without leaving a gap. By Wednesday, things were normal again. We were back to being friends. Friends who had kissed on three occasions—that day in his family's summerhouse, again that day when he drove me home, and the night of our first and only date. It's been two weeks since we sat on Bayer's Cliff and swapped milkshakes. Taking things slow with Davi has left me wondering if he likes me as much as I like him, enough to take our relationship to the next natural stage.

"Hey." He stops walking and turns to face me. His pinched, tension-filled expression worries me.

"Is everything okay?" I ask.

"Yeah. I just feel like we haven't really spent time alone since our date."

"Me too. I guess we've just been busy—me with the musical and you with football and debate."

"Yeah. But it's not like I haven't wanted to spend time with you or ask you out again or . . ." He draws in a long breath and releases it. "I've just been dealing with some stuff."

There. Another sign everything is not okay with Davi. Something is going on, but he refuses to tell me what, and I know better than to ask. I want to believe he'll talk to me when he's ready.

"Listen, Enore." He takes my hand. "I like you a lot. You make me really happy, and I swear I think about you all the time."

It feels so good to hear those words, to have them silence my doubts.

"I think about you too," I say. "All the time."

It's true. Davi is on my mind a lot—while I'm doing homework, rehearsing for the musical, helping my mom in the kitchen, watching reality shows with Esosa. The memory of him is like the warmth that lingers after a long hug.

"It's been really hard since my dad died," I tell him. "But you make me happy, Davi. And I was really sure I wouldn't be happy for a very long time."

I look at the way moonlight reflects on his face, the way it makes him appear almost celestial. We inch toward each other, tilt our heads, and align our lips. The urge I've been suppressing for weeks, all in the name of respectfully taking things slow, is no longer manageable. When our lips touch, I moan and press my chest against his. My fingers dig into his hair, rubbing his scalp and pulling his face closer to mine. We kiss deeply, break apart for air, and then continue again. When we finally separate, our chests moving quickly as we catch our breaths, Davi squeezes my hand and whispers my name.

"Yeah?" I answer.

"Will you . . ." His fingers shake. His palm turns damp. He chuckles, likely trying to downplay his sudden nervousness, but it's a broken, weak sound, so he stops and becomes sober. "Will you be my . . . girlfriend? I know we've only gone on one date and—"

"Yes," I cut in. "Yes. Absolutely. Definitely."

"Really? Because I've wanted to ask you for a long time, but I got nervous. Really nervous. I didn't know what you'd say."

"I've been waiting to say yes."

He smiles and pulls me in for a hug.

I bury my face in his chest, breathe in the clean scent of soap on his shirt, and make a conscious decision to dwell in this moment and disregard the reality of hiding a boyfriend from my mother.

Chapter Twenty-Eight

HOMECOMING MARKS THE START OF NEW beginnings—the beginning of a new school year, the beginning of a new football season. That's what Blake enthusiastically explained to me yesterday at lunch. Now I spot him on the field, running with a football tucked under his armpit, Davi a few feet ahead of him.

I know nothing about football. It isn't a sport people follow in Nigeria. We prefer soccer. I hoped Zane would provide some insight during the game, but he's leaning back against the bleachers, looking at the field but not really looking at it. His stare is bored and detached. He might be as clueless as I am.

"I'm just here for support," he says, twisting a ring on his finger. "I have no idea what's going on—never have, never will. Ara knows better than me. Ask her."

Ara is sitting on the other side of Zane, her face tight with concentration while she watches the players on the field. This is what she does—ignores me. I could be right beside her, and she wouldn't say a word to me—maybe a few irritated glances, but not a word. Because she hates me and has essentially marked us enemies, I should avoid her. In fact, that's one of my rules.

Rule #5: In the unfortunate event that you make an enemy, try by all means to stay away from them.

But with Ara and me both in the musical and in the same friend group, we are unfortunately always in proximity.

I sigh, annoyed I'll have to sit through the whole game clueless about what's going on. There's no one else to explain things. Bethany is in a blue and white uniform, shaking pompoms and cheering with her squad, and Sybil is on the sidelines, taking pictures of the game for the school newspaper. I want to support Davi, but that's impossible when I don't even understand the objective of the game. I'll have to resort to copying the crowd—cheering and grunting when they do. If I get my timing right, I can fool just about anyone.

"Hey, Enore."

At the mention of my name, my head snaps up. Cole stands with his hands in his pockets.

"Is this spot taken?"

"Um . . . no." I shuffle closer to Zane, and Cole sits beside me.

"I've missed a few minutes," he says. "Give me an update?"

I laugh. "I wouldn't know where to start. I don't know a thing about football."

"Isn't your boyfriend on the team?"

Boyfriend. It's only been official for a week, and I'm still turning the word around in my head, examining it, finding it truly hard to believe it's applicable to me. I have a boyfriend. Davi Santiago—the cutest, sweetest boy—is my boyfriend. I smile at the thought.

"I could explain the game if you like," Cole says.

"Yes, please. Tell me everything."

He does. Well, as much as I can grasp in my first lesson and in one sitting. During halftime, the homecoming court comes out on the field. This is, by far, my favorite part of the game—the glittering plastic crowns, the formal attire, the satin sashes with titles that mean nothing outside the realm of high school. Blake—the crowned homecoming king—stands with Casey Rowell, homecoming queen. The whole ceremony is elaborate, and I love every minute of it. The band, in perfect formation, plays a classical rendition of "Blank Space" by Taylor Swift, and the cheerleaders perform a complex routine that involves flips and somersaults. It's incredible, and the audience buzzes with energy, fully hyped for the second half.

My eyes stay on Davi throughout the duration of the game. With a little more understanding of how things work, I can say Davi is really good. I leap to my feet and cheer when he scores a touchdown. Despite the rowdy crowd on the bleachers, he sees me—looks right at me—and smiles. I was wrong before. This is my favorite part of the game.

I love being with Davi, being his girlfriend. Whenever I'm with him, I feel most like myself. The pressure to be the perfect daughter and the shining example for my sister doesn't exist when I'm with Davi. He gives me room to just be Enore—the viral sensation, the star of the school musical, the girl who sometimes cries on his shoulder because she misses her dad, the girl who is cautiously but fondly enjoying the new experiences in her new home. It's nice to have a safe place to explore these new versions of myself. And that's what Davi is—my safe place.

Sometimes, it takes a lot of effort to forget how different our backgrounds are and also how enigmatic he often is. He never tells me where he goes on Sundays, right after he watches me sing in the choir. He's unreachable for hours, and when he finally texts me, his vibe is off. Then there's the issue of his mom. All my questions about her are still unanswered. Frankly, I have no idea what's going on with Davi, but I wish he could see me as his safe place too.

Clearly, he doesn't.

SCHOOLS IN NIGERIA DON'T HAVE DANCES LIKE homecoming and prom. Esosa and I have only experienced a school dance vicariously, through characters in movies. And if it wasn't for Auntie Sara, that wouldn't have changed.

"The homecoming dance is a rite of passage," she explained to our mother last week. "They have to go."

"The time they will use for that nonsense is the time they can use to study and prepare for their futures," Mom said while flipping through her medical textbook, indirectly showing what she expects us to do, a visual subliminal message if you will.

"Ivie, they're teenagers," Auntie Sara went on, "and they're good kids. They deserve to have some fun."

"Fun?" My mother lifted an eyebrow and curled her lips. I was sure she was going to give a lecture about how fun is a pathway to foolery. It's one of her top three lectures. Regrettably, I have it memorized.

"A little fun won't hurt anyone." Auntie Sara matched Mom's coldness with a warm smile. "And if it makes you feel better, Adrian is going too. They'll all be together."

After thinking for a moment, Mom looked between me and Esosa and nodded slowly. "Okay. They can go."

At those words, basically magic words, Esosa and I glanced at each other and smiled. The plan, Esosa's plan, had worked perfectly.

It wasn't very complex. We simply asked Mom if we could go to the homecoming dance. But we made sure Auntie Sara was present when we did. Auntie Sara, a true advocate for teenagers living their best life, took care of the rest.

Now we're in the school gymnasium turned banquet hall. Strings of light and lit paper lanterns dangle from the ceiling and decorate the dim space with bright specks, a tie-in to the theme—A Night of a Thousand Stars. There is an enormous crescent moon at the photo station. People have been taking turns sitting or lying on it for the perfect IG-worthy shot. Currently, Esosa, in her ruffled fuchsia dress, is perched on the curve of the moon, smiling at the camera. I'm swaying with Davi on the dance floor, our arms around each other.

"Did I already tell you how beautiful you look?" he asks.

"Yeah," I laugh. "I think ten times already."

"Well, you do, and I can't get over it." He takes my hand and spins me around. My royal blue dress flares round my thighs in a circle, and I giggle.

When Esosa and I went shopping with Auntie Sara, it was the first dress I tried on. My sister raved about how the color was perfect for my complexion. She was right. The short spaghetti strap dress with a sweetheart neckline looked stunning on me, and now, with Davi, I feel even more beautiful. He pulls me in to his chest, and I kiss his cheek.

"You look very handsome too. I've told you that, right?"

"About ten times already. But who's counting?"

He's wearing a navy blue suit with a white T-shirt and white sneakers to match. The outfit is both formal and casual, and I love it.

"How are rehearsals going?" he asks.

"Good. Progressive."

It's been three weeks since Mr. Roland proposed a change to the musical. For the first few days, we worked together, incorporating parts of my culture into the script—the language, food, and clothes. At first, the idea of working solo with Mr. Roland was unnerving. But he's proven to be tolerable and sometimes even pleasant to be around. When he talks about musicals, his face lights up. There's almost something childlike about his disposition. It's been refreshing to see that side of him. But getting that rare glimpse hasn't made him lenient with me during rehearsals. He's still the strict, no-nonsense director who calls me out when I miss a dance step or forget my lines.

I suppose it's fair.

"Is it fun?"

I squint and consider Davi's question. "Um . . . well, it's a lot of work. A lot more than I thought."

"Yeah. But it all pays off on opening night."

"Well, it's a lot of work regardless—a lot of work for just a high school play."

"But don't you enjoy it—the process?"

Again, I squint while thinking, and my stare moves above his shoulder and to the people at the refreshment tables, filling their cups with drinks and their plates with finger food. I wonder if the punch is spiked. This might be my first school dance, but I've watched enough movies to know some rebel might have emptied a bottle of vodka into the punch. To be safe, I'm following a very important rule on my list and have also instructed Esosa to do the same.

Rule #7: Never drink the punch at a school dance. ✓

"Hey," Davi says, nudging me gently. "You okay? You kinda spaced out."

"Sorry." I blink sharply and focus on the question he asked. "I love singing. That part, I enjoy."

"And the rest?"

I shrug. "I'm still getting into it."

The slow song ends, and an upbeat one begins. It's a popular song, and everyone rushes to the dance floor to jump and scream the lyrics rather than dance.

"Hey," Davi says into my ear. "Wanna get out of here?"

I look at the hyper teenagers who might or might not have drunk spiked punch and nod. "Yes. Let's go."

He takes my hand and leads me through the crowd. The moment we step through the back door of the gymnasium, fresh air hits our faces, and we sigh.

Hand in hand, we climb the bleachers and sit at the very top, looking at the football field where Davi scored the winning touch-down last night. The open, quiet space is the perfect respite from the supervised commotion inside.

"This is nice," I say as my head drops to his shoulder.

"Yeah. It is."

"I know I said it before, but you were amazing yesterday during the game."

"Thanks. I'm not gonna lie. I'm counting down the days until this season is over and I can focus on other things. Maybe join another club. Maybe Model UN."

I tap his leg. "Hang in there. Just a few more weeks."

"Yeah." His arm comes around me. "Anyway, I want to take you somewhere."

"Okay. Where?"

"To New York City."

I lift my head and watch him through narrowed eyes. "You want to take me to New York?"

"Yeah. To see a show on Broadway."

My eyes shrink even further. Now I can only see him through a sliver of space. "You're not serious."

"I am."

"New York City?"

He nods.

"A Broadway show?"

Again, he nods. "You ever seen one?"

I shake my head. "I have never even been to the city."

"Would you like to, then?"

"Well . . . yes." I laugh.

"Okay. Good. I'll get tickets to a show."

He's acting like going to New York City is the equivalent of crossing the street when it's in fact a one-hour train ride from Bellwood.

"We'll see an afternoon show," he goes on nonchalantly. "We'll take a train there and then one back home."

I watch him expectantly, waiting for him to crack a smile—a sign he's joking. But that doesn't happen. He continues planning our day in the city—where we'll eat before and after the show and the sights we'll see. Soon, pure excitement replaces my expectation for a punch line. The idea of me and Davi in New York City—miles away from my mother, enjoying the sort of freedom I've never experienced—is thrilling.

When I lived in Nigeria, I never craved freedom the way I do here. Back there, my parents, my mom especially, limited my life to school, church, home, and the market. In America, it's different. Freedom seems like low-hanging fruit, easier for me to grab, especially with friends to cover for me and an aunt willing to advocate for me. The more things I experience—first kiss, first date, first school dance—the more freedom I crave.

"So?" Davi asks. "Are you in?"

I think briefly, then nod. "Yes. Let's go."

He kisses me, and I don't think about the how—how I might convince my mother to let me go into the city. But then again, with Davi, I never think about the how. With him, the hows seem irrelevant and so do the consequences of my actions.

And maybe that's just part of being a reckless teenager.

Chapter Twenty-Nine

RECENTLY, I'VE BECOME THE KIND OF PERSON WHO lies frequently. I am a liar.

Recognizing this new trait doesn't make me want to change. A part of me has gotten comfortable lying. And the reward lying brings appeases the part of me that feels guilty and ashamed.

Today, the reward is quality time with Davi.

He holds my hands as the train nears Grand Central Station. "Are you excited?" he asks.

"Very."

A lie made this trip into the city on a Saturday morning possible. And so did some strategic planning, courtesy of Esosa. Two weeks ago, after the homecoming dance, I told her Davi wanted to take me to see a Broadway show. She instantly came up with a brilliant plan—invite Bethany and Sybil to our house to meet our mom.

Initially, I was on defense. Our mother isn't like Sybil's, who dotes over me whenever I go over, offering snacks, asking me questions about school and my plans for university, and basically begging me to stay for dinner. My mom is more the why-are-your-friends-in-my-house-and-when-are-they-leaving type.

In Nigeria, she allowed Tolu, Abby, and Osas to come over for study sessions, but she wasn't the most hospitable host. She walked past my open bedroom door frequently to ensure we were reading and doing nothing else. She never offered them snacks or made conversation. And she hardly smiled. My dad, however, would come out of his office to say hello. He would tell jokes, then give us money to buy *small chops* from the vendor across the street. He was our respite during every study session—the only reason my friends had some fun whenever they came to my house. He balanced my mom. His softness rounded out her sharp edges. Without him to be a buffer, I was hesitant about Bethany and Sybil coming over, but Esosa reminded me it was necessary. If I planned on going to New York City with Davi, my cover story, a.k.a. spending the day studying at Sybil's house, had to be so solid my mom wouldn't question it. That could only happen if she met my friends and saw they were upstanding members of society and unquestionably good influences on me.

The visit was a crucial part of the plan, and with Bethany not mentioning her extracurricular activity as a social media influencer and Sybil speaking nonstop about her plans to attend Yale for prelaw, it was a pleasant visit. My mom was impressed, so impressed she retreated to the kitchen and returned with a platter of crackers, finely sliced cheese, and fruits. It was definitely something she picked up from the store. But regardless, the gesture shocked me and Esosa. We looked at each other with wide eyes and then at our mother.

"It was nice meeting you girls," she said, smiling. "But you'll have to excuse me. I have some studying to do." She went to her room and left us alone in the living room. Sybil and Bethany then raved about how pretty and sweet she was.

The visit certainly went well and was as effective as Esosa predicted. Last night, when I told Mom I would spend Saturday studying at Sybil's, she didn't object.

"After we're done studying, we're going to the movies," I added while holding my breath.

"Okay," she replied. "But be careful."

It took me a few seconds to fully absorb her reply. My mom had permitted me to go to the movies without an interrogation or a lecture. Esosa had been right. Meeting my friends made her less inquisitive about my whereabouts, and I couldn't have been more grateful for my sister's genius.

Davi didn't have to go through the same hurdles to spend today with me, and I hope one day, I won't have to lie to my mom about the major aspects of my life like a new interest I'm nurturing or a boy I really like. But that idea seems far-fetched. My mom has always been a parent, not a friend—not someone I can confide in. It's hard to imagine a future where she could be everything my dad once was to me.

Davi and I get off the train and walk through Grand Central Station. Only seconds in New York City, and I'm hyperaware of the sense of urgency in the air. Bellwood has a relaxed vibe, so instantly, I feel alert here. Even on a Saturday, people move with purpose. But I linger and observe the building's stunning architecture—the arched windows, the grand staircase, and the high turquoise ceiling with constellations painted on it.

When we step out of the station, I tilt my head backward and take in the expanse of skyscrapers. Then something tightens in my chest, and I squeeze Davi's hand, imagining, just for a moment, that it's my father's hand and he's right here with me.

For a brief while, this was his dream—New York City, the concrete jungle, as Alicia Keys and others have called it. He held on to this dream for as long as he could, but then his grip grew weak, and he let go.

"Hey," Davi says. "You okay?"

I release a deep breath, and my father's loose leather watch sways against my wrist; suddenly, I'm reminded of its existence—of the part of him I always carry with me.

"Yeah," I tell Davi. "I'm okay." I blink sharply, refocus on him, and force a small smile. "Just a little hungry."

"How about we grab a quick bite before the show?" He glances at his Apple Watch. "We have some time. What do you feel like?"

"Well, everyone is always going on about New York pizza, so how about that?"

"I know just the place."

We have lunch at Uncle Paul's Pizza. The Margherita pizza is the best I've ever had. The crust is thin and crispy, and the tomato sauce is savory and slightly tangy. Once we're stuffed with pizza and chicken wings, we walk the short distance to Times Square.

Stunned, I look from one billboard to another. My attention is being pulled in so many directions, I have to spin around to capture my surroundings. Without a doubt, I'm the perfect image of a dazed tourist.

I pull my phone from my purse, prepared to take pictures, then quickly realize I can't have any evidence of this day. The risk of my mom stumbling on it is too high. I sigh and tuck my phone into my bag. When I look at Davi, he has his phone aimed at me.

"What are you doing?" I ask, hiding my face behind my hands.

"Did you see the way your face lit up? I had to capture it on camera." He draws the phone closer to my face. "Come on. Smile. No need to be shy."

I drop my hands instantly. "I'm not shy."

"Then strike a pose. And make it a good one."

There's a lot going on around me. The commotion of Times Square is distracting. The crowd is daunting. Maybe I am shy, somewhat cautious about my little presence in this massive, iconic place. But the challenge in Davi's eyes is the perfect motivation. I brace my hands on my hips and strike a pose. It's nothing worthy of a magazine cover, but it's goofy enough to make Davi laugh. After he's taken several pictures of me, he presses his cheek against mine and snaps a few selfies.

We eventually make it to the Lunt-Fontanne Theatre, a two-story building with the show's banner hanging from it.

"*Midnight's Muse*," I say, looking at Davi.

"Yeah," he replies. "I've never seen it, but I've heard it's really good."

Inside, the theater is grand, far more extravagant than Bellwood High's. There are three levels of seats that are already packed, but an usher directs us to seats on the fifth row of the ground level. We're so close to the stage.

"These are good seats," I whisper to Davi. "Really, really good seats. How much did they cost?"

"Don't worry about it. I've got connections."

I arch an eyebrow, waiting for the whole truth.

"Fine." He huffs. "My dad's client and friend gave them to me. He's some big-shot entrepreneur who always has Broadway tickets. So don't worry about it. They didn't cost me an arm and a leg."

I sigh, relieved. "Okay. Good."

"But if they had cost me an arm and a leg, it would have been worth it." He leans into me. "You're worth it." His lips brush mine, and just as I kiss him, the lights in the theater dim, and the stage curtains part.

THROUGHOUT THE PERFORMANCE, I'M SPEECHLESS. I forget Davi is sitting beside me. I forget he's holding my hand until he squeezes it. I forget the lies I told to be here, in this seat, looking at the stage. The story unfolds beautifully with dazzling lights, a captivating cast, dance-worthy musical numbers, and a lead that leaves me absolutely floored.

I have never seen a musical live, so I didn't know it could be so spectacular. Is the possibility of creating a show this incredible the reason Mr. Roland disregards our amateur status and pushes us so much?

It all makes sense now, and I want to smack myself for not understanding it before, for not seeing the bigger picture.

During the intermission, while I'm drinking a soda, Davi brings my attention to the program.

"Here," he says, pointing at the names of the cast. "Look."

After reading the lead's name, I grab the paper from him and bring it closer to my face. "Amarachi Okoye." I look at Davi in disbelief. "She's Nigerian. The lead. The lady playing the lead is Nigerian."

He nods. "Yeah."

I look at the name again, the non-Western name.

She's the lead in a Broadway show.

This fact doesn't completely hit me until I'm seated again, watching her perform the closing number. She sings the last note, and the lights onstage go out. The crowd applauds, and tears that gathered in my eyes during that final song fall.

Weeks ago, as I auditioned, something happened. While singing, a new passion grew inside of me. Within seconds, it became big and ferocious. It sank its claws in me, resolute to never let go. But I, too afraid of what it might demand of me, pulled at each claw and weakened its grip. First, by questioning my ability to be the lead. Then by quitting on the first day of rehearsal. Then by downplaying my enthusiasm for the musical, never getting too excited about it, reducing it to only being a high school play. For weeks, I've been dulling that drip, but now I feel it. That passion for singing and being onstage takes hold of me again. And I don't fight it. I don't want to fight it because, for the first time, I see the possibility of what it could be.

A career. A life. For someone like me.

ON THE TRAIN RIDE HOME, I STUDY DAVI, REALLY trying to figure him out.

"Hey," he says when he catches me watching. "You okay?"

I tilt my head from side to side, inspecting his face from new angles. "Why did you take me to see a show?"

He shrugs. "So you could see it can be more than just a high school musical. If you want it to be. I needed you to see it. It was easier to show you than explain it to you."

Well, it's safe to say his plan worked.

"And why the play we saw? Why did you choose it?"

"Because of the lead. I saw her in an interview. Learned she was Nigerian. Thought it might be cool for you."

I nod. "You know I've watched a lot of movies. Teen movies, I mean."

"Yeah." He laughs softly. "I know."

"A Black girl being the lead is rare. And a Nigerian girl . . . well, that hasn't been done yet. But when I saw her name on that program, then saw her on that stage—at the center of the story, commanding the attention of the crowd, receiving a standing ovation—it was like looking at myself, seeing myself." A deep breath rushes out of me. "It was like seeing everything I can be—everything that's possible for me as a Black girl, a Nigerian, an immigrant."

He wraps his arm around my shoulders, and I rest my head on his chest.

"Broadway," I say, just as the train comes to our stop. "I think that's what I want to do with my life."

Chapter Thirty

THREE WEEKS INTO OCTOBER, AND BELLWOOD HAS transformed. Fall, which truly seems like pure magic, paints the small town in copper, mustard, and auburn. The combination creates an ambiance of warmth that makes the cool air tolerable. Esosa misses the summer. She complains about the cold. And according to Adrian, the cold hasn't even started yet.

I don't mind the weather. It's definitely the coldest I've ever experienced, a stark difference from Nigeria's smothering heat. But the cozy knitted sweaters and hot drinks make up for the cold.

As I bring a cup of pumpkin spice latte to my lips, Sybil and Bethany watch me close, waiting for my verdict.

"So?" Sybil leans into the table, her dark eyes set on me. "What do you think?"

We're at Sip & Gist, a cute café with a countryside cottage aesthetic. After learning I had never drunk a pumpkin spice latte, they insisted we go to the café that serves the best in town. Though I suspect they have an ulterior motive, because the best café in Bellwood is also where Ara works. The situation is giving make-up-and-be-friends vibes.

I don't have a reason to make up with Ara, because I've never had a problem with her. The problem has been on her end, and I don't particularly understand why, especially since Sybil and Bethany confirmed she doesn't have a reason to hate me. I'm dating her ex-boyfriend, but she could not care less. I got the lead in the musical, but she never really wanted it to begin with. So what exactly is her problem with me?

I push my confusion aside, set my cup down, and smile. "It's really delicious."

"Right?" they both say in sync. "The best."

As they sip their own drinks, Ara walks to the table with our order of pastries.

"Here you go." Her signature monotone is intact. She places a piece of pecan pie in front of Bethany, an almond croissant in front of Sybil, and a raspberry Danish in front of me. She sits in the empty chair after distributing the order. "How's it going?"

"Good. We're just catching up," Sybil says, more chipper than usual. "Enore saw her first Broadway show yesterday. That's cool. Right, Ara?" Mentioning my name so abruptly and then directing a question at Ara isn't the slickest attempt at whatever it is she's trying to do.

Bethany must think so too, because she gives Sybil a side glance before clearing her throat. "Anyway, what did you see?"

"*Midnight's Muse*," I answer.

"Oh, I heard that's really good. How'd you like it?"

"It was . . ." I think back to everything I experienced only hours ago—the sensational show, the emotions I felt from seeing a Nigerian girl onstage, the possibility that awoke in me. I'm still on a high from the experience. "It was magnificent—the best thing I have ever seen in my life."

"Well, damn," Sybil says. "Look at the way your face lit up."

"Yeah," Bethany adds. "The instant glow."

"Well, I loved it—everything about it." I focus on the pastry on my plate while pondering. "There's this school. Davi told me about it. It's called Juilliard. Have you heard of it?" I look at them.

"Well, yeah. Who hasn't?" Sybil laughs.

"I think I want to go there." Last night, I spent hours reading about it. It seems like the perfect fit for me, more perfect than any academic institution.

"Juilliard." Ara's monotone breaks through my thoughts. "It's the best performing arts school in the country. You know that, right?" She gives me a once-over, then looks through the café's bay window, her stare distant. "My mom went there."

"Your mom?" I ask.

"Yeah," Sybil answers. "Ara's mom is, like, a total Broadway star. But she's retired now."

Bethany gives Sybil another side glance. Obviously, she wanted that response to come from Ara.

"You know you have to audition to get into Juilliard, right?" Ara says. "And the half-ass performance you've been giving at rehearsal won't cut it." She pushes her chair back and leaves without another word.

Sybil and Bethany share a look of shock and disappointment before turning to me. "We're so—"

"No." I hold up a hand, stopping their apology. "She's right."

The delivery could have been different, but it doesn't change the fact that Ara is 100 percent right.

Chapter Thirty-One

I HATE TO ADMIT IT, BUT ARA MOTIVATED ME.

Since our brief conversation at Sip & Gist, I've stepped up my game at rehearsals. I suppose I can credit that to her and the Broadway show Davi and I saw a week ago.

Since then, I've become fully immersed in the musical. I perform without reservation. I stay an extra thirty minutes to practice after rehearsals end. I ask Mr. Roland for feedback, even when he says he has none. The other day, after I ran through the ball scene, he told me I was exceptional. I still get a high from that compliment.

The truth is, I'm the happiest when I'm performing. When I'm onstage, there's this insuppressible thrill that makes me certain I'm doing exactly what I'm meant to. Nothing I've accomplished academically—excellent grades, honor awards—has given me that feeling. The idea of pursuing a career in medicine doesn't give me that feeling.

After seeing that Broadway show, I realized I can't possibly be a doctor. I haven't told my mom this yet. Earlier this week, she watched me apply to four universities. Each of my chosen majors fell under science. She doesn't know there's another school I want to attend. She doesn't know that today, only hours ago, I applied to Juilliard.

Davi stayed on the phone the whole time, supporting me until the moment I hit the Submit button.

Now we wait. Anxiously.

"Hey," Esosa says. She struts into my room and props a hand on her hip. "Guess who I am."

She's wearing a strapless pink gown with matching elbow-length gloves. She runs a finger along her faux diamond necklace and winks. "Figured it out yet?"

Her platinum blond wig really brings the look together and gives me a clear answer. "Marilyn Monroe."

"Correct!" She claps. "Do you like it?"

"I love it."

"Thank God." She exhales. "Because it was very last minute. Halloween night, and there was basically nothing left at the custom shop. But Zane helped me put this together—a pink dress there, a blond wig here, some jewelry, and we have Ms. Monroe."

At the mention of Zane's name, I squint and study Esosa's face for any signs of the crush Bethany mentioned weeks ago. Unfortunately, her face gives nothing away.

"What exactly are you supposed to be?" she asks.

I spin around, and my blue dress flares around my knees. "Isn't it obvious?" I touch the blue bow on my hair. "I'm Wendy. From *Peter Pan*."

Esosa's face is blank. She isn't impressed. Neither were Tolu, Abby, and Osas when I showed them my costume over video call minutes ago.

"I am painfully underwhelmed," Tolu said. "At this point, you should just stay in your house and play ludo."

Abby and Osas voiced their agreement, which motivated me to

cut the call short. For some reason, I thought Esosa would understand why I had to wear such a boring costume. I was wrong.

"Seriously?" she says, annoyed. "Are you joking right now? Our
first Halloween ever, and you couldn't choose a better costume?
Wendy? From *Peter Pan*? Couldn't you at least find a sexy Tinker
Bell costume? Gosh! Have those movies you've been watching
taught you nothing?"

*Actually, while watching Mean Girls, I learned Halloween is the
one night a year when a girl can dress like a total slut, and no other girls
can say anything about it. The hardcore girls just wear lingerie and some
form of animal ears.*

As it stands, I can't leave my house wearing lingerie and bunny
ears. I can't even leave dressed like a witch or any other demonic
entity. God knows it took a miracle and a lot of convincing from
Auntie Sara before Mom let us attend Blake's Halloween party.

Halloween is a western tradition, one most Nigerians consider
demonic. There's no Halloween in Nigeria, not when many of
the people there are already highly superstitious, and as a result,
extremely religious and rigorous with their prayer regimen.

"So you want to dress like a witch just for fun and celebrate a holiday that's dedicated to witchcraft, *shebi*?" Mom said while watching
me and Esosa with a mixture of confusion and annoyance. "Dressing like a witch is now considered fun for you both, *abi*?"

"Well, they don't have to dress like witches," Auntie Sara, our
advocate, interjected gently. "They could dress up as anything they
like. Even a doctor." That, I had to admit, was a good touch. "Besides,
it's not like they'll be sitting around a fire, chanting and calling on

spirits and all that stuff." She laughed, but Mom's face remained straight. "Adrian will be going too. He'll drive them to the party and bring them home. It'll be fun."

"I still don't understand why fun is such an essential part of a child's development in this country. They have no responsibilities. The one thing they are required to do is go to school and get good marks. So why the constant need for respite? You are acting as if they labor at a farm from dawn to dusk. Ah-ah."

"Well, the kids do work hard at school to get good grades. And you know what they say, all work and no play . . ." It was a basic point, but I sensed it was Auntie Sara's last attempt.

"Okay." My mom spat out the word. "As long as Adrian is there, they can go."

Because our mom's permission was subject to change, I knew we couldn't make the wrong costume choice. We couldn't dress like a witch, a zombie, a vampire, or a sexy bunny. With this in mind, I gave myself two costume options—Wendy or a hot dog. With Davi deciding to dress like Peter Pan, the choice was simple.

"So let me understand," I say to Esosa. "You want me to dress up like a sexy Tinker Bell, while you look like an elegant beauty-pageant contestant? Do you want Mommy to say I can't go to the party?"

"Look, all I'm saying is that you could have put a little more effort and creativity into your costume."

"This costume is a necessary precaution."

"More like unnecessary caution," she mutters.

"Whatever." I roll my eyes and walk through my bedroom door. "Let's just go."

"Hey," Esosa whispers as she shuffles behind me. "From this angle, your ass looks really good."

I pause and turn to look at her. "Really?"

She shoots two thumbs up. "Really."

Well, at least there's that.

Chapter Thirty-Two

THE HOUSE PARTY. IS A TEEN MOVIE EVEN A TEEN movie without a house party?

I would like to argue it hardly is.

Time and time again, I've seen the same scene—a house cramped with unchaperoned teenagers who are ready to let loose. They consume alcohol. Sometimes even drugs. Friendships end and friendships begin. There are hookups and breakups. And usually, the cops show up.

Each scene I've watched has been cautionary and aspirational. Of course, I don't want to be the drunk girl who pukes on her crush right after she kisses him. But I wouldn't mind being the girl killing every game of beer pong and dancing on the kitchen counter while everyone cheers her on.

Yes, it's a known fact that shit always goes down at house parties. It's typically a pivotal point in the movie—the high before the dreaded low. In the movie *Booksmart*, Molly—an uptight bookworm—lets loose for one night before graduation. She goes to a party at her crush's house. She plays beer pong with him; they connect over Harry Potter, and she's positive they're going to hook up. But minutes later, she finds him kissing someone else. She's heartbroken. But it doesn't end there. She also has a huge falling-out with her best friend.

As I walk into Blake's large contemporary-style house, the only one of its kind I've seen in Bellwood, I try not to think of the low point that typically occurs at house parties. I'm too excited to be paranoid or overly cautious. Like everyone who comes to a party, I just want to have fun.

At past eight, the house is already crowded. Because of the occasion, it's difficult to recognize people. Masks and face paint do a good job of disguising identities. Though I suspect a girl in a skintight Catwoman suit and a BeDazzled black mask is Tamara. Her signature Afro is the only evidence I need.

"All right!" Esosa claps. "Let's get this party started!" Because of her formal attire, she looks out of place, like she should be sipping champagne at an elegant black-tie event.

"Okay. I'm gonna go find Katie," Adrian says. "Apparently she's dressed like 'Oops! . . . I Did It Again' Britney. The queen of pop and the king of pop. A match made in heaven." He runs a hand over his slicked hair. Three loose curls remain where he strategically placed them earlier—right in front of his forehead, the perfect touch to his Michael Jackson costume. He spins around, releases a high-pitched "he-he," and moonwalks away from me and Esosa.

"Isn't the queen of pop Madonna?" I ask.

"Yeah. But let him have it," Esosa says. "He's had a crush on Katie for what seems like forever. If he thinks he has even a little chance with her, let him have it."

I snort under my breath, then yelp when arms abruptly come around my waist.

"Hello, Wendy."

I release a deep sigh and relax against Davi's chest. "Hello, Peter Pan."

He trails kisses along my neck, and warmth creeps up my spine.

"Okay. We're in public." Esosa scrunches her nose. "Respect yourselves."

"How about you respect yourself by giving us some space?" I wave my hand at her, shooing her off.

"Whatever." She scans the room and smirks. "Actually, there's somewhere else I'd rather be, anyway." After pulling her gloves up and pursing her glossed lips, she struts toward Zane.

I guess her crush is still intact.

"Hey." Davi kisses my cheek and draws my attention from Esosa. "You okay?"

"Um . . . yeah." Seeing my little sister in flirtation/seduction mode is uncomfortable, to say the least.

"Do you want to get a drink?"

"Okay." Maybe that will help shake my discomfort.

We shuffle past the crowd in the hallway and make it to the kitchen. Blake is behind the counter acting as the bartender.

"Wendy! Peter!" he shouts when he sees me and Davi. "A cheesy couples' costume. Now, if that isn't a sign of true love, what the hell is?"

"It's adorable," Sybil says, smiling. She's wearing a long blond wig and a pink mini dress that's skintight. Her over-the-top makeup exaggerates her lips and heightens her cheekbones, making them look razor sharp. Black lines cover most of her body—her arms, chest, and neck—as if a surgeon marked down the parts of her body going under the knife.

I squint, trying to figure out her costume.

"Botched Barbie," she says. "I'm a botched Barbie."

I'm caught between laughing and marveling at her pure genius. "Wow."

"Creative, right?" Bethany says. "Ara and I couldn't be bothered." She sips from a plastic cup and shrugs.

They're both wearing the Bellwood cheer uniform. The only sign they're dressed for Halloween is their makeup—the dark circles around their eyes, the trail of blood painted at the corners of their lips, and the very realistic gunshot wound in the middle of their foreheads. This is the kind of costume that would have kept me and Esosa at home, where our mother would have carried out an extensive lecture followed by an avid prayer session for the salvation of our souls.

"I'd like to add that this is their second year going as murdered cheerleaders." Blake shakes his head, unimpressed by their effort.

"And you're a cowboy," Ara says. "I'm pretty sure you went as a cowboy for Halloween every year in middle school."

"What? I love cowboys. You, on the other hand, are just lazy. Big difference." He laughs as Ara rolls her eyes. "Anyway . . . let's get wasted." After aggressively shaking a stainless steel cocktail shaker, he fills six shot glasses with green liquid. "Here you go," he says, extending glasses to me and Davi.

"Um . . . is there alcohol in it?" It's a stupid question. I saw him pour vodka into the shaker. But I'm honestly hoping it was somehow Sprite.

"Yeah. There's vodka in it. And a few other ingredients." He winks. "It's my specialty drink."

So no, not Sprite.

"I've never had alcohol before," I admit, without considering how childish I might sound.

"You don't have to," Davi says. "I could get you a Coke. We could have that instead."

There's no trace of judgment on his face or on anyone else's. Well, except for Ara's. I swear judgment and disdain are imprinted on her face.

"Yeah. I could get you a Coke if you want," Blake adds.

"Um . . . no. Don't worry about it." I take the glass in his hand.

"Are you sure? I could make you something else—a mocktail."

I consider his offer and remind myself that tonight, I want to have fun.

"It's fine," I say. "I'll have this."

We all lift our shot glasses and, at Blake's command, down our drinks. I close my eyes and wince as the sweet and sour liquid fills my mouth. The burn of alcohol turns warm as it goes down my throat. When I open my eyes, everyone is watching me, likely waiting to see if I'll double over and throw up. To their surprise, I extend my empty glass to Blake and say, "Fill it up."

"All right!" Blake claps and mixes another drink.

"Here." Davi opens the box of pizza on the counter. "Eat while you drink, so you don't get light-headed or anything."

"Thanks." I grab a slice and have a few bites before taking one last shot.

I'm definitely not drunk. Well, I don't think I am. But my limbs feel loose, and my head feels a little empty. The loud music pulsates in a way it didn't when I initially walked in. I wrap my arms around

Davi and sway along with the other people in the crowded corridor. I'm completely caught up in him until someone mentions my name. Davi stops dancing, and his stare shifts above my head.

"Hey." He places his hands on my hips and stops me from swaying. "I think that's your mom. Well, from the family pictures you've showed me, I'm guessing it's her."

"What?" I laugh, confused.

"Your mom," he persists. "She's here. Behind you."

Still laughing, because I'm convinced Davi is making no sense, I turn around. The instant I come face-to-face with my mother, a chuckle gets caught in my throat like something I can neither swallow or cough up. I gawk at her, speechless.

What is she doing here—at Blake's party? Her eyebrows are furrowed as she looks from me to Davi. She's furious.

"Um . . . Ms. Adesuwa." Davi's voice shakes as he addresses my mom and attempts to hold her downright intimidating stare. "It's nice to . . . um . . . meet you. I'm Davi."

Although I've met Davi's dad, I was positive Davi would never meet my mom. At least not anytime soon. But for some reason, my mom is at this party, looking at Davi.

"Where are your sister and your cousin?" she asks without saying a word to Davi. Her voice is low and steely, rather than the alternative—loud and terrifying. Regardless, the people in proximity look at her questioningly.

"Um . . ." I glance around. "I don't know. They're somewhere here." I only pray Esosa is not in a corner kissing Zane. This is not the time to explore her crush.

"Find them," my mom says. "And meet me in the car. Now." She glares at Davi; her eyes shift from his head to his toe, then she turns around and walks toward the front door.

My heart beats erratically. Sweat covers my forehead. I can't believe this is happening. I look away from everyone who's staring at me. I have to find Esosa and Adrian before she comes back and really makes a scene.

"Esosa," I call out as I rush toward the kitchen.

"Hey," Davi says, following. "What was that about?"

I don't answer him because I don't know myself. But truthfully, my priority at the moment isn't my curiosity. It's finding Esosa.

"Have you seen my sister?" I ask Bethany.

"Yeah. Outside. By the pool."

"Thanks." I march through the sliding glass door, and of course, Esosa is sitting at the edge of the pool with Zane. The enormous pink bow on the back of her dress is the first thing I see, and then Zane's arm around her shoulder. "Sosa." I'm panting when I reach her.

"Hey." Her expansive smile drops the moment she notices the look on my face. "What is it?"

"Mom. She's here."

"What do you mean, she's here?"

"As in she's outside, waiting to take us home. We have to find Adrian and go."

"But I don't understand. What is she even doing here?"

I sigh, annoyed. "I don't know. But it doesn't matter right now. We have to go."

Thankfully, she asks no more questions. With Zane's help, she stands, then rolls down her dress; it goes from a mini dress on her thighs to its original length at her feet.

"Okay. Let's find Adrian." She takes a step forward with me, then stops abruptly and turns to Zane. Even with the chaos of the situation, her lips stretch into the sweetest smile. "This was fun."

"Yeah," Zane agrees, grinning. "It was. See you around?"

"Yeah. Absolutely."

"Oh, come on." I grab my sister's hand and pull her along. "We have to look for Adrian."

It doesn't take much to find my cousin. He's sitting on the stairs, his head between his legs.

"What's wrong with you?" Esosa asks him.

"Don't feel so good. My stomach." He groans. "Is my mom here? I called. Told her to come get me?"

Esosa and I look at each other and sigh. I guess that explains the current situation.

"Come on. Let's go." Esosa hunches down, places an arm around him, and helps him to stand.

"I've got it," Davi says. He takes Esosa's place, allowing Adrian to rest his weight on him.

We all walk through the door and then outside. I see my mom at the curb, inside Uncle Davis's Mercedes. Esosa opens the backseat door, and Adrian enters the car slowly. When the door shuts with my sister and cousin inside, Davi turns to me.

"Are you going to be okay?" His concerned eyes search mine.

"I have to go." I can't possibly stand on the curb of this street and have a conversation with him while my livid mother waits inside the car. That won't make any of this better. "I'll see you on Monday."

I open the passenger door and enter the car. The silence that greets me once I shut the door is daunting. My mother doesn't look at me. She doesn't say a word. Neither does Esosa. It seems like even Adrian has the good sense to hold off on groaning until he's escaped the tension in the car.

I guess this is it, then, the dreaded low that comes after the high of a house party.

Chapter Thirty-Three

AS I WALK INTO THE HOUSE, I REMIND MYSELF MOM didn't see me kiss Davi. That has to count for something. But seriously, who am I fooling? She saw me holding him, probably staring into his eyes like a lovesick puppy. Kiss or no kiss, I'm in trouble.

She stands in the middle of the living room and stares at the floor. Esosa and I glance at each other, communicating our shared panic. Silence stretches, and the tension in the room increases. After a long while, what seems like an eternity, Mom clears her throat and lifts her head.

"Who was that boy you were with?"

My teeth dig into my lip. "Um . . . he was a . . . a . . . friend."

"A friend?" She squints and watches me closely. "Come *o*, Enore. Do you take me for a fool? Eh?"

The answer is no, but I'm not supposed to answer that. I'm only supposed to answer one question.

"Who was that boy you were with?"

I can't lie, not when she's looking at me like she already knows the truth.

I sigh and whisper, "My boyfriend."

"Your what? What did you just say?"

I'm positive she heard me, but she's making me repeat myself. So I do. And her features harden.

"Esosa," she says.

My sister flinches at the mention of her name.

"Go to your room."

"What? Why?"

"Now! I don't want to say it again."

"Okay." Esosa looks at me apologetically, then rushes down the hallway and closes her bedroom door.

I wonder if Esosa's dismissal was necessary. Maybe Mom thought it was. Maybe she's trying to protect her from the bad example I've become. That's probably what she sees as she looks at me—a bad example, her upstanding, play-by-the-rules daughter who has gone rogue.

"Since when?" she asks. "When did you start all this boyfriend nonsense, eh?"

"A few weeks ago."

She closes her eyes and presses a finger to her temple while breathing deeply and slowly. "All those times you told me you were studying at your friend's house, what were you really doing?" Her eyes flash open. She waits for the answer but already knows it. "You were with him, weren't you?" At my silence, a.k.a. my admission, she shakes her head. She's disappointed, but after a closer look, it's clear she's confused.

Maybe she expected this from Esosa, the daughter with an uninhibited passion she's been trying to stifle for years. But she never expected this from me. All my life, no character trait signaled I would be the defiant child.

"Why, Enore?"

I huff and say the only thing that comes to my mind, regardless of how stupid it may sound. "I like him."

Juvenile, I know. But what else am I supposed to say? For the first time in weeks, I can't lie to divert my mom from the truth. Without my sister and friends to be accomplices or Auntie Sara to be an advocate for teenage fun and freedom, the only thing I can do is tell the truth.

"He's nice," I add.

"You like him. He's nice." She chuckles slowly, and the sound is taunting. "Enore, are you mad? Have you lost your mind? Against my wishes, you have a boyfriend, and your stupid defense is that you like him. He's nice. Frankly, I don't care if he is Christ reincarnated. You cannot date—no boyfriends. You are a child, for God's sake."

"I am almost eighteen." It's a bold statement, one that could escalate things between me and my mom. I immediately regret saying it.

The concept of adulthood being marked by eighteen candles is very American, and somehow that concept has unconsciously infiltrated my mind. I blame it on the teen movies; they made me believe the milestone birthday equates freedom, freedom to make my own choices as an adult. Unfortunately, that isn't my reality.

"You're almost eighteen. And so what?" Mom says. "You think you are now an adult, right?" Her lips fold into a tight grimace. "So, these are the things you are learning from your useless friends? This is the nonsense they have pumped into your head—'in America, once we are eighteen, we are adults and can do whatever we want.' They have taught you the American way, right? *Sisi Americanah*. That's who you are now, *abi*? That's why you have the audacity, the effrontery, to disobey me. To lie to me. To stand in front of me and start spilling this rubbish from your mouth. Isn't it?"

"Mom, I—"

241

She lifts her hand, silencing me. "I don't recognize you. I am standing here, looking at you, and still I do not recognize you." Gradually, the hand drops. "You leave school without my permission—disappear for hours. You lie repeatedly to me. You date a boy against my wishes. You drink."

My eyes widen with shock.

"You think I did not smell it—the alcohol on your breath? This is the example you're now setting for your younger sister."

Ashamed, I let my eyes fall. I can't look at her, not when she's calling me out on everything I've done wrong in the past few weeks. And those are only the things she knows of.

Did I go too far? It all started with the musical, and then things spiraled. The first lie was the hardest. And then it became easier. The more freedom I got, the more experiences I had, the more lies I got away with, the more daring I became. I got carried away, determined to satisfy the part of me that had been repressed for so long.

"Enore, whatever you have going on with that boy ends tonight."

It's not like I didn't see this coming. It's the only way this night can end, with me being forced to cut ties with Davi.

"From now on, it is school, home, and choir practice once a week. That's it."

Before Davi, that schedule would have suited me fine. But it doesn't anymore. She doesn't understand the impact he's had on me—how until him, my father's death was like a thorn in my chest, constantly prodding at me. Being with Davi eases that pain. Being with him makes me happy, really happy—not the mask I wear to relieve my family's worries and convince the world I'm okay. Being with Davi allowed me to discover a part of myself I never even knew existed. From my mother's perspective, his influence is probably all negative. But I need her to see otherwise. I need to change her mind somehow.

"Mommy, please." My voice shakes as I hold back a cry. "I know I've lied and done some things, and I . . . I'm sorry. Really. But Davi is . . . he's on the football team and the debate team. He's smart and funny and so kind, and he makes me feel . . ." I search for the right word.

If I can just find it and express to her what he means to me, maybe she'll change her mind. Then I'll tell her everything—no more lies. I'll come clean about the musical. About Broadway. About Juilliard. We'll sit down and talk. I'll make her understand I can't imagine doing anything but musical theater for the rest of my life. And we'll take it from there.

"He inspires me," I finally say. That perfectly sums it up.

"Inspires you to what?" my mother asks through clenched teeth. "To lie to me? To drink?"

"What? No. He's not like—"

"I don't want to hear a word from you, Enore. Not another word!"

Just like that, the conversation is over.

There is no room for understanding, compromise, or reconciliation. There's no room for the truth. It was stupid to think otherwise, because no matter how well I lay down my case, a school musical and Juilliard and a boy I care for deeply will always translate to absurdity to my mother.

Chapter Thirty-Four

SCHOOL, HOME, AND CHURCH. FOR THE PAST TWO weeks, that has been my schedule. The only reason I still go to rehearsals is because it's under the guise of math club. It's the one thing that's still intact, the one thing keeping me grounded—steady. And every day, I'm terrified Mom will find out about it and I'll lose it too. I've already lost Davi. Our relationship is basically over. I haven't broken up with him officially. It's a difficult thing to do. Davi has been nothing but kind to me. I can't imagine hurting him. But even without the official statement, the confirmation, it's obvious our relationship is not what it used to be.

On Sunday, the day after the Halloween party, things were noticeably tense between us. I replied to his text messages with one-word answers.

DAVI: Hey. Are you okay?
ME: Yeah.
DAVI: You sure?
ME: Yeah.
DAVI: Okay. How are things with your mom?
ME: Fine.
DAVI: Did she find out about us? Dating?
ME: Yeah.
DAVI: Oh.

He didn't ask what this meant for our relationship. I think he was scared of the answer. And frankly, I was scared of delivering the answer and officially ending things. So, we said nothing else. On Monday, however, I could hardly keep eye contact with him. Whenever he held my hand, I pulled away after a few seconds. The image of my furious, disapproving mother made it impossible to enjoy moments with him.

Before my mom, being in a relationship with Davi felt like living in a cocoon. We were shut out from the world. Well, at least my world, which is where the true threat existed. But now, with my mom knowing about him and disapproving, the cocoon is gone. We're exposed to our biggest threat.

We still eat lunch together. We walk the halls together. But nothing is the same. Our kisses are brief, forced, and uncomfortable. In the moments when I hold his gaze, I see uncertainty in his eyes— questions he wants to ask but is too afraid to. He doesn't ask, so I don't answer. And there are no official words, no confirmation our relationship is over.

Today, rehearsal runs twenty minutes longer than usual. After Mr. Roland dismisses everyone, I climb down from the stage and walk to a seat in the first row, where I tossed my bag earlier. As I fling the strap over my shoulder, Ara appears in front of me, wearing her signature expression.

"Um . . . yes?" I say, confused and frankly low on patience. I just need to get home and start my English essay.

"What the hell is wrong with you?" she asks.

"Excuse me?" Maybe I misheard her because even that's too much for Ara. "What did you just say?"

She repeats her question, enunciates each word.

Okay. I guess I heard her right the first time.

"I've been watching you during rehearsals," she continues.

"All right." I'm not sure what to say to that.

"In the past couple of days, your performance has had a steady and tragic decline. Like, it's hard to watch."

"Okay. Then how about you don't watch. I'm sure you have better things to do," I hiss, then walk away.

I was wrong before. I'm not low on patience. I just don't have any at all. Ara is the last person who should rate my performance. I already know I haven't been giving my best lately. Since the argument with my mom, it's been difficult to devote my full focus to singing on key, dancing on beat, or acting convincingly. The musical is the one thing I still have for myself, but I'm ruining it.

"Hey." Ara appears in front of me again, stopping me in my tracks.

Frustrated, I grunt. "What do you want?"

"Look. I didn't mean to be harsh or anything, but . . ."

Her features soften in a way I've never seen before. Honestly, it's like seeing a magician who's known for one trick, do something else. I'm sure there's an audience who would appreciate the new way Ara's face transforms, but I just want to go home and lock myself in my room.

"Listen," I sigh. "I don't have the time or energy for whatever this is." I take a step forward, and she moves in front of me again.

"Why are you making this so difficult?" She grunts like she has a right to be frustrated. "I'm trying to help you."

I'm not even in the mood for laughing, but I laugh regardless, because Ara has just said the funniest thing I've heard in a long time. "You. Want to help me."

"You're talented, Enore."

Slowly, my chuckles stop. I don't know what to do with that compliment. If I could, I would hold a microscope over it and conduct an examination to make sure it's a compliment and not an ulterior motive coated in a lie.

"I'm being honest."

I scoff. "Sure you are."

"You don't believe me?"

"Have you given me a reason to? You've been nothing but rude since the moment we met, and now you're throwing a random compliment at me and you want me to believe you?"

As if I knew this would happen, I'm prepared.

Rule #8: If a mean girl is suddenly nice to you, be suspicious. Be very suspicious.

"Look, Enore. I know you don't have a lot of reason to believe I have the best intentions, but I do."

"Right. And if Mindy and Jodi hadn't fallen for Whitney's fake kindness and accepted her invitation to a party, they wouldn't have been humiliated in front of their senior class."

"Um . . ." Ara frowns. "What?"

I realize she might not understand my reference to the movie *The Outcasts*. Well, unless she's seen it. But with the look of confusion on her face, she likely hasn't.

"Never mind," I tell her. "Just forget it. I have to go. And it would be great if you stopped jumping in front of me."

"Fine." She throws her hands up in surrender, steps aside, and I walk away with no inference.

Rule #8: If a mean girl is suddenly nice to you, be suspicious. Be very suspicious. ✓

It's late—almost six—and the school is more active than it should be. Students and teachers walk the halls. In the distance, I see Sybil's parents enter the gymnasium. What's going on? As I'm about to stop Felicia from English lit and ask, a hand falls on my shoulder. Reflexively, I flinch before turning around and facing Mr. Roland.

"Enore, you're just in time," he says, smiling.

"Just in time for what?"

With wide eyes, he looks above my head. "That?"

I turn around to see what he's staring at, and again, I flinch. "What in the world is that?" I'm shaking and sweating while looking at the enormous poster on the wall, the poster with my face on it and the words *Cinders and Embers Starring Enore Enchanted*.

"A poster for the musical, obviously."

"Yes. But why is my face on it?"

"Well, you are the star of the musical. And a bonus is your status as an internet star."

"I'm not an internet star."

"Of course you are. With that viral video of yours."

Tension builds in my head, and I shut my eyes and rub my temple.

"I thought tonight was the perfect time to hang it up—right before the parents arrive."

My eyes fly open, then shift to the gymnasium doors. "Parents? What are you talking about?"

"Well, it's parent-teacher night. And I'm looking forward to meeting your mom. I'm sure she'll lose it when she sees your face on this stunning poster."

That much is guaranteed.

My heart pounds. This is bad. But maybe there's nothing to worry about. With all the studying she's been doing lately, my mom likely won't come. Unless Auntie Sara prompts her to. And something tells me she will.

"You have to take that down."

"Take it down?" Mr. Roland steps back and looks at the poster. "Why? Doesn't it look good here? Do you think it would look better somewhere else?"

"Um . . . yeah." I glance around, then point at the stairway at the far end of the hall. It's the perfect secluded corner. "How about there?"

"What? The stairway?" He laughs. "You're funny. No. It's perfect right here. All the parents can see it when they walk in. They won't miss it."

That's exactly what I'm scared of. Sweat covers my forehead as I breathe deeply.

"My goodness." Mr. Roland leans into my face and studies me. "You don't look so good."

I wipe my head with the back of my hand. "I'm fine."

"I beg to differ. Come along." He takes my arm and leads me down the hallway.

"Where are we going?"

"To the gym to get you a cold beverage. Looks like you need one."

"What? No," I say, dragging my feet. "I'm fine."

It's bad enough my mom will see the poster when she walks into school, but I can't be in the gym when she arrives or I'll risk being publicly scolded. And the embarrassment alone could be detrimental to my mental health.

"We like to make parent-teacher night a bit special, especially the first one of the year," Mr. Roland explains when we enter the gym. "That way, it's more of an attraction for the parents."

With soft lighting and classical music in the background, the gym looks a lot like a cool lounge space. Unlike the homecoming dance, the ambiance is calm and elegant for the mature crowd.

Mr. Roland brings me to the refreshment table and hands me a chilled water bottle.

"Thanks." As I take a sip, I hear my name and turn around. "Mrs. Hathaway," I say to Sybil's mom. "Hi. How are you?"

"Wonderful, dear," she replies. "Is that you up on that poster?"

"Um . . . yeah."

"Stunning, dear. Absolutely stunning. Can't wait to see you on that stage."

The halfhearted smile I hold in place during the exchange falls when she turns away. I need to get out of here, preferably before my mom arrives.

"Thanks for the water, Mr. Roland. But I should go now."

"Nonsense. You should stay—mingle with parents, tell them about the musical, and get them to invite their friends."

"Isn't that something you should do?"

"Yes, but I think it would hit better if it came from you—the star."

I really wish he would stop calling me that.

"Come on." He hooks his arm into mine and leads me across the room and toward a group of people.

I spend the next twenty minutes forcing a smile, talking to parents about the musical, watching the door for my mother, and plotting my escape. Unfortunately for me, Mr. Roland, as if sensing my desire to run, hasn't unhooked his arm from mine. Gosh, what kind of *wahala* is this?

The gym fills up more, and while glancing at the door for what seems like the hundredth time, I see Auntie Sara, Uncle Davis, and my mom walk through. I gasp and alarm Mr. Roland and the couple we're speaking to.

"Um . . ." I clear my throat. "Sorry. Excuse me, but I have to go . . . um . . . to the restroom."

"Can't it wait? We're telling Mr. and Mrs. Benson about the fabulous musical."

"Unfortunately, no." I force my arm from Mr. Roland's tight grip and rush away.

The crowd of parents and teachers helps me stay hidden. If I'm slick enough, I can make it out of here without running into my family. All I have to do is keep my eyes on them while moving. It's likely they've already seen the poster. If my mom's wrath is going to come down on me, it won't be here. It's the perfect setting for another public humiliation, and I'm not having it.

"Hey, where do you think you're going?" Mr. Roland's voice makes me freeze. His hand on my shoulder prevents me from running through the doors, which are only a few feet away.

"Um . . . I have homework to do." I turn to him and manage an innocent smile. "At home. So I should go."

"Okay. I get it." He rolls his eyes. "You don't want to hang out with a bunch of parents and teachers all night. Noted. But can we just do another five minutes of publicity? Trust me, you've been doing well so far."

"I'm sorry, but I—"

"Enore? What are you doing here?"

I know that voice. It's my mom's. So much for a slick escape.

After expelling a deep breath, I turn around. Uncle Davis and Auntie Sara stand with her, their little entourage of three that should be four.

Before I can speak, Mr. Roland, the person who made this disaster possible, steps forward. "You must be Enore's mother." He gasps in a melodramatic way that warrants an eye roll. "The resemblance is striking." With a wide smile, he looks between me and my mom, then extends his hand. "I'm Mr. Roland. The theater director at Bellwood High."

"Oh. Nice to meet you." She shakes his hand with a polite but fake smile. Knowing my mom, she's probably wondering why she's meeting the school's theater director rather than a math or science teacher.

"I must tell you," Mr. Roland goes on, "your daughter is bringing something very special to our musical this year. Not only does she sing like an angel, but her acting isn't so bad either." He laughs, but the joke, if it is one, doesn't land.

Uncle Davis, Auntie Sara, and my mom look at each other for clarification. They missed it. Somehow, they missed the poster. But now, because Mr. Roland is feeling very chatty and overly friendly, they're going to find out the truth. My head is suddenly weightless and fuzzy. I'm going to faint—right here, on the gym floor where the sweat of countless teenagers has landed.

"Enore, honey." Auntie Sara's smooth voice breaks through the fuzziness in my head. Her grip on my arm is tender. "Are you okay? You look a little out of it. Maybe you need to sit down."

"Home," I manage to say. If I can cut this conversation short, I can spin a good cover story to explain away what they've just heard.

"Okay, dear. Let's get you home." She puts an arm around my shoulders and steers me from Mr. Roland, and I think I've succeeded in getting my family away from the chatterbox until my mom shakes her head.

"I'm sorry. I don't quite understand. What is this about a musical?"

"Yes, *Cinders and Embers*, our modern spin on the Cinderella story. Enore is the star, but she must have told you so much about it already."

Slowly, my mother arches an eyebrow and turns to me. My teeth dig into my lip, and even when I taste blood, I don't let go.

"We just put the poster up today, and it's stunning. I'm sure you saw it in the hallway on your way in."

Instantly, my mom spins around and marches toward the doors. Uncle Davis paces behind her, and after letting me go and ensuring I'm steady, Auntie Sara does the same. All three of them stand in the center of the hallway, facing the poster.

I look at Mr. Roland, who believes he's been a good informant. "You should look for another lead."

His smile drops quickly, but I walk away before he can say a word.

In the hallway, I hold my breath while approaching my mom. I'm certain I'm about to receive the public humiliation I hoped to avoid, but she turns to me with an impassive expression and says, "Let's go home."

Finally, after many failed attempts, I get to go home. But it definitely won't provide the escape I hoped for.

Chapter Thirty-Five

WHEN I CLOSE THE FRONT DOOR BEHIND ME, ESOSA steps out of her room.

"There you are," she sighs. "I've been—" She looks between me and Mom and frowns, likely sensing the tension. "Is everything okay?"

"Esosa, go to your room," Mom says.

"Okay, then. I guess not." She backs away while watching me. Her lips mouth, *Are you okay?*

I shake my head as she enters her room and shuts the door.

Silence extends for well over a minute. Mom paces around the living room with her head low, while I stand unmoving. Lately, we've had a lot of moments like this. I hate it.

"Math club." She stops walking and looks at me. "Was there ever a math club?"

Slowly, I shake my head.

"All that time, you were at rehearsals for this play?"

I nod.

Neither of us says a word as she paces around again. My nails dig into my palm. Maybe I should fill the uncomfortable silence with an explanation or maybe, before anything else, an apology.

"Mommy, I'm sorry. Sorry for lying." After a deep breath, I start with the explanation. "I auditioned for the musical and didn't expect to get the lead. But I did, and it was exciting. I wanted to tell you, but . . . well, I was scared you'd make me quit."

She stops moving. This could be a good sign, a sign she's listening and maybe even open to what I'm saying.

"I couldn't imagine quitting. Mommy, I love it. It's . . . it's not just about singing. It's acting and dancing and performing. And it's incredible." My voice swells as my enthusiasm comes through. "It's what I want to do with my life."

She frowns, but I muster the courage to say more, to tell her the whole truth. I'm terrified of her reaction but won't let fear stop me.

"Mom, there's a school. It's called Juilliard. It's for performing arts. I can learn everything there, everything I need. That's where I want to go. For university." My heart beats fast. "I . . . I sent in an application."

"You applied? For the school?"

"Yes," I whisper.

"Without telling me?"

I nod.

She releases a loud, rough breath and shakes her head. "I can't do this anymore. I just cannot. It's too much."

"Can't do what?"

She throws her arms up. "This. This country. Trying to build a life here. Taking care of you and Esosa alone. I cannot do it anymore." Her shoulders slump. "Your father should be here. He was better at all this than me. Better at interacting with your friends whenever they visited. Better at keeping the order. Better at parenting you and Esosa." She rubs her teary eyes. "He was my balance. I don't know how to stand steady without him. I am falling, failing without him here."

"What? Mommy, no. You aren't."

"Twice. I failed my USMLE Step 1 twice. Back home, I was a doctor for over ten years, respected in my field. But here, I can't even pass a common exam." Her lips roll into her mouth as if she's holding back a cry. "You do whatever you please as long as it makes you happy. You forget I came to this country too. That I lost your father too. That I am struggling and in pain and trying to keep this family together. That I feel alone. So, so alone." She hunches over, her hands braced on her hips as she pants.

I've never seen my mom like this. I wasn't even sure this version of her existed. When my father died, she cried and mourned, but her optimism made those moments brief. She helped me and Esosa through each day with her endless encouragement: *It's going to be okay. We're going to make it through this. America will be a new start. We'll be happy there.*

It's only now I recognize her optimism as false, a fragile strength she used to disguise her grief and fear. Why didn't I see it before? How could I have been so blind?

"And as if all this wasn't hard enough," she continues, "in the past few months, you've skipped school. Dated a boy behind my back. Lied to my face repeatedly about your involvement in a useless play. And now you're talking all this nonsense about going to a performing arts school." She lifts her head and watches me sternly.

Guilty of everything she's mentioned, I can't open my mouth to say a word. What's there to say, anyway? Sorry for being an additional source of stress in your life? Sorry for prioritizing my grief and struggle and failing to see yours? Sorry for being the daughter you no longer trust?

I could apologize for all these things, but I sense we've come to a point where an apology no longer matters.

"Since we came to this country, you've become someone different," she says to me. "I hardly recognize you. This girl, the one standing in front of me, isn't the girl your father and I raised. You are not the person your father knew." She shakes her head. "If he was here right now, he would be more than just disappointed in you. He would be heartbroken by you."

Those words have the force of a punch, hitting me so hard, I stumble back. Tears well up in my eyes and blur my vision until everything in the room turns to smudges of colors.

He was only ever proud of me. I can't think of a time when he expressed disappointment in me. But now my mom paints the perfect scenario that would warrant his disappointment, and shame settles on me, a weight on my chest that makes my breaths short and quick. Tears soak my cheeks and keep falling.

"We're going back to Nigeria," my mom says.

"We're what?" Esosa shouts.

My sister's loud voice and the unexpected announcement make me blink hard. My blurry vision clears. The room comes into focus again. My sister is standing at her open bedroom door, her eyes wide with shock.

"What do you mean, we're going back to Nigeria?" she asks.

"You both will finish the semester here, then we will leave for Nigeria during the Christmas holiday."

"No. No. No. No," Esosa protests.

"I can still get my job back there. We have family there—my sister and brother. They can help me with the two of you."

"We have family here. Uncle Davis. Auntie Sara."

"Well, I'm not in total support of their style of parenting—the way they let you children run around and do as you please. There'll be none of that once we get home."

"Home?" Esosa shouts, her voice shaking. "This is home. It's been our home for months. We go to school here. We have friends here. We have lives here. We can't just leave, right, Enore?" She looks at me for support but doesn't find it.

Mom is right. We have to go back. Things were easier there. I knew the role I was meant to play and never deviated from it, never felt the need to be anything other than what was expected of me. The temptation for something more started here. I realized my passion here. I found the resources to nurture it here. I became a liar here. I disappointed my parents here.

Determined to make her case, even with no support, Esosa continues to protest. "I love my country and all that, but people are literally trying to leave Nigeria, and we want to go back? What? You have to be joking."

"That's enough," Mom says, holding her hand up. "Enough. I've been thinking about this for a long time, and I've made my final decision. We're going back to Nigeria in a few weeks. Start packing and say your goodbyes." With that, she marches to her room and shuts the door.

"Seriously," Esosa says to me. "You just stood there? You couldn't say anything?" She walks to me and shoves my shoulder. "Not even a word? Do you realize what's going to happen? She isn't bluffing."

"I know she isn't."

"Then why didn't you say anything?" She wipes her wet eyes. "Huh? Why didn't you?"

I shrug and walk away, quiet as I enter my room and close the door.

Chapter Thirty-Six

I COULDN'T IMAGINE BREAKING UP WITH DAVI, AND now I'll have to say goodbye to him for good.

It's likely I'll never see him again. It's likely once I'm gone, he'll move on and forget about the weeks we dated. I won't forget, though. I think I'll carry him with me forever, tucked away somewhere deep in my mind, behind a door I'll forever be afraid to open because of all the things that might fall out, things I can never have—Juilliard, Broadway. It's likely the what-ifs of my life will haunt me forever, but I'll learn to live with them.

"Hey. Enore."

My head snaps up, away from the biology textbook I have opened on the library table. "Um . . ." I clear my throat after seeing Davi standing above me. "Hi."

"I've been looking for you. What are you doing here? It's lunch."

"Just catching up on some studying." I'm trying to convey some coolness, but my voice shakes.

He watches me without a word. I wonder if he notices my puffy eyes, the evidence I spent last night crying. After the conversation with my mom, it was all I could do. This morning, I held an ice pack over my eyes before leaving for school, but I doubt it made much of a difference.

After a long pause, Davi pulls out the chair beside me and sits. "What's going on with you? Huh?" he asks softly.

I look away from him. If I'm going to lie, my eyes can't give anything away. "I'm fine."

"Ara just told me you quit the musical. Why?"

"I didn't want to do it anymore. It was interfering with my schoolwork."

After another long pause, he shifts closer to me and holds my hand. "This has something to do with your mom, doesn't it? She found out about the musical and made you quit."

With the cautious look in his eyes and the slight tremor in his voice, I know he's calculating his words, careful not to mention what else my mother recently found out. He's still afraid of the answer—of what her knowing means for our relationship. And I'm still afraid of delivering the answer—of breaking his heart as well as mine.

"Enore." His voice is sweet, tender. "Did you tell her what the musical means to you?"

"It doesn't matter," I say. "The musical, Juilliard. It's not happening. It will never happen."

"But—"

"There are no buts." Only what-ifs. That's all there will ever be, the fantasy of what could have been. I grab my books and stand. Tears gather at the corners of my eyes. Before they fall, I need to excuse myself and rush into a bathroom stall. "Sorry. But I have to go."

"Wait." Davi stands quickly. "Juilliard. It's your dream. You can't just give it up. You have to talk to your mom. Make her understand. Make her see this is what you want."

"What I want doesn't matter, Davi. My family is . . . is . . . broken. What I want doesn't matter." It never should have.

And if I had stuck to my original plan, followed the rules, and stayed on that straight and narrow path, I wouldn't have discovered a passion I was once conveniently oblivious to. I wouldn't have self-ishly pursued it to the extent where I couldn't see my mother's pain and struggle. I wouldn't have disappointed her or my father.

"Enore, listen to me." The determined look in Davi's eyes is a sign he's about to give a pep talk I don't want to hear. "You have to stop hiding who you are from her."

"Hiding who I am? Really?" Those words feel so wrong coming from him, because he's preaching something he doesn't practice. "First of all, you don't know what it's like to be me. Our cultures and our upbringings are so different. So please save the speech where you tell me to defy my mom and do whatever I please. Because, for the last time, it doesn't work like that for me.

"And second, you're the one who's hiding—too afraid to tell Blake you'd rather join every academic club than play football. Too afraid to tell me the truth about your mom."

The librarian at the front desk presses a finger to her lips, but I ignore the gesture and the fact that I might be disturbing Cooper Clark, the only other student in the library.

"You've kept things from me," I tell Davi, my voice low and pained. "I've told you so much. About my dad. About moving here. Do you understand how hard that was for me—to trust you, to rely on you? And for months, you completely shut me out. You've ignored every question I've asked about her. I've been open and vulnerable with you, and you've been hiding who you are from me."

My chest is pounding. For a while, all I hear is my rapid breathing and the librarian's aggressive "shh." And then school bell chimes, indicating the end of the lunch period.

The hurt is clear in Davi's eyes as he watches me. Maybe I said too much, crossed a line. Maybe everything I said was necessary.

"We can't see each other anymore," I add. "We're done."

There it is. Finally. The breakup. Though not the goodbye. With the overwhelming ache that reverberates through me, I know I can only manage to do one today.

I clench my books against my chest and rush away from him.

Chapter Thirty-Seven

A FEW WEEKS AGO, WHEN I IMAGINED MY FIRST Thanksgiving in America, I didn't imagine my sister wouldn't be speaking to me. I didn't imagine Davi would no longer be my boyfriend or that things between me and my mom would be so tense, I could hardly look her in the eyes. I didn't imagine my first Thanksgiving in America would also be my last.

My entire family is around the table in the formal dining room. Today, the main house doesn't seem too big. That's because we're all together, including my cousin Naomi, who's home from college. Thanksgiving is her favorite holiday, and when she got home last night, she instantly went into preparation mode. That meant going over the extensive Thanksgiving menu, rearranging the fall-themed decorations her mom already put out and assigning me, Esosa, and Adrian to our specific Thanksgiving prep duties. The girl is not only meticulous, she's an impressive multitasker too. Today, she woke everyone at the crack of dawn, and between bossing us around and ensuring things stayed on schedule, she baked four pies—sweet potato, pecan, pumpkin, and apple. With her excitement, I didn't have the heart to tell her I don't like pie. When the time comes, I'll likely have to smile while forcing a piece down my throat. Until then, I'll enjoy the fried dumplings and herb stuffing I can't get enough of.

The impressive spread on the table is a combination of American,

Japanese, and Nigerian food. Briefly, I wonder what Davi's Thanksgiving table might look like. Then I push the thought away.

"Please pass the jollof," Adrian says with a big grin.

"I'm scared if I do, there'll be none left for the rest of us," Esosa says.

"Well, it's not like we're short on food, so come on. Hand it over."

After rolling her eyes, Esosa extends the dish of rice to him.

Dinner continues with the adults speaking among themselves and Naomi interjecting, assertively expressing the brilliance she's gained from three months in college. Esosa isn't talking to me and doesn't say much these days anyway, not even to Adrian. Her eyes shift between her plate and her phone, while Adrian's eyes shift around the table in search of what to eat next. The only reason he's not speaking is because his mouth is full to the brim.

When dinner is over, Naomi and I sprawl out on the couch in the living room and watch highlights of the Macy's Thanksgiving Day Parade. Esosa is upstairs in Adrian's room, while the adults are having tea in the den. I avoided eating my slice of pie by telling Naomi I was too full. But knowing my cousin, she'll likely hold me down and try to shove a piece into my mouth before the day ends.

"Hey." She turns to me, and I'm scared the time for pie has finally come. "I'm really sorry you're leaving," she says instead. She sits up and tousles her long, curly hair. "It's really messed up."

I try to hold a neutral expression like I do whenever someone brings up the topic. "My mom thinks it's for the best." It's the response I've learned to recite.

"Yeah, but it still sucks. With me being at college, we haven't really had much time together. But I at least thought we had all the time in the world. I thought maybe you could come down to Cambridge one weekend. To visit. None of my friends believe Enore Enchanted is my cousin." She rolls her eyes. "Oh, that reminds me." She pulls her phone out of her pocket and presses her face against mine. "Come on. Smile."

When she tickles me, I laugh for the first time in days. It's forced—prompted by Naomi's wriggling fingers rather than emotions—but it feels good regardless.

"Ahh. There you go." She takes a few selfies, then swipes through each. "This one's my favorite." She shows me a picture where we're both laughing with our mouths open. When she looks up, she watches me for a long while, then sighs. "I'm sorry you have to go. But we'll stay in touch, right? We'll talk, and I'll come visit. I promise."

I don't know my cousin very well. She visited Nigeria with her family once, years ago. And for the two weeks, we got along well. Then when my family and I moved to America, she had to go to college. She texted a few times while away, but our conversations were usually brief. All our lives, our interactions have been brief. Now I wonder if we'll ever get to build a relationship. I think if given the chance, an extensive period to know each other, we could be more than cousins. We already have one thing in common.

"I love your movies," I tell her.

"My movies?"

"Yeah. The collection of teen movies."

"Ahh." She smiles. "You found the box."

"Adrian gave it to me. They helped."

"Helped? With what?"

"High school."

She squints and nods slowly. "Yeah. I could see how. Would you like to take some with you when you . . . leave? Maybe some of your favorites?"

"No. That's okay. I won't need them there."

We go back to watching highlights from the parade. The Santa Claus float appears just as Uncle Davis enters the room. He clears his throat while standing over me and Naomi.

"Um . . . hey, guys." He glances at the television and then back at us. "Naomi, can I please have a moment with your cousin?"

Naomi looks between me and her father and then stands. "Sure. I'm due for another slice of pie, anyway."

When she leaves the room, Uncle Davis sits beside me. With his thumbs twiddling, he gives me sidelong glances while keeping his head straight, toward the TV. I've never seen my uncle so uncomfortable. Is he preparing to deliver bad news, trying to find the guts to say something difficult?

"Uncle? Is everything okay?"

He turns to me slowly and sighs. "Enore, I feel like I have failed you and Esosa."

"Huh? What are you talking about?"

After a long pause, he continues. "I never thought things would end up like this—with your mother deciding to return to Nigeria. To me, the decision is absurd. I've spoken to her extensively, tried to make her change her mind, but . . ." He runs his hand over his face and huffs. "She's set on leaving."

"That isn't your fault, Uncle. I'm the one who pushed her to that decision." Me and only me. "I lied to her—so many times."

"Enore, you did not always make the right decisions. But maybe you would have with some guidance from me. I should have been more present as you adjusted to everything, especially school."

"You have been present. You pick me up from choir practice. And on Sundays, we always go out for frozen yogurt."

"But I've been tiptoeing around you and Esosa, afraid to say the wrong things. You two have already been through so much. I just wanted to find ways to make you both happy."

"And you have."

"I should have done more, especially since I knew the real reason your father wanted you to come to America."

"The real reason?" I shuffle closer to my uncle. "What do you mean?"

"Do you know how long I begged your father to move to America? Years. He was always opposed to the idea. I think moving, especially at his age, frightened him. Your mother was a doctor at a top hospital, your father loved his job and had other thriving side businesses. He was comfortable in Nigeria and scared moving to another country would mean starting all over again. He wasn't ready for that."

"But then he agreed to move," I say.

"Yes, because of you."

"Me?"

My uncle nods. "He thought you had an exceptional talent. He thought America would provide the resources to nurture that talent and give you a broad range of career choices. That's why he wanted to come. For you."

I'm not sure how to process that information. My father was willing to give up everything, including his comfortable and stable life, for me. I'm shocked by his selflessness and even more shocked by how much he believed in me. I didn't truly understand the extent of it until now.

"Enore." Uncle Davis holds my hands. "I'm sorry I didn't do enough to fulfill his wishes. Maybe if I had been more involved, more present, you would have confided in me—told me about the musical and Juilliard. If I had known about everything, we would have navigated things together. I would have spoken to your mother and tried to help her understand your choices. Maybe things would be different right now."

Maybes aren't certainties. They're imaginary realities.

This is my first and last Thanksgiving in America. My mother is disappointed in me. My sister isn't speaking to me. I am no longer in the school musical. I will never attend Juilliard. Davi is no longer my boyfriend. These are the facts, my reality.

I can't entertain anything else.

Chapter Thirty-Eight

IT'S A SATURDAY AFTERNOON, AND I'M SPRAWLED ON my bed, looking at the open suitcase on the floor. There's nothing inside it, but there will be once I decide what to take and what to leave behind. In a couple of weeks, I'll be on a plane back to Nigeria. The Broadway program I stuck to the mirror on my dresser won't be coming with me. Neither will the *Hamilton* DVD Davi bought me. If I could somehow leave behind memories, I would do that too. I would forget Sybil, Bethany, Blake, Zane, and Davi. I would forget my audition, my first date, and New York City. It would be easier that way—a lot less painful.

My friends in Nigeria were shocked to learn I'd be returning. But Osas and Abby's shock turned to joy when they realized they'd see me again. Tolu's shock, however, stayed intact. She came up with an escape plan that was elaborate and ridiculous. I had to tell her I would not fake my death. At the thought of that absurd conversation, I shake my head.

When my phone buzzes, I roll on my bed and grab it from the nightstand. I'm surprised to see Davi's name on the screen. It's December 1. I haven't spoken to him—in person, over the phone, or via text—in almost three weeks. I no longer go to the cafeteria during lunch, and I avoid making eye contact with him in class or in the hallway. Sybil and Bethany tried to mend things between us, in their own way.

"What the hell is going on?" Bethany said when they cornered me in the bathroom two days after the breakup. "Why did you end things with Davi? He's miserable."

"And apparently, you are too," Sybil added. "No offense, but you look truly miserable."

"And while we're at it, why are you avoiding us? I mean, I thought we were friends. Like, one minute, we're hanging out, and the next, you're MIA? Can't even return a text?"

"Yeah," Sybil said. "And while we're at it, the musical. Like, why?"

I looked between them, uncomfortable. I wasn't sure if they were conducting an ambush or an intervention, but the sound of the school bell saved me from being subjected to the confrontation any further. When I ran out of the restroom with a rushed "Have to get to class," I'm sure it was the final act to end our friendship. More bridges burned. Two less goodbyes to say.

The phone buzzes in my hand. Another incoming text from Davi. Why is he reaching out to me? After the way we left things, I didn't expect it. But maybe he's finally processed what happened, gathered his thoughts, and is texting to give me a piece of his mind. That possibility is terrifying. But ultimately, my curiosity outweighs my fear, and I slide my thumb on the screen.

The message opens.

DAVI: Hey. Can I take you somewhere? Just give me one hour. I'm outside your place.

"What the hell?" I mutter to myself. I'm on edge, biting my nails as my heart thumps. He shouldn't be outside my house, proposing an outing. We broke up. We aren't supposed to see each other anymore. Well, I'm not supposed to see him.

I look at my phone when it buzzes again.

DAVI: Please Enore.

I stare at his text. I imagine him saying my name the way he always did—soft, as if it's breakable, as if tenderness is an essential part of the pronunciation. Slowly, whatever resolve I wanted to exercise disappears.

ME: On my way.

I send the message without thinking things through. When it comes to Davi, there's an act-and-damn-the-consequences pattern I thought I had broken, but here history goes repeating itself. I grab a coat from the closet, put on sneakers, and walk out of my room.

My mom isn't home. She's having a spa day at the insistence of Auntie Sara. Esosa is in her room, her new favorite place. I consider tiptoeing out of the house, but it wouldn't make a difference. She doesn't really care what I do these days. With things as they are, no one will know I left the house and with Davi, of all people.

The brisk cold hits me the moment I step outside. December in Bellwood is no joke. I shove my hands deep into my pockets and run to Davi's car, which is parked in front of the main house. Once I'm inside, I wrestle with the wind to shut the door. It closes with a loud thud, and I exhale as the heat from the ventilation warms my face.

"Hi," Davi says, smiling or trying to maintain some sad semblance of a smile.

"Hi."

Our first words to each other in what seems like months. I've missed him. But that's really an understatement. I've thought of him constantly and cried when the heartbreak seemed unbearable.

In the last few weeks, I've had to deal with so much—the reality of moving back to Nigeria, giving up my dreams, and no longer having Davi in my life. I wonder how much more loss I can take, how many more goodbyes I can say, before finally losing my mind.

"Thanks for coming," he says, his voice small. "I know you probably didn't want to."

"Um . . . don't worry about it. It's fine."

Things are awkward. It was never like this between us, even when we were strangers.

"So . . ." I pull the seat belt over my chest. "Where are we going?"

"Um . . ." He clears his throat and grips the steering wheel. "To see my mom."

His response is so unexpected, I gasp. I have questions, but hold off on asking.

He drives for twenty minutes without saying a word. The music on the radio fills the silence until the car slows down in front of a white three-story building. He pulls into a parking spot and turns off the engine.

"Where are we?" I follow his gaze to a gold plank fixed on the building. There are four words engraved in it. WELLYBEE'S MENTAL HEALTH CENTER. I turn to Davi, confused. "I thought we were going to see your mom."

"Yeah." After a long pause, he looks at me. "She's in there—has been since September."

I hold my breath while waiting for further explanation. After another long pause, it comes.

"She has bipolar disorder," he says. "For years, she managed it with the right meds. But early this year, she went off her meds with no one knowing. And things got a bit out of hand at home. She had episodes. They scared Natalie." He presses his hand to his forehead and huffs. "Grams and Dad thought they could handle it—get her back on her meds. But for months, things just kept getting worse. Home didn't feel safe anymore." He taps his fingers against the steering wheel. "That's around the time I started dating Ara. She was going through some things too. Her grandma, who was basically her best friend, died. So yeah . . . I guess we were just hurting and built this codependent relationship that was really kind of toxic." He stares into the distance, his eyes glazed with tears. "She was an amazing mom before everything. Natalie adored her. She loved performing arts and had this children's studio in town. Little Big Star."

I remember the studio beside the dry cleaners, the one I've stood outside countless times. "She owns that place?"

"Yeah. But her partner has been running things since she's been here. After things got out of hand at home, Dad persuaded her to check herself into the center. It wasn't easy, but she agreed. Dad used my college money to set her up here. That's why we're selling the summerhouse."

"Oh." I nod. "Is this where you come every Sunday? Right after I sing in the choir?"

"Yeah. That's when me, Dad, and Natalie usually visit her."

All the pieces of the puzzle fall into place.

"Why didn't you tell me any of this before?"

He shrugs. "I wanted to. Trust me, I did. You kept bringing her up, and I felt so bad for blowing you off, but I had just met you. I liked you a lot. We started dating. I guess I didn't want you judging me or anything."

"I would never." I touch his hand gently. "Never," I say sternly, and hope he believes me. "I wish you trusted me enough to tell me earlier."

"Yeah. So do I." He holds my hand, and his tight grip shakes. "Um . . . I would like to introduce you to her. If you don't mind. She's much better now. Doctors said she'll be home for Christmas. Natalie is counting down the days." He searches my eyes. "So? Would you like to meet her?"

"Will she be okay having me here? Visiting her?"

"Yeah. She's not ashamed of people knowing about her disorder. She was once. She tried so hard to hide it because she was ashamed. She isn't anymore. And I think it's helped her."

"Okay, then." I smile. "I would love to meet her."

DAVI HAS HIS MOTHER'S EYES. IT'S THEIR BEST FEATURE, captivating and expressive. She lights up when she sees him, drops the book she's reading, and stands from a rocking chair.

"Hey, you." She holds him in a tight hug. "This is a surprise. I was expecting you tomorrow."

"Thought I would shake things up a little." Davi pulls away from her, strokes her long dark hair, and kisses her forehead.

Watching the sweet gestures doubles my feelings for him.

He really is incredible. I think I could love him. I think I do love him. I want to slap the thought out of my head, because loving Davi is a terrible idea. I can't love him when there isn't a future for us.

"Enore." His mother stretches a hand to me. "Davi has told me so much about you."

"Really?" I say while shaking her hand. "He has?"

"Of course, every chance he gets."

Davi doesn't deny it.

"I've been dying to meet you and to hear that voice of yours. He showed me a video, but I'm sure it doesn't compare to an in-person performance. So? What do you say?"

"Wait. What?" I chuckle awkwardly. "You want me to sing?"

"Well, you have an audience who would appreciate some entertainment." She gestures around the massive recreation room, where patients are occupied with different activities. "I'll play, and you'll sing." She marches to the piano in the center of the room, sits on the bench, and waves me over.

"Um . . ." I look at Davi, hoping he'll save me from performing, but he places his hands on my shoulders and nudges me toward the piano.

"Come on," he says. "Give them a little show. Be generous with your gift."

I freeze at his words that sound familiar. *Be generous with your gift.* I've heard them before, though phrased differently. "Don't be stingy with your gift," my father always said to me. And I swear those words mean to me what "with great power comes great responsibility" means to Peter Parker. *Don't be stingy with your gift.* I thought I'd only hear that phrase in my memories, when I revisit moments with my father. But here Davi is, almost reciting it. I think it's now, in this very moment, despite being certain there's no future for us, that I fall for Davi.

"What do you want to sing?" his mother asks.

"Um . . . I really don't know."

"Well, music is therapeutic—healing. Especially in a place like this. So why don't you sing something that has always had a calming effect on you? Does anything come to mind?"

It doesn't take me long to decide.

"Do you know 'With Love' by Christina Grimmie?"

She shakes her head. "But it's fine. You sing, and I'll follow along."

After inhaling and expelling a deep breath, I sing the first notes. The keys on the piano accompany my voice. The bustle in the room quiets.

I've always sung this song with my father in mind. This time, however, I sing and think of Davi. I forget where we are and about the people around us, including his mother. I only focus on him.

Davi shook up my world. He was tough when he needed to be, honest even when I didn't want to hear it, and tender when I needed it most. When we were getting to know each other, he asked me something: "What are you into? What's your passion?"

He was the first person to ask me that. And even though I didn't have the answer back at the time absolutely clueless about myself—he guided me to the answer. He saw something in me and didn't stop drawing my attention to it until I saw it too. I don't know if he loves me, but everything he's done, every action since the day we met, has been with love.

Chapter Thirty-Nine

DAVI STOPS THE CAR IN FRONT OF THE MAIN HOUSE. We look at each other and smile, and it's like things between us never changed, like there was no conversation in the library.

"Your mom is like a ray of sunshine. Thanks for letting me meet her."

"Thanks for being so cool with everything—singing and all. I know you didn't really want to."

"Well, I'm glad I did. It was fun."

Our eyes stay on each other, but with nothing else to say, we fall silent. That's when all the tension creeps in and infiltrates the light atmosphere we kept during the ride home. I dig my teeth in my lip, while Davi's shoulders turn stiff.

"Enore." He runs his fingers through his hair, tousling the curls. "You breaking up with me." He pauses and thinks. "It's because your mom found out about us, isn't it? She made you do it."

"Yeah." But even without my mom giving me the command, our relationship would have ended eventually—as soon I got on a plane to Nigeria.

"Do you think I could meet her—talk to her. Maybe if she got to know me and see how—"

"Davi." I sigh, let out so much air, my body shrinks and folds into itself. "It's more complicated than that. My life, right now, is so much more complicated than that."

"Yeah. I know. And I didn't mean to act like I get what you're going through. Or to shove my advice about talking to your mom down your throat. You're right. We're different in a lot of ways, and I don't understand what it's like for you. But I hope you'll give me a chance to learn because . . ." A curl falls over his forehead; it dangles, covering his right eye until he pushes it backward and looks at me. "I love you, Enore."

My dad used to tell me that love is an action. He repeated that often, drilled it into my head and Esosa's. And as if his reminders weren't enough, he showed us exactly what he meant. He treated my mom like a queen. He respected and supported her. He was kind and selfless, placing her needs ahead of his. He did all that to show me and Esosa how to identify love, so it was always clear to us. Today, more than ever, I appreciate his lessons. Because the moment Davi says he loves me, I refer to my memories and look for the evidence. And there's a substantial amount, enough to support his claim and enough to convince me.

Tears fill my eyes, but I can't decide if they're triggered by happiness or another emotion, one that makes this moment less enjoyable. Davi is watching me anxiously, waiting for my response. I should tell him I love him. Because I do. And if I say it, we would kiss as if our lives depended on it. We would be so enamored with each other, everything would seem possible—us, Juilliard, a future in America. And when we finally pull apart, panting and grinning like lovesick fools, I would remember the various complications in my life—my mother's disapproval and, of course, our return to Nigeria. In one moment, we would be ecstatic and the next, I would have to break the difficult news to him.

I could play out that hypothetical outcome, or I could spare us both and break the news to him right now.

"I'm going back to Nigeria once the semester is over. My whole family is."

He frowns and shrinks back. His mouth falls open, but nothing comes out. After a beat, he shakes his head. "Wait. For good?"

I nod.

"But why?"

"Everything—my father's death, the move here—has been difficult for my mom. She's been struggling. And she found out I'd been lying about the musical and Juilliard. And dating you."

He nods slowly.

"Now she thinks it's best for us to go back to Nigeria."

"You just got here, and now you're leaving?" His head falls into his palms. "This can't be happening."

It's probably resonating with him that once I'm gone, we'll likely never see each other again. It seems wrong to feel the way we do about each other, only to end up on different sides of the world.

When Davi's eyes, dull with sadness, meet mine, I press my lips together and hold back a cry.

"What are we going to do?" he asks.

"There's nothing to do."

"Don't you want to stay?"

"Of course I do. But what I want doesn't matter. I'm going to Nigeria, Davi. That's that."

He slumps in his chair. Neither of us says a word. We make peace with the utterly hopeless situation, because that's all there is to do. When a white flake lands on the windscreen, I squint and focus on it. Snow. Big bits fall from the sky. It's the first time I've seen snow, and it comes at this very moment. If I was overly sentimental, I would interpret the timing as a sign, a sign to be hopeful and see my situation with a little less pessimism. I shake my head because the last thing I want to do is entertain hope, not when my mom has already bought our tickets to Nigeria.

Before the tears I've been fighting back fall, I open the passenger door. "I have to go."

"But—"

"I'll see you at school." At least for a few more weeks. "Bye." I climb out before he can say anything.

Snow hits my face as I rush toward the guesthouse. The sound of a dribbling basketball gets louder as I get closer. Adrian throws a ball into a hoop and celebrates by clapping. Before he turns around and sees me, I rub the tears from my eyes.

"Where did you go?" he asks.

"Just stepped out for a bit."

"Right." He dribbles the ball, then tucks it in his armpit. His black jacket is so puffy, he looks three times his normal size.

"Are our moms back yet?"

"Nope."

"Oh. Okay." I sigh with relief, then walk home. "See you later."

"So you guys are really leaving?"

I pause and turn to him. "Yes."

"Well, that sucks. I like having you guys around."

I look at him, frown, and then look away.

"Wait. What was that?" he asks.

"What was what?"

"That look. That look you just gave me." He walks closer to me. "And don't you even deny it, 'cause I saw it."

I suppose denial would be pointless. "I just find it hard to believe you like having me around. Esosa, yes. But not me."

"Why not you?"

"Well, you're closer to her. You have been since we got here. We hardly even interact."

"Yeah, that's 'cause you don't want to interact with me. How many times did I ask you to hang out with me and Esosa during the summer? You said no every time. And I totally get you were going through things. But it still kinda came across like you didn't really like me."

I gasp. "What? That isn't true."

Now he gives me the same look I gave him.

"Okay. Fine. I wasn't the most social person when I first came. Understandably, right?"

"Yeah. Understandably. But when you became a social butterfly, you never once fluttered to me."

I want to take this conversation seriously, but with a statement like that, I'm not sure I can. I burst out laughing, and he does too.

"Seriously?" I ask.

"Well, you get my point."

"Yeah." I stop laughing and nod. "I do. And I'm sorry. I guess I just got carried away with other things."

"The musical, your new friends, your boyfriend."

"Yeah. I'm really sorry."

"Well, we've still got time."

"Only a few weeks," I say.

"Better than nothing." He tosses the ball to me and although I fumble, I manage to hold it. "Down for a game?"

"Are you joking? It's snowing and freezing."

"If you move around enough, you won't feel the cold." He bounces on his feet. "Okay, show me what you've got."

"Um . . . that would be nothing. I don't know how to play basketball."

"Lucky for you, you've got a damn good teacher, so go on."

I dribble the ball like an amateur and gain more confidence once Adrian gives me some tips. Somehow, I get the ball into the net. The celebration I have with my cousin after scoring is the one thing preventing me from completely breaking down.

My fingers are cold. My nose is runny. But I'll stay out here a little longer to avoid the empty suitcase in my room.

Chapter Forty

THERE ARE FIVE PIECES OF CLOTHES IN THE ONCE empty suitcase. By the end of today, there'll be more. I plan to leave a lot of clothes behind. After all, I don't need knitted sweaters and winter coats in Nigeria. It's only December 8, but in a few weeks, shortly after Christmas, we'll be on a plane back. Esosa still has not made peace with this. And she's still not talking to me. Instead, she communicates with long hisses and intense eyeballing. I hope things between us return to normal once we're in Nigeria.

Normal. It seems like such a strange word, because the meaning keeps changing. For so long, normal was Nigeria. The routine of my everyday life was practically embedded in my DNA, coded in me. Then that normal was disrupted. And a continent away, I had to adjust to a new normal. Now I'll have to adapt again. What will it be like to return—to reclaim Nigeria, Benin City, as home again? The old routine no longer exists, not without my father. I'll have to create another one—map out a new normal.

I'm my yellow sundress into the suitcase when the doorbell rings. I pause and listen for any movement that indicates someone is going to answer it. My mom is in her room, talking to her sister in Nigeria and finalizing the details of our move. She likely didn't hear the bell. Esosa likely didn't hear it either, since she prefers tuning the world out with headphones these days. I sigh and toss the dress on the bed.

I don't think about who could be at the door. Our visitors are typically Uncle Davis, Auntie Sara, and Adrian. However, when I pull the door open, I'm shocked to see Ara.

Ara. Of all people.

"Hey," she says.

"Um . . . hi."

It's quiet, and I wait for her to explain what she's doing at my house, but she doesn't say a word. Instead, she tugs the hem of the knee-length *ankara* dress she's wearing. It's the opening outfit for the musical. Cassandra, the main character, enters center stage with a suitcase and looks at her surroundings with awe. "Wow," she says. "Finally. I'm here. New York City."

It's been weeks since I quit, but I still remember every detail of the musical, including the fact that tonight is opening night. Now I'm even more confused why Ara is at my doorstep.

"Um . . . could we talk?" Her voice is unusually calm, and so is her demeanor.

"Why?" My eyes shift over her dress again. "Shouldn't you be at school . . . at the musical?"

"Yeah." She flicks the flare of her dress and laughs awkwardly. "I definitely should be." Slowly, her awkward chuckle stops. Her eyebrows pinch together. "But I don't want to do it."

"You don't want to do what?"

"The musical. I don't want to do it. I honestly would rather jump off a cliff."

"That's extreme."

"Well, it's the truth." She wraps her arms around herself and shivers. "It's freezing out here. Think we could take this inside? Please?"

After considering her for a moment, I step aside, and she steps in.

"Is there someplace we could talk?"

"Yeah." I turn around and walk to my room. She follows behind me.

I shut the door once we're inside, and Ara looks around. Her eyes settle on the open suitcase on my bed.

"I heard you're going back to Nigeria," she says, turning to me.

"Yeah."

"Cool . . . um . . . I mean, not cool. Depending on your stance on the subject."

I watch her as my confusion grows. "Ara, it's an hour until showtime. You shouldn't be here. In fact, why are you even here?"

"I'm not cut out for musical theater," she blurts. "I hate it, actually. I hate it so freakin' much. I did it for years, but I can't anymore. I seriously can't." She hunches over, her hands on her knees, and hyperventilates.

"Here," I say, leading her to the bed. "Sit. Take it easy."

Slowly, her breathing returns to normal.

"Do you want some water?"

"No. I . . . I'm okay."

Clearly, she isn't. I forget we aren't friends and sit beside her. My hand rests on hers, and she doesn't pull away.

"What's going on, Ara?"

After a long pause, she sighs. "You know my mom's, like, this Broadway star, right?"

"Yeah."

When Sybil mentioned it a few weeks ago, I did some research, and *star* is truly the right word. Ara's mom, Caroline Forbes, is a

Tony-winning actress who has appeared in fifteen Broadway productions.

"Well, ever since I was a kid, she's wanted me to follow in her footsteps. I'm talking dance classes, singing classes, and acting classes since I was six. If it was up to her, I would have gone to some performing arts school in the city. But my grandma . . ." Ara smiles faintly. "She knew musical theater wasn't my thing and stopped my mom from sending me to performing arts school. I stuck with the annual high school musical just as a compromise—to get my mom off my back. And for a long time, that was enough. But earlier this year . . ." She blinks fast, pushing back tears. "My grandma died."

I go from touching Ara's hand lightly to holding it.

"My grandma was my best friend. I was beyond devastated when she died, and my mom could hardly get out of bed. I just wanted to make her happy. That's why I wanted the lead spot in the musical so bad. That's why I was so upset when you got it instead. That's why I've been such a bitch to you." She lowers her gaze and blows out a breath. "I'm really sorry about that, Enore."

"Oh. Okay. Yeah. Thanks." I'm stunned. I never expected an apology from Ara or an explanation for her behavior. It feels good to have both.

"Vying for the lead every year hasn't done me any good," she continues. "Because my mom made me apply to Juilliard and Carnegie Mellon, and it's like I'm back exactly where I started—following footsteps I don't want to follow, and . . . and . . ."

"And you can't do it anymore."

She shakes her head. "I was backstage—dressed and in full makeup, and it just didn't feel right. I mean, it never has. But every year when I got the lead, I just pulled through. This year is different. I peeked between the curtains and looked at the gathering audience, and it became so clear."

"What did?"

"My life—my future—how miserable it will be. Say, hypothetically, I get into Juilliard. And somehow make it and become a Broadway success. Then what? I spend my life trying to pull through every performance, suppressing everything I want just to make my mom happy? Yeah. I can't do that." She squints, and her eyes wander around the room. "You know what's crazy? I don't even know what I really want to do with my life. I don't know what I'm passionate about."

There was a time when I was just as clueless. I'm not anymore, but it doesn't matter—not when there's a suitcase I need to fill, not when I don't know how to dispel obligation and guilt. Ara has somehow done it.

"My mom is a doctor," I say. "She wants me to be one too."

"A doctor?" Ara scowls. "Has she seen you perform? You belong on a stage, Enore. I've watched you during rehearsals. You're . . ." She thinks, then smiles. "Spectacular."

I know rule number eight instructs me to be suspicious when a mean girl is suddenly nice to me. I had my guard up when Ara gave me a compliment in the theater, but this time is different. Ara and I are having a real conversation for the first time since we've known each other. There's no tension or animosity. She's being vulnerable, and I'm realizing how much we have in common.

"It feels right," I tell her. "When I'm onstage, performing, it feels right."

"Then it's what you're meant to do."

"I'm going back to Nigeria soon.

"Well, you have tonight." She gestures to the dress she's wearing. "This role was made for you. Mr. Roland literally crafted it for you. He's likely freaking out right now, seeing that I'm MIA. But trust me, he would rather have you on that stage than me."

"My mom. I can't . . ."

"Aren't you tired too?" Ara asks. "Of trying to follow someone's footsteps?"

Actually, I *am* exhausted. Lately, when I think about my future, there's no excitement or hope. Instead, I feel powerless, like a puppet, like there are strings tethered to my arms and legs, propelling me to act in accordance to someone's will. I imagine what my life would look like if the strings aren't cut. After university, I would get into medical school. I would become a surgeon. I would spend the rest of my life struggling in my career while suppressing my passion and happiness until it's totally snuffed out. I see it clearly—my life, my future, how miserable it will be if I do what's expected of me.

"Here." Ara turns her back to me. "Help me take this off."

I pull the zipper down, and the dress loosens against her body.

"Think you could lend me something to wear?"

"Um . . . yeah." I go to my closet and grab a set of blue sweats from the hanger, part of the clothes I planned on leaving in America. "Here."

"Thanks." She changes quickly, then extends the dress to me. "Go on. Put it on. Showtime is in less than an hour."

The dress dangles between us. Ara waits for me to take it, while I try to convince myself not to. I could ask her to leave, act like our conversation never happened, and go back to packing. I could do exactly what's expected of me. But then the image of that miserable future comes to my head, and I grab the dress quickly. When it's on, Ara pulls the zipper up, and we walk out of the room. Midway down the hallway, I pause, and Ara turns to look at me.

"Come on. We have to go."

"Not yet," I say. "Not without telling my mom first." Over the past few months, I've lied and hid who I am from her. I won't do that anymore. "Would you mind waiting in the living room for a minute?"

"Yeah. Sure."

When Ara is out of sight, I knock on my mom's bedroom door and wait.

"Yes? Come in."

I turn the knob and step inside. She's looking through her closet, likely doing what I was minutes ago. When she turns to me, she frowns.

"What are you wearing and where are you going?"

I suppose this is my moment of truth.

"Enore?"

My nails dig into my sweaty palm. I'm terrified, but words somehow find their way out. "Daddy loved it when I sang. He was proud whenever I did. He pushed me to sing. I think it's because he knew it's what I'm meant to do."

Those first sentences take a lot out of me. I pause and catch my breath.

"In the past few months, I haven't been myself. I've lied to you. And I'm so sorry, Mommy." Tears fill my eyes, and I blink until they all fall and my vision clears. "I think I was just trying to find myself, find my purpose. And I had to do that without you. I had to separate myself from your expectations, so I could see things clearly. Still, Daddy wouldn't be proud of me for lying. But I think . . . I know he would be proud of me for finally seeing what he saw in me."

She folds her arms, tilts her head, and watches me without a word.

"Mommy, I don't want to be a doctor or even a lawyer or an engineer. I am positive any of those careers will make me miserable." I look at my dress. "I worked very hard to be in this musical—rehearsed every day. And I loved every minute.

"When I'm on that stage, it feels right. It makes me happy. So I'm going to go now—to perform. We're leaving for Nigeria soon, and I wish we weren't. But since we are, I have to do this. Because I don't know if I'll ever get a chance to again."

I wait for her to say something. She says nothing. Her arms stay crossed over her chest, and her narrowed eyes remain fixed on me.

"I'm sorry I've disappointed you, Mom. I'm so sorry."

I turn to leave, but before I walk out of the room, Esosa rushes in.

"I'm going with Enore." She pants through a wide grin. "I know you said I couldn't, but makeup is my passion and . . ." She looks at me and shakes her head. "Sorry. It's not about me. The point is, I'm going because I signed up to do the makeup, and it's likely everyone looks a mess without me. So . . . see you later."

We walk out of Mom's room without being stopped.

"You ready?" Ara asks. "Our ride is waiting."

"Yeah. Let's go."

It's freezing outside, and none of us are dressed appropriately, especially me. Ara runs ahead, while Esosa and I follow behind her.

"I can't believe you did that," my sister says. "It was legendary."

"So, you're talking to me again?"

"Well, you left me high and dry, not even backing me up about staying. But you've made up for it."

I throw an arm around my sister's shoulders and pull her close. "Well, I've missed you."

"Makes sense. I'm a highly miss-able person."

I can't help but laugh. When we reach a silver Toyota, I turn to Ara. "That's our ride?"

She shrugs. "He insisted."

I look through the window at Davi's face, and my heart skips several beats.

"They insisted too."

Bethany and Sybil are in the backseat, waving at me.

I've been avoiding all of them for weeks, but they're here, conducting some sort of rescue mission. It completely warms my heart.

"Come on," Ara says. "We gotta go." She opens the passenger door and urges me to get in.

When I settle into the seat, I glance at Davi. "Hi."

He smiles. "Hey."

Esosa and Ara settle into the back, sharing the small space with Bethany and Sybil.

"I can't believe you guys came."

"We were plan B," Sybil says. "If Ara couldn't convince you, we were gonna drag you out of that house."

As we laugh, Davi pulls out of the driveway. He speeds and cuts the ten-minute drive in half. When he stops the car in front of the school, everyone in the back rushes out, but I stay inside.

"Come on," Ara says. "Move it."

"Can you give me a minute?" I ask.

"Um . . . yeah. Sure. But make it fast." She backs away and enters the building.

When it's just me and Davi, a fluttering sensation starts in my chest. "Thank you," I whisper. "For coming to get me."

He nods, his hands still on the steering wheel. "Yeah. It was nothing. I'm just glad you decided to come."

"Yeah."

It's awkward between us. There's no denying that. But I'm trying to push through the awkwardness so we can be us again. Especially now, as I'm about to get onstage, I just want us to be *us*—the Davi and Enore sitting on the bleachers exchanging food, the Davi and Enore running through New York City without a care. But it seems impossible to break through the haze of tension. Disappointed, I push the door open. But just as I'm about to step out, he holds my hand.

"You're going to be amazing, Enore."

His words cut through the tension, and I don't think. I just lean forward and kiss him. It might as well be our first kiss, the way our lips move cautiously before rushing to match our eagerness. His tongue slips into my mouth, and I grip his hair. I'm breathless but refuse to come up for air because I've missed this so much. I've missed him.

We only pull apart when Ara shouts my name.

"You should probably go," Davi says, laughing. "Or she'll come down here."

"Yeah." I step out of the car, then look at him. "I love you too, by the way."

Even though there's no future for us. Even though we'll likely never see each other after I leave.

I love him.

Chapter Forty-One

OVER THE LAST FEW MONTHS, I HAVE EXPERIENCED some moments of sheer terror. Like when the doctors delivered my father's diagnosis, when my father died, and when we left the only home we had ever known in pursuit of another. Now, as I pace around backstage in full makeup, I add another moment of sheer terror to my list.

"We go on in one! One minute! One minute, people!" Mr. Roland shouts.

He's experienced enough uncertainty and anxiety over this musical—first with me quitting and then with the understudy disappearing on opening night, only to show up with me minutes before the show starts. He conducted an intense and brief interrogation when he saw me in the opening scene costume.

"Can you do this? Do you remember everything?" When I confidently answered yes, he was more than happy to put me on.

Now, madness ensues backstage. The crew is running around, ensuring things are in place. There are too many voices coming from too many directions. Someone is complaining about their wardrobe, while another is rehearsing their lines aloud. Mr. Roland is giving people both directions and threats. The commotion makes me more nervous. I draw in a deep breath and blow it out.

"Hey," Cole says, giving me a roguish smile. He's already in character, looking the part of a millionaire playboy with his aviator sunglasses and fitted suit.

During one of the early rehearsals, Mr. Roland explained that Cole needed to give off a "Chuck Bass level of smugness." I say he's doing exactly that.

"You look good," I tell him.

"So do you. You're gonna do great."

"Thanks." I force a smile and remind myself I'll be onstage alone for three minutes before he joins me. Three minutes. That's not bad. I can do that.

"Okay," Mr. Roland speaks into the microphone attached to his headset. "Let's go."

The curtains part slowly. The backdrop of New York City is stunning. The audience doesn't make a sound. The music starts. I know exactly what I'm supposed to do—the lines, the moves, the song. Before Mr. Roland nudges me forward, I grip the suitcase and march onstage.

The lights are bright, blinding. Were they this bright during rehearsals? Maybe. There's no time to debate about it right now. I have to deliver my first line.

"Wow," I say. "Finally. I'm here. New York City." My voice is small and shaky. Even with my microphone, it likely didn't travel to the back of the theater. The music starts before I can dwell on my mistake. I'm supposed to sing now, but my throat tightens up. Even when I open my mouth, nothing comes out.

I scan the audience fervently. I'm unsure what I'm searching for until it hits me.

My dad.

He isn't here. And his leather watch around my wrist, the one I begged Mr. Roland to let me wear during the musical, isn't enough to make him seem present. I want to close my eyes and picture him in the audience, smiling proudly at me. I thought I had broken this habit. But no. For the biggest performance of my life, I need my dad. And if I can't close my eyes throughout the show and picture him, then I can't sing.

With the suitcase still in my hand, I turn around and rush backstage. Mr. Roland calls after me, but I don't stop running until I'm in my dressing room. I shut the door and sit in front of the mirror. Tears fill my eyes. I'm an idiot. I really thought I could do it, but standing in front of that audience without seeing him was more overwhelming than expected. I sigh, and my face falls into my hands. When the door creaks open, I look up.

I expect to see Mr. Roland's scowling face. It's an utter shock when my mother's face appears instead. I sit upright and frown.

"Mommy?"

She enters the room and closes the door.

"What are you doing here?"

"Well, I came to see a musical. My very first, by the way. What I did not expect to see was my daughter running off the stage. With the way you spoke at home, frankly more confident than I have ever heard you speak in your life, I thought you would get up there and put on a real show, eh?" She searches my eyes. "What happened?"

I shrug. "You won't understand."

"Ah. Okay." She drags a chair, pulls it next to me, and sits. "Then help me understand."

I watch her hesitantly.

"Ah-ah. Speak *na*," she urges. "Talk."

I huff. "He isn't here. Daddy. I can't do it without him. Before, he was always there—in the audience. But now he isn't."

"And so you can't sing?"

I shake my head. "He should be here."

"But he isn't. And I wish I could tell you he's watching over us or he's here in spirit, but I don't know that." She rolls her eyes. "Besides, it is a little cliché. Don't you think?"

"Yeah. A little," I mumble while looking at my fidgeting fingers.

"Enore. *Lare*." She takes my hands in hers. "Think about what your father left behind—what he gave you, what he gave us before he passed."

"I don't understand."

"Well, he gave me two beautiful daughters. A lifetime of wonderful memories. And one of the greatest loves I have ever felt. What did he give you?"

I sort through my memories of him, and the answer is clear. "He gave me a lot of things," I say. "Including confidence. In my gift. Every time he told me I was a great singer, every time he was the first to stand and clap after my solos in church, every time he told me I sounded better than the singers on the radio, he gave me confidence."

"Then hold on to what he gave you. That's how you hold on to him. That's how you keep him here."

I nod and tears come down my cheeks. My mother extends her arms and holds me tight. More tears fall, but not just from me.

"Just because I didn't say you were a great singer or stand on my feet after each of your solos or say you sounded better than the singers on the radio doesn't mean I didn't think you were exceptional." She pulls back and wipes my wet cheeks, then hers. "I saw it too—that very special thing inside you. It scared me."

"Scared you?"

She nods. "It seemed unsafe, unpredictable. I wanted to protect you—to make sure your future was secure. Being a doctor or even a lawyer would have provided that."

"Either of those options would make me miserable."

"Yes."

I'm shocked she agrees.

"You know, the main reason your father wanted us to come to America was for you and Esosa. He said you both could be absolutely anything here. He used to rant about all the possibilities. He dreamed big dreams for you both, much bigger than I could ever conceive. Fear always limited me. I've always wanted to play things safe."

I study her. "Are you still afraid?"

Is fear one of the reasons she wants us to return to Nigeria?

Her eyes wander as she thinks; when they settle on me, she smiles. "Yes. I'm still a little afraid. But I just realized your father left me with something else."

"What?"

"His boldness. His audacity. Esosa has a lot of it."

We both laugh.

"Yeah," I say. "She does. I don't have much of it."

"Of course you do." Her voice is stern as she takes my hands and prompts me to stand. "You are his daughter. You have the very best of him." She holds my face between her hands. "He would be so proud of you."

"Really? You think so?"

"I am positive." She kisses my forehead. "*Oya.*" She opens the door and gestures for me to step out. "Go. That your Mr. Roland is acting like a chicken with its head cut off."

I laugh, and just before stepping through the door, I hug her. "Thank you, Mommy."

She strokes my cheek when I step back. "I am too," she says. "Proud of you."

When I rushed offstage and into the dressing room, I expected someone to come in and urge me to come out—either Mr. Roland with force or Davi with sweet words. In the movie *Tall Girl 2*, Jodi, the lead in the school musical, has an anxiety attack and runs to the dressing room before the show starts. The person who encourages her to get onstage is Kimmy, her understudy and nemesis.

In my case, another intervention from Ara seemed more likely. I never, in a million years, thought my mom would be in the dressing room, encouraging me to perform. But I'm glad she showed up. Because I think she's the only person who could have given me exactly what I needed to go onstage and give a performance worth a standing ovation.

Chapter Forty-Two

I CLOSE MY EYES AND LIFT MY FACE TO THE SKY, enjoying the sun's warmth. It's the first time in months that I've felt the sun on my skin. Winter was brutal. Esosa complained every single day. I, on the other hand, have a greater appreciation for all the seasons. At first, I was certain nothing could beat summer, and then fall came. The colors and ambiance made it a real contender for my favorite. During winter, I stared out of windows a lot, always watching snow fall or admiring the way layers of it covered rooftops and tree branches. It was absolutely picturesque. But now it's spring, the first day of April, and my new favorite thing is helping Auntie Sara in the garden, planting, and then watching the gradual process of flowers bloom.

Metaphorically, the cycle of the seasons is reminiscent of my life in the past year.

Summer: my father is alive, and my family is whole and happy.

Fall: my father gets diagnosed and we watch him slowly grow ill, weaker and weaker every day.

Winter: he dies and we mourn.

Spring: there's hope.

Just last week, my mom learned she passed the USMLE Step 1. It took her three tries, but she did it. She still has a long way to go before she can practice medicine in America. There are a few more tests and a residency program, but she's determined. Deciding to stay in America even though things weren't perfect was hard. She did it for me and Esosa, so we could have a future with the endless possibilities our father hoped for. Passing her exam gave her a future too. She said for the first time since we immigrated, she felt grounded in America.

"Hey," Davi says, shuffling along the bleachers until we're side by side, our knees touching. "Are you ready?"

I look at my phone and then at his. My heart thumps—brisk and hard, like it fully intends to break free. Our futures are literally in our hands. With a few taps, we'll see if we got accepted into our dream colleges. I cringe at the thought of rejection.

"Hey." Davi takes my clammy hand. "It's going to be okay. No matter what happens, we'll get through it."

"Okay." I breathe deeply and look at the track field, where a gym class is in progress. At the beginning of the school year, we sat in this exact spot, exchanging home-cooked meals and talking about the teen movies I watched. It seems like so much has happened since then. It took some convincing from Auntie Sara, the certified advocate for teenagers living their best life, for Mom to agree to meet Davi. The whole family gathered for dinner in January, the week of my eighteenth birthday, and there was a formal introduction. Davi came with flowers, a box of chocolates, and a plate of his grandmother's *pão de queijo*. Throughout dinner, he talked about his plans to attend Columbia University and study political science. He made a great first impression.

Mom has significantly warmed up to him. Though she refuses to acknowledge he's my boyfriend. She calls him my friend. And sometimes, my little friend. Regardless, she knows Davi and I are serious, as serious as two teenagers can be when their future is uncertain. Once we graduate and summer ends, we'll go to our respective colleges. I'll miss the routine we've established—sitting side by side during class, having lunch together, driving home together. But if Davi gets into Columbia and I get into Juilliard, we'll only be a short subway ride from each other. We could establish a new routine. My fingers are crossed.

I think back to my Juilliard audition in early January. Ara and her mom helped me prepare for it. I think Ara was happy to introduce her mom to someone who actually wants a Broadway career, and her mom was more than happy to be a mentor. With their guidance, I prepared the song "She Used to Be Mine" from the musical *Waitress*. It's a big, emotional song, and I did my absolute best. And now, I'm hoping for the best.

"Do you want to do it together, or one at a time?" Davi asks.

"Together," I answer. "Definitely together."

"Yeah. Okay."

We look down at our phones, and our fingers work against the screens.

A moment of silence passes, then Davi and I look at each other.

"So?" he asks. "Did you . . ."

I sigh and press my eyes closed. Tears are on the verge of falling, but I hold them back. "Yeah. I got in." I can't celebrate. Not yet. "What about you?"

He shows me his phone screen. "Accepted."

A sigh of relief rushes out of me, and then immediately after, I laugh. "Oh my God!"

Davi and I hold each other, our grip tight.

"This is wild," he says.

"It's incredible."

When we pull apart, we look at each other, and that's when the tears I've been holding in fall. Suddenly, I think back to the first rule I broke.

Rule #1: Avoid interacting with or befriending anyone who is popular.

Breaking that one rule led to me breaking more—four, to be exact.

Rule #2: Control your heart and your hormones. No crushes. And absolutely no boyfriends.

Rule #3: Don't do anything to draw attention to yourself. Keep a low profile.

Rule #4: Don't make any enemies or start a rivalry.

Rule #5: In the unfortunate event that you make an enemy, try by all means to stay away from them.

Even with my effort and determination, I broke multiple rules—the ones I set for myself and also the ones my mom set for me. But maybe they were the right rules to break, necessary acts of rebellion to get me to where I am now. My father, aware of how structured and obedient I was, used to give me one piece of advice repeatedly. The day before school began, while writing my list of high school dos and don'ts, I wrote his advice as a rule.

Rule #9: Don't be afraid to break the right rules. ✓

I know he would be proud of me, proud to see his daughter divert off the straight and narrow path paved with practicality and obligation to create her own way.

I'm proud of myself too. As there isn't an exact blueprint to navigating high school, there isn't a blueprint to surviving loss. Grief can be consuming. It can dig a hole inside a person, uprooting hope and joy until all that's left is a void. Sometimes the void seems bottomless, like nothing can ever fill it. But that isn't true. It fills slowly, like droplets of water falling into a bucket. It takes time. Every day, I fill the void inside me with moments with Davi, moments when I sing on a stage or in the choir, moments when Esosa and I laugh so hard our stomachs hurt, moments when my mom and I go on long walks and just talk, moments with my friends.

I'm only eighteen. I will live a big life—meet interesting people, have wonderful experiences, do incredible things, and have my own family one day—and that hole, that void, will keep filling up with all the beauty in my life.

"Okay," Davi shouts. "Let's celebrate! With some food." He opens his backpack and pulls out a container. "I've got *coxinhas* and *brigadeiros*. My mom made them."

"Oh. Hand it over." I reach out to take the container, but he pulls away.

"Not so fast. You know how this works." He nods at my bag on the bleacher. "Show me what you've got."

"Fine." I laugh while unzipping my bag. "I've got jollof rice and *suya*."

"Ahh. All right. Now you're talking." The grin on his face is wide.

As we exchange containers, I wonder about the alternative to the future we now have.

"What if we hadn't gotten in?" Those words leave a bad taste in my mouth.

"Well . . ." He thinks for a moment, then shakes his head. "Then that would have really sucked, and this would have been comfort food."

"I prefer celebratory food."

"Same."

We toast with our cans of cherry Coke and eat while watching the gym class on the field.

"Hey," Davi says. "You never told me what your favorite teen movie is."

I chew and swallow a piece of coxinha, then clear my throat. "I actually don't know. I loved a lot of them—*Sugar & Spice, Sierra Burgess Is a Loser, She's All That.* But a favorite?" I think, then shrug. "I don't know."

"Come on. You've watched all those movies and don't have a favorite?" He arches an eyebrow and stares pointedly at me.

"Well, I didn't really think about it until now. But yeah." I nod slowly as an answer comes to me. "I do have a favorite."

"Okay. Which one?"

"This one." The one when I—a dark-skinned girl with box braids and a non-American accent—am the star, alongside a boy with hazel-green eyes and a golden-brown complexion. "This, us, is my favorite teen movie."

Davi smiles while nodding. "Yeah." He throws an arm around my shoulders and draws me into his side. "This is my favorite one too."

It's a perfect spring day in Bellwood. Outside Bellwood High, students run around a track field, while a coach urges them to move faster by blowing a whistle. I'm sitting on the bleachers with my boyfriend. We're having lunch. His arm is around me. I'm happy. Really happy.

I take this movie-perfect moment and store it in my mind, along with other wonderful memories I've made over the last few months. And then mentally, I cross out the last rule on my list.

~~Rule #10: Try your best to make some good memories.~~

I've made many.

Acknowledgments

The immigrant experience is framed both by fear and excitement. When I moved from Nigeria to Canada at the age of eleven, the idea of a new home and a new beginning thrilled me. At the same time, the newness and uncertainty frightened me. I didn't deal with these emotions. Instead, I ignored them and all the other emotions that came with immigrating. I adjusted to my new home while on autopilot—without truly comprehending the impact the huge change had on me. I only started to process in my early twenties when I read books that reflected my experience as a Nigerian immigrant. When I set out to write *With Love, Miss Americanah*, I wanted to delve into my experience further. The process was therapeutic for me but also fun. I enjoyed writing each character and telling Enore's story, which to some degree is mine.

When searching for a home for this book, I prayed for an editor that would completely understand the story and the characters and me. And thanks to my agent, Kevan Lyon, for submitting this book to Foyinsi at Feiwel & Friends. I couldn't have asked for a better editor. The first draft of this book was okay. But the final draft, shaped by her insight and attention to detail, was incredible. Thank you, Foyinsi. Thank you also to the amazing editorial and design team at Feiwel & Friends.

Writing a book isn't an easy thing to do. There were times when I got frustrated and was tempted to throw my laptop out the window, but my family's support kept me from having a total meltdown. A huge thank you to them. To the readers who chose to spend their time with this book, thank you so much. I'm grateful to share this story with you.

With Love, Miss Americanah is the fourth book I've written. Every time I finish a book, a part of me worries I might have used up all of my words and creativity and won't have enough to tell the next story. But then I start to write another book and then complete it, and there is still so much left in me to pour out. God alone deserves credit for this. Time and time again, he equips me with everything I need to tell a story. I am more than grateful. Thank You.

Thank you for reading this Feiwel & Friends book.
The friends who made

With Love,
MISS
AMERICANAH

possible are:

Jean Feiwel, Publisher

Liz Szabla, VP, Associate Publisher

Rich Deas, Senior Creative Director

Anna Roberto, Executive Editor

Holly West, Senior Editor

Kat Brzozowski, Senior Editor

Dawn Ryan, Executive Managing Editor

Emily Settle, Editor

Rachel Diebel, Editor

Foyinsi Adegbonmire, Editor

Brittany Groves, Assistant Editor

Ilana Worrell, Senior Production Editor

Follow us on Facebook or visit us online at mackids.com.
Our books are friends for life.